MW00532407

R. FRANKLIN JAMES

to. *The Return Of The Fallen Angels Book Club* is well crafted, the writing is top-notch and you can see just far the author has come from her first book. The confidence in writing shows every step of the way."
—*Mystery Sequels.com*

STICKS AND STONES

4 Stars: "Readers are sure to be captured by this plot-twisting, exciting mystery. It is a real page turner and I certainly am going to keep reading this series."
—Cyclamen, *Long and Short Reviews*

"Who knew a simple nursery rhyme could be so dangerous? Someone knows. Someone has all the answers Hollis seeks. You'll want to keep turning the pages to see if Hollis survives long enough to uncover the truth."
—*I Love a Mystery Reviews*

"*Sticks & Stones* is a great read, a fun legal mystery about a great researcher who really knows her stuff…. There was even a light romance, which did not overpower the plot."
—*Mystery Sequels*

THE FALLEN ANGELS BOOK CLUB

"Hollis is a character you sorta warm up to, you have to get past her cool exterior and suddenly you realize you REALLY like her and care what happens to her. "
—Bless Their Hearts Mom Blog

"R. Franklin James' new book has everything a reader could ask for in a good mystery: intriguing plot, fascinating characters, and a few shockers thrown in along the way."
—Shirley Kennedy, romance novelist

5 Stars: "Although I had my suspicions of one character, the solution to the mystery surprised me. And that, my friends, is the mark of a good mystery."
—*Self-Taught Cook Blog*

"A fast paced plot with many twists coupled with a smart and determined protagonist make this a most enjoyable read."
—Kathleen Delaney, author of the Ellen McKenzie mysteries

"The author manages to reel the reader in with her delightful storytelling and likable characters.... a great first book that lovers of the old-fashioned detective genre surely will appreciate!"
—Fenny, *Hotchpotch Blog*

"A satisfying, clean mystery with several twists that kept me guessing, and also left me anxious for the next book in the Hollis Morgan Mystery series."
—W.V. Stitcher

"I love a good mystery and this is one of the better ones I have read in awhile. A fun story for sure!!!"
—Kathleen Kelly, *Celtic Lady's Reviews*

"The story line was interesting, as were the characters.... I really liked the author's way of writing.... If you love a good murder mystery, you should get a copy of this book."
—Vicki, *I'd Rather Be at the Beach Blog*

"This book allows the reader to take part in the investigation; I felt my suspicions sift as each new clue was revealed. This is a remarkable, well-rounded mystery and I HIGHLY recommend this to anyone who enjoys crime fiction."
—Heather Coulter, *Books, Books, and More Books*

"This first book written by Ms. James is a winner for anyone who enjoys a clean mystery which will keep you guessing until the end about 'whodunit.'"
—My Home of Books Blog

"This book is full of murder, mystery and of course mayhem. Thoroughly entertaining and a fast read, I can't wait for the next book in the series. Excellent debut novel, Ms. James!"
—Tammy & Michelle, Nook Users' Book Club

"This is R. Franklin James' debut novel, a fact which I find hard to believe. She has created a character I love in Hollis Morgan, and a great plot …. I'm going to follow the series and R. Franklin James. I've found a winner."
—*Views from the Countryside Blog*

"Highly inventive… a wonderful thriller. The tension mounts as Hollis becomes the target of the killer, putting her life in great peril."
—*Vic's Media Room*

"An enjoyable first book in the new series featuring Hollis Morgan. Hollis is a good heroine as she is smart, determined and resourceful."
—Barbara Cothern, *Portland Book Review*

"A delightful read. It certainly contained mystery, murder and mayhem…. Like any good mystery, there was a mystery within a mystery and I found [Hollis'] exchanges with the older folks at the center refreshing and decidedly touching…. The reader could feel Hollis's fear with each event and her determination to clear her name. Very well written and very well thought out! Well done, Ms. James, well done!"
—Beth, *Art From the Heart Blog*

The
Bell Tolls

The Bell Tolls

A HOLLIS MORGAN MYSTERY

R. FRANKLIN JAMES

CAVEL PRESS

Seattle, WA

CAMEL
PRESS

Camel Press
PO Box 70515
Seattle, WA 98127

For more information go to: www.camelpress.com
www.rfranklinjames.com

Cover design by Sabrina Sun

The Bell Tolls
Copyright © 2017 by R. Franklin James

ISBN: 978-1-60381-217-7 (Trade Paper)
ISBN: 978-1-60381-218-4 (eBook)

Library of Congress Control Number: 2017903848

Printed in the United States of America

Acknowledgments

T O Catherine Treadgold and Jennifer McCord at Camel Press, this book is so much better because of you.

To Joyce Pope, Barbara Lawrence, Carol Oliveira, and Geri Nibbs, the world is so much better because of you.

To Leonard, I'm so much better because of you.

Also by the author

The Fallen Angels Book Club

Sticks & Stones

The Return of the Fallen Angels Book Club

The Trade List

CHAPTER ONE

———∽∽———

Monday Morning

Hollis Morgan, senior probate attorney. It had a nice ring to it.

She turned on the lights in George Ravel's office and placed her box of personal items on the credenza under the window that overlooked San Francisco Bay. No, not George's office; it was *her* office now. She could feel the smile of accomplishment play on her lips. She'd earned it. George had been gone for almost three months, but he'd made sure that she, as his protégée, would move up into his spot on the status pole of Dodson, Dodson and Doyle, or Triple D, as its employees referred to it.

Even with the sun barely peeking over the Berkeley hills, from her position on the Seventh Floor, she could see the East Bay Bridge toll plaza already backing up with commuters slowly edging into San Francisco. She was glad she worked in the East Bay.

If there had been any internal political angst over her promotion to senior attorney after only a year as an associate, she hadn't picked up on it. Everyone seemed unfazed. But then, with George gone, she was the only probate attorney in the firm. Triple D was a well-established law firm in downtown Oakland. Small in size, it specialized in nurturing its clients and caring for their every legal need.

"Want some help?" offered Tiffany, receptionist and all-around ace employee. She stood in the doorway, carrying an armful of law books. Though wearing a sleeveless, charcoal-gray dress and pearls, she had blonde, high-school-cheerleader looks that belied a sharp, intuitive mind.

Hollis looked up and smiled. "Yes, thank you." She brushed a lock of thick auburn hair out of her eyes. "You're here early."

She rubbed at a patch of dust on her black wool pants. Though no match for Tiffany's tall, shapely frame, Hollis at five-foot-three could hold her own in the looks department. Still, fashion was not her forte.

Tiffany put the books on the floor in the corner of the office. "Like I said, I came to help. I woke up early and couldn't get back to sleep, and I knew you'd be here." She looked around the room. "It doesn't take long for an office to take on the character of its new occupant, does it? Pretty soon we'll be betting each other over whether we can remember who occupied the office before you." She sighed.

Hollis frowned at the receptionist's dismal expression. "You okay?"

Tiffany looked puzzled. "What? Oh, yeah ... yeah, I'm fine." She turned back onto the hallway. "Come on, let's keep going. You've got a busy day."

Hollis fell in step behind her, and for the next thirty minutes they spoke little as they shuttled boxes back and forth from her old office. She paused a moment, remembering the first day she came to Triple D as a paralegal. After serving eighteen months in prison, she was distrustful of the system that put her there, and yet she had wanted nothing more than to finish law school and get her life back. Triple D and the Fallen Angels had been her rescue.

She smiled to herself. Once a Fallen Angel, always a Fallen Angel. She, Rena, Gene, Richard, and Michael comprised the Fallen Angels Book Club. The group was more than just a book club, it had been a lifesaver for all involved. The name said it all: they had fallen—flouting the rules of law-abiding society—been punished, and were now white-collar ex-felons. They'd overcome society's stigma as well as their own guilt to redeem themselves and earn a second chance. It still surprised her that after several years, the club was still going strong. They'd skipped meeting this month, only because the majority couldn't make it. But the members had already chosen the next book for discussion. Hollis was looking forward to getting together.

The phone rang, and Tiffany dashed out into the lobby to answer. Hollis went back to arranging files in the cabinet.

"Hollis," Tiffany called from her desk, "it's for you. I put the call through to your line. That blinking light is yours." Hollis picked up the phone.

"Ms. Morgan," she heard, "this is Odelia Larson. I work for Matthias Bell as his personal secretary." The voice was stern and clipped.

"Yes, Odelia, I recognize your voice." Hollis smiled to herself. Odelia Larson refused to give up the formality of using her full name, even though they had met several times. Odelia insisted on calling her "Ms. Morgan," and feeling contrary, Hollis insisted on calling Odelia Larson, "Odelia."

"I called to inform you that Mr. Bell passed away on Saturday."

"Oh." Hollis leaned back in her chair. "What happened?"

"It was a heart attack; he went into the hospital on Saturday afternoon. It … it didn't take long." Odelia lowered her voice. "I have the death certificate from the hospital. What time can we expect you?"

"Pardon me, expect me for what?"

Odelia hesitated, and for the first time since Hollis had known her, she seemed uncertain how to proceed.

"He ... he left a note for you. Well, not for you. He left a note for me to tell you where to find his instructions for carrying out his ... his wishes."

Her words were halting. She took in a full gulp of air.

Hollis glanced at the wall clock. "I can be there at eleven. Does that work for you?"

"Yes, yes, that will be fine."

Hollis' brow wrinkled. Matthias Bell wasn't one of her favorite people. She'd inherited him from Avery Mitchell, a senior attorney she'd been assigned to when she first came to work at Triple D. He'd been passed on to George Ravel when Avery left, and now, she realized, he was her client. As a paralegal, she'd met Bell a few times. His secretive manner had amused her but irritated her bosses. She'd only spoken with him briefly since she'd become an attorney, and that was to prepare an amendment to his trust. He'd been transferring a small parcel of real estate, but he'd bombarded her with questions filled with such suspicion, it was only after she reminded him that he'd come to her that he backed down. The last time she'd seen him was almost two years ago.

Within a few minutes, Hollis was able to pick over the moving boxes and locate his client folder. Matthias Bell was eighty-four years old. He was a wealthy man as a result of a modest inheritance from his parents, who both died when he was forty. Successful investments, since they appeared to have given him the financial security and cushion to own a mini-mansion in San Francisco. Then there was a condo in Chicago, a house in the Caymans, a small yacht, and miscellaneous land holdings scattered throughout the states. He wasn't frail, but his history of a bad heart had slowed him down, and lately he'd mostly stayed at home.

She flipped through the file to the pages of the trust. It wasn't a complicated document. Bell left the bulk of his estate to his remaining relatives, a much younger sister in Iowa, and a niece who resided in the Bay Area.

She noticed the time in the Midwest and pulled out the contact sheet to get in touch with his sister. After several rings, a woman picked up.

Gloria Bell Haver's response to her brother's death was cool.

"Matt and I weren't close. I haven't seen him in … gee, I guess ten years. His heart, huh? It was never good." There was a rustle of what sounded like the newspaper. "Fortunately, I have my own money, because I would hate to have to count on him. Is there a lot of paperwork? Can my attorney handle things?"

Hollis was used to all types of beneficiary responses, and while Bell's sister seemed more callous than most, she wasn't shocked.

"Absolutely," she said, "Give me their contact information and I'll work through them." Hollis paused, then asked, "And the funeral arrangements?"

"Damn, that's right," Haver muttered, and then said, "I'm supposed to visit friends in the Bahamas day after tomorrow. I can't change my plans now. Like I said, Matthias and I were not close. We didn't get along well, and if you knew him at all, you'd know he hated hypocrites. Let me get you my lawyer's name." She put the phone down.

A moment later, she came back on the line and read off the information. "Er, can attorneys set up funerals?"

Hollis shook her head in amazement. "I'm sure your attorney can handle things. What about your daughter?"

"Yes, I should tell my daughter, Constance. I think she had a marginal relationship with her uncle, formed by their mutual love of money. But I doubt she'll want to be bothered with a funeral, either. Is there anything else?"

"Nope," Hollis said. "I can take it from here. Just have a nice trip."

She turned back to Bell's file, adding notes from her

conversation with his sister and the phone number of Haver's attorney. She'd picked up the phone to call when her phone rang in her hand.

It was Odelia.

"Ms. Morgan, I'm … I'm sorry to bother you again. I know you said eleven o'clock but … but …."

"Odelia, what is it? What's the matter?" Hollis urged.

"Can you come *now*?"

CHAPTER TWO

—~~—

Monday Afternoon

THE BELL MANSION—BECAUSE AS HOLLIS stood in front of its wrought-iron gate, she could not think of it as a *house*—was located in San Francisco's Pacific Heights District. She'd only been there once before to drop off papers for his signature. The tall, narrow, white-stone edifice had surprisingly few windows. The ones that did open onto the street were covered in dark drapes. The residence stood as the man had, aloof and overbearing. Its landscaping might have been the work of a still-life painter—pruned and contrived.

Hollis paused to steel herself and rang the bell.

Odelia immediately opened the door.

"Ms. Morgan," the older woman said, "thank you for coming so quickly." She pointed her to a large living room to the right of the oversized entry.

Odelia Larson had aged well. From Bell's file, Hollis knew her to be in her late sixties. She had let her hair go totally gray, but it was cut in a modern style and complemented her blue eyes. Medium height, she always stood as if at attention. Hollis had never seen her in a relaxed slouch.

They entered the tastefully furnished, rose-colored living room. Its high ceilings were encircled with white molding, where small cherubs cavorted among grapes on twisted vines. It was a large room with an oversized marble fireplace. A huge portrait of an imperious-looking man dressed like an eighteenth-century lord stared out into the room. Her former boss, Avery Mitchell, had told her that it was Bell's father, who died in 1950.

She'd stopped in the doorway when she spotted a young man sitting in a chair in the corner. Hollis turned to Odelia with a questioning look.

"Oh, Ms. Morgan," Odelia said, "this is a reporter from the *San Lucian Daily*. He came after I spoke with you, and honestly," her voice dropped to a whisper, "he's been snooping around here for a story, and I didn't know what to do with him. Could you …?"

Hollis looked closely at the man, dressed in jeans, a white polo shirt, and a black linen sports coat. He appeared to be in his thirties, with thinning brown hair gelled into short spikes on the top of his head. He stood.

"Hi," he said, "my name is Kip Lyles. I'm a reporter for the *Daily*. I was in the emergency room when they brought Bell in, and I heard about his death." He came toward her with his hand outstretched. "Are you his attorney?"

Hollis shook his hand. "I didn't know the *Daily* was so on top of things. My name is Hollis Morgan, and yes, I'm Bell's probate attorney. Why are you here?"

He chuckled. "I'm the only reporter for the *Daily*. Mike Piper is the new editor. He was hired after Tony Nyland retired. Fortunately, I'm a trust fund baby, and I can afford to work for a small-town paper."

She waited without speaking for him to finish. He had said a lot without answering her question. He eventually caught on.

"Oh, I'm here to get background. Matthias Bell was a prominent citizen."

Hollis smothered a snicker. The *Daily* was four print pages long, with slightly longer online news content. In fact, it wasn't a daily, and hadn't been since the recession. It came out once a week on Wednesdays. They kept the name *Daily* on their masthead because they claimed to be on top of the news every day. She could imagine that Bell's death on their front page would be the equivalent of the collapsing of the upper deck of the Bay Bridge during the Loma Prieta Earthquake.

"Well, Mr. Lyles—"

"Kip."

"Well, Kip, I'm not sure what kind of background you're looking for. He died of a heart attack, and he was eighty-four years old. He's survived by a sister and niece. The rest of his life and business story you can probably Google." Hollis spoke with a little impatience. She was ready to move on.

"Okay." He nodded. "How large is his estate? Did he own a lot of assets? How did he make his money?" He grinned. "See, if I'm going to do a story, I have to get it in by tonight to make the Wednesday issue."

Hollis glanced at Odelia, so pale she might have been on the verge of a heart attack. Hollis walked over to her and led her to a nearby chair. She sat and gave Hollis a grateful look.

"I think you and I should speak later," Hollis said to the reporter. "Ms. Larson was a long-time employee, and this is a shock for her. I'm sure you understand." She led him firmly by his elbow out into the vestibule and gave him her business card. "Call my office tomorrow and make an appointment for us to talk." She didn't want to take the time for a meeting, so a call would be the compromise.

He took the obvious hint and let himself out the front door. Hollis saw him get into his Toyota and drive away. Taking a breath, she returned to the living room, where Odelia was staring off into space.

Hollis looked around. She had never been past the first floor. "Odelia, there will need to be a formal appraisal. How large is the house?"

"What?" Odelia broke out of her reverie. "Oh, there are twenty-seven rooms," she replied. "And besides me, there is a full-time cook and a housekeeper. That's one reason it was important for you to come as soon as possible. I wasn't counting on that young man being here. He's been a pest."

"He's gone. I'm meeting with him later. And Odelia, I've already met the other staff."

In fact, she'd enjoyed the other staff much more than she had Odelia. Angie, the cook, was from the South and served the best shrimp and grits Hollis had ever tasted. During her last visit, while she waited for Bell to finish a call so they could continue their meeting, Angie hadn't minded Hollis' visit to the kitchen. The cook had chatted amiably and let her sample a bread pudding that must have been delivered from heaven.

Hollis took the chair next to an end table and closest to a window that provided the single source of light. "I have to admit, I'm curious. What's the urgency?"

Odelia Larson slipped her hand into a pocket in her skirt and retrieved a beige envelope. She offered it to Hollis, who could see her firm's name on it. But before Hollis could take possession, Odelia pulled it back.

"Wait, before you read it, let me explain the circumstances under which I'm presenting it to you."

The familiar note of formality in Odelia's voice caused Hollis to resist her mounting impatience. She lowered her outstretched hand.

"All right, what is it you're supposed to tell me?"

Odelia straightened up to her full height. Even seated, she towered over Hollis.

"Mr. Bell was a very precise man. He could be demanding, but he was fair. He required the upmost loyalty and—"

"Odelia, I knew Matthias Bell. He left instructions with us

years ago in the event of his death." Hollis patted her briefcase. "What are these other circumstances you need to tell me about?"

She sighed. "Yes, of course. I'm sorry for drifting, but this has all come so sudden, and Mr. Bell wanted you to be contacted immediately in the case of … in the case of his death. Of course, you would have your own instructions." She held the letter in her lap. "We … the staff don't know where we stand. I mean what provisions were actually made to …. Well, Mr. Bell always assured me that we would be taken care of, but—"

"I think I understand your concerns." Hollis leaned back in her seat and counted to five before she spoke. "Perhaps if you could just give me his note, I could reassure you there is no need to worry." She pointed to the letter.

Odelia nodded, ignoring Hollis' hand. "Yes, yes, I'm being silly." She straightened her shoulders. "First, I will show you to the library, where you can read this letter containing his instructions and where you will be directed to the location of a box. Oh, and Mr. Bell wanted me to assure you that I have no information whatsoever to provide about his instructions. In fact, once you have been given his directions, I will be going home, and in a few weeks, I'm going to visit with my daughter and son-in-law in Chicago. The other staff members have also been informed and are prepared to leave immediately. So … there it is."

Her trembling hand still gripped the letter. They both rose and Odelia led her to an adjacent room, the library.

"I'll leave you to read it alone. But I'll be close by," Odelia said. One hand held the doorknob; the other held out the envelope.

It was all Hollis could do not to snatch the letter out of her hand.

"Thank you, I shouldn't be long."

Odelia bowed her head and backed out of the room, shutting the door with a loud click.

Hollis took a typewritten sheet out of her briefcase and placed it in front of her. She quickly read through Bell's original instructions for the second time; they were fairly straightforward. Then she reached for the most recent envelope and pulled out two sheets of paper, covered in Bell's almost unintelligible handwriting.

November 3, 2014

Dear Ms. Morgan,

I'm not sure when you will be reading this letter. Years, months, or days from now. It is ironic that I must rely on a young female attorney to settle my affairs and put things right. You see, I find working with ambitious females distasteful, but here you are. To your credit, had we been given enough time to know each other properly, I think I might have liked you. I like straightforward people, male or female. And more importantly, I find you trustworthy. But enough of this preface. Let me get to the substance of my instructions.

Hollis looked up and shook her head. Bell had chosen his words deliberately to taunt her. She went back to reading.

Miss Larson has been told to take you to my library. Tell her to leave. Go to my desk's lowest drawer and reach in the back for a black velvet box. Use the key your firm was holding for me to open it. Inside you will find three blank severance checks. Fill in the amounts for each person as shown on the yellow card at the bottom of the box and distribute them to my staff with my best wishes.

Also, I owe a special gift of gratitude to the Cornerstone Church in Daly City. Upon my death, provide them with a generous check. I will leave the amount to your discretion.

Now, as to my further instruction, I do not intend to

explain the rationale for my behavior. Your role is to simply follow my directions. When the house is empty of staff, take the key and go to the safe located behind my father's portrait in the living room. Use the combination in the bottom of this box. Inside the safe you will find a metal box. Use the key to open it. Inside are four large envelopes. Each envelope contains a contact sheet. You are to return the contents of the envelope to the party indicated. In some cases, there may be a need to disperse cash, in which case, as I've stated in my trust, use the proceeds from my estate to settle any demands you deem appropriate.

I'm tired of writing. So, I must leave you on your own to follow my instructions. If you make a mess of things, then the joke is on me.

M.M.B

Hollis raised her eyebrows at the abrupt ending, but she supposed there was little more for him to say. She was mildly surprised at his bequeath to a church, since he'd always ranted about the uselessness of religion, but it wasn't unusual for the elderly to cover all their bases.

If not for Bell's advanced legal directive giving Odelia Larson the authority to provide any miscellaneous communications in the event of his demise, she would have questioned the letter. But it was no wonder he and Odelia got along so well; they both had the same off-putting personalities and tone. Fortunately, her intuition had told her to bring Bell's key with her. She took a small manila envelope out of her briefcase and shook its contents, a flat gold key, into her hand.

She glanced at the summary page that she'd retrieved from Bell's trust files, which was pretty standard. It required her to ask staff for their keys to the house, then to make sure that it, and its contents, were readied for sale as soon as deemed feasible. As executors, Triple D was to liquidate his assets for distribution to his beneficiaries.

It didn't take long to retrieve the black velvet box. It lay on top of a stack of correspondence at the front of the drawer. She located the blank checks. They were already written out; all she had to do was date them. Opening the door to the hallway, she found Odelia sitting thin-lipped and prim in a hall chair. She stood as Hollis walked over.

"Odelia," Hollis said, "when did you say Mr. Bell gave you this letter for me? It's dated some years ago."

Odelia Larson's brow wrinkled. "Yes, well, that's when he entrusted it to me for safekeeping." She pursed her lips in thought. "Let me see, it was before he left for New York … or was it after? No, it was before. I remember because we were having the carpets cleaned so it was in the spring. So a few …. No, it wasn't then. I'm sorry, Ms. Morgan, this has me all flustered. He just told me to give it to you in the event of his death, so I did."

Hollis counted to ten before speaking. "Had he been ill? The tone of his letter seems to anticipate some health issue."

"No," she said, "I don't think so. Although you know Mr. Bell was a very private man, and while he counted on me tremendously, he may have kept something like his health to himself."

Hollis nodded in agreement. Bell was not one to express any personal feelings, and the state of his health would likely never be shared.

"Odelia, Mr. Bell left a severance check for you." Hollis handed over the six-figure check. "He wanted me to thank you for your many years of loyal service and to give you his best wishes." She added the latter, thinking it would be a nice touch.

Hollis noticed Odelia's stern expression and thin, pressed lips.

"He told me he'd made provisions for us." She reached for the check but hardly looked at it. A rush of red climbed up her neck. "A hundred thousand dollars … I … I don't know what to say."

Hollis smiled. "I can imagine his generosity has caught you off guard."

"What?" Odelia's head jerked up, and she snapped, "No, you've got it wrong. He owed me close to a quarter million. He promised me. He said he would set me up in a house in Daly City." She waved the check in front of Hollis' face. "He *owed* me."

Oh, great.

Hollis' brain scrambled to come up with a proper response, but she could only mumble, "I'm sorry, but this is all I have for you."

Odelia took a giant step into Hollis' personal space. "You're a lawyer, right? Well, I can get a lawyer, too." She pulled the sweater she was wearing over her chest. "I'm leaving, so you're on your own."

She started down the hallway.

Hollis grimaced. "Er, Odelia … Mrs. Larson, according to the instructions Mr. Bell left for us, I must ask you and the rest of the staff to turn in your keys immediately. He wants us to put the house on the market right away. I'll need your keys before you go. All your keys, please."

HOLLIS WANDERED AROUND THE ROOM, waiting for Odelia to return. A short time later she did, carting two small boxes of personal items. Then she abruptly left, tossing her keys on the hallway carpet. Hollis was on guard with the remaining distribution of the checks. Fortunately, the other staff had already packed their things. Angie was tearfully pleased and the housekeeper appeared to be satisfied. There was no problem collecting their keys.

"I can tell you why Mrs. Larson's upset," Angie said in response to Hollis' question about Odelia's reaction. "She called herself a professional, and we were the workers." She chuckled, "I guess she's been humbled."

After waving goodbye, Hollis glanced at her phone for the time. She had a three o'clock conference call and about forty minutes to make it back to the office. She went into the living room and quickly realized that she would need a small ladder in order to reach behind the portrait over the fireplace.

The things I do for clients.

She found a stool in the kitchen pantry and carried it into the living room. Climbing to the top step, she could only reach the bottom of the portrait frame. She tugged; it was stuck.

Pulling from both sides of the frame, she still couldn't get it to give way. She slid the stool to the opposite end and repeated her effort.

It wouldn't budge.

More than a little frustrated, Hollis knew she would need a ladder or a taller person to help. She gathered her purse, locked up the house, and headed back to the office.

An hour later, when Hollis pulled into her parking spot in Triple D's garage, she was pretty much over her meeting with Odelia Larson. The day was almost gone, and she tried not to think of the cases sitting in her basket. When she reached Triple D's lobby, she leaned over the reception counter and spoke to Tiffany.

"Can you come with me on an errand tomorrow?" Hollis asked. "Penny is at paralegal training, and you're the only one here I can think of who might be able to help me."

Tiffany turned her head to the right and to the left. "Are you asking *me* for help, Hollis?"

Hollis smiled. "Yes, I'll explain later. I'm almost late for a conference call, but I was hoping tomorrow morning you would come back with me to the Matthias Bell estate. Bell was a difficult man and evidently he went to a great deal of trouble to put several envelopes in a safe over the fireplace. But I can't reach it since I'm height-challenged." She put a wide clown grin on her face. "But you're five feet eight."

The receptionist mustered a weak smile and said in a low tone, "Sure, I don't mind. I'll get one of the interns to cover the front desk."

Hollis' eyes narrowed. "What's the matter? You don't have to, you know. You've been asking if I could find something different for you to do, and I thought you might like to see what my world looks like. I should be able to get one of the guys to come. I'd ask Vince, but he took two days off to finish his finals."

"I said I would do it." Tiffany waved her hand and almost knocked over her Starbucks Venti, catching it mid-fall before losing too much of its contents over her desk. She quickly snatched up a few napkins and contained the spill. Her cheeks turned red.

"Tiffany, you haven't been yourself lately. Come on, tell me, what's going on?"

Tiffany looked up and opened her mouth as if about to speak, but she closed it again and shook her head.

"Maybe later, but not right now." Her voice stronger, she glanced at the lobby clock. "You'd better get to your office. You're going to be late for your conference call."

CHAPTER THREE

Tuesday

THE NEXT MORNING TIFFANY COULDN'T get anyone to sit in for her at the reception desk until nine. Hollis was eager to start out sooner, but she used the time to put a couple of files on Penny's desk for processing. At a few minutes before nine, she was getting ready to leave when her phone buzzed.

"Hollis," Tiffany said, "a Mr. Lyles is here. He said he doesn't have an appointment, but he just wanted to pop in."

Hollis was amused by the irritation in Tiffany's voice. The receptionist hated clients who "popped" in to see their attorneys.

"I'll speak with him in the lobby," she said and then added, "I'm ready to go. We'll leave as soon as I finish with Mr. Lyles."

Hollis grabbed her briefcase and purse and strode to the lobby. Lyles leaned over Tiffany's desk.

"Mr. Lyles," she said pointedly, shifting her briefcase to her left hand so she could shake his with her right, "you must have X-ray vision. I just came into the office for a few minutes before setting off on an appointment. This is not a good time. My paralegal told me you called and that she scheduled a phone appointment for later this week."

His beaming smile was clearly an attempt at charm. It was wasted on her.

He laughed. "I thought you were going to call me Kip. No matter, I was just hoping for a quick quote for this Wednesday's paper. Or maybe something more than a quote?"

Tiffany was motioning that she was ready to go. The intern covering her desk was already intercepting calls.

"Look Mr. Lyles ... Kip," Hollis snapped, "the only quote I have for you right now is: no comment." Noticing his flinch, she softened her tone. "Look, why don't you make this a two-part story? Keep your loyal San Lucian readers on the edge of their seats." She edged toward the door. "This week, just write about Bell's background, and next week you can detail his recent good works and business dealings. And there's his funeral. Maybe that will generate some interest."

Lyles looked skeptical. "Well, that's an idea for this Wednesday. Perhaps we can talk about part two when we meet on Friday? A phone call is not really adequate."

A weekly paper had to have pretty flexible deadlines. But rather than extend the conversation, she wanted to get back to the Bell mansion without this human mosquito following her.

"All right, I'll see you Friday at four."

HOLLIS AND TIFFANY DROVE LARGELY in quiet. San Lucian was a compact community in the East Bay nestled between San Leandro and San Lorenzo. Its tree-lined streets were clustered at the base of rolling hills that crested with views of the Golden Gate, San Francisco Bay, and San Mateo Bridges framing the city. Hollis glanced over at Tiffany's stiff figure. She stared straight ahead.

Hollis honored Tiffany's silence. She hated it when people tried to draw her out, particularly when she clearly wasn't interested in talking. She respected Tiffany's preference to keep what was bothering her to herself, but it was hard.

The Bell living room was just as Hollis had left it, with the stool standing in front of the fireplace.

"You want me to pull at it from the side middle?" Tiffany asked. She could reach from the ladder's second step.

Hollis held the ladder steady. "Yeah, tug at it, but brace yourself in case it pulls open fast."

Tiffany nodded and yanked at the gold-scrolled portrait frame. It came away easily from the wall. "There's a safe all right. Do you have the combination?"

Hollis took a slip of paper from the pocket in her slacks and called out, "Okay, it's not too complicated. Go back and forth left and right with each number. Left to 12, right to 25, left to 19, right to 45."

"Hmmm, that's Christmas 1945," Tiffany offered.

The door gave an audible pop.

"There's just a metal box." Tiffany reached in, lifted out a gray metal document box with a padlock, and handed it to Hollis. Closing the safe, she pushed the framed portrait back over the opening and stepped down.

Hollis placed the box on the coffee table.

Tiffany leaned over her shoulder. "I hope you have a key. That lock looks like something they'd use at Fort Knox."

It was an ordinary legal letter-sized box, but Tiffany was right, the lock seemed oversized for the container, and while the box wasn't particularly heavy, Hollis could tell it was full. Sitting on the sofa, she pulled it toward her. She dug in her pocket for the key and inserted it in the lock.

There were four thick manila envelopes, each with a name across the middle written in black Sharpie. Hollis and Tiffany glanced at each other in surprise.

"It's going to take a while to go through all this," Hollis said, putting the envelopes back in the box and locking it again. "I'm going to take the envelopes back to the office and open them there."

"Sure," Tiffany agreed, "they may be confidential." Although she worked for a law firm, she had no problem staying out of client issues. She'd told Hollis that she tended to think that the less she knew the better.

In a few minutes, they had made sure the house was secure and were driving back to the office.

"Now, do you want to tell me what's been bothering you?" Hollis ventured, sneaking a quick side glance at the stoic-looking receptionist.

Tiffany sighed but said nothing.

Hollis said, "I'm not one for sharing, but I'm willing to listen, and you know it won't go any further."

Tiffany turned to face her. "How old do you think I am?"

Hollis frowned. "Ah … I never thought about it. I'm not very good at guessing ages."

Tiffany continued to stare at her.

"Well, I'd guess, er, twenty-four?"

Tiffany's lips tightened, and she slammed her back against her seat and said with exasperation, "Point made."

Despite Hollis' urging, she refused to engage in an explanation of what point had been made, and when they returned to the office, she acted as if nothing had been said.

Tiffany nodded at the intern to let her know that she could return to the administrative office. Slipping her purse into a bottom drawer, she sat down in the chair.

"Hollis, do you want me to log those envelopes in?"

"Er, yes." Hollis placed the box on top of the counter and lifted out each envelope for Tiffany to time-stamp and log in.

It didn't take long, and Hollis was ready to move on to her office. "You know, Tiffany, about the other … we can always talk and—"

"Of course." Tiffany gave her a forced smile and pointed to the ringing phone line before picking it up.

Hollis nodded and went to her office.

She saw the small stack of pink message slips sitting in the middle of her desk and quickly pushed them aside. Her curiosity was piqued. Placing the security box on the floor, she took out the first envelope. The name on the outside wasn't familiar: Anthony Cantone.

The envelope had a simple clasp, and she dumped the contents. On top was a sheet of paper with an address and phone number. Behind that was an accountant's log sheet with a list of dates and associated dollar amounts. The entries dated back four years.

She focused on the dozen or so black and white prints of canceled checks, airline tickets, and hotel receipts and frowned. The dates on the documents varied, but the most recent was three years prior. Turning to her computer keyboard, she clicked on the firm's PeopleSearch icon and typed in Anthony Cantone's name. The PeopleSearch database was the firm's answer to background checking using public information. Education, vital statistics, law-enforcement encounters, and in some cases links to newspaper articles would spill out and provide a snapshot of a person's life. After a few moments of searching, fifteen records scrolled down the page.

Born in Long Beach, California, Cantone was forty-six years old and currently lived in Piedmont, California. He owned an architectural firm located in Carmel Village that had been in operation there for the last eight years. He and his wife of nine years, Constance, had two children: a son, Noah, nine and a daughter, Frances, seven.

Tapping on her door jamb diverted her attention.

"Excuse me, Hollis." Her paralegal Penny approached, holding two appeal volumes. "Can I see you about the Irving case you gave me to research?"

Hollis glanced up. "I thought you were in training." She went back to her screen.

"I was. The class is over." She tilted her head. "You do know it's almost six o'clock? Everybody is gone for the day."

Hollis noted the time in the corner of her computer monitor.

"What? Oh, great! I was supposed to get home early." She chewed her bottom lip. "Look, I have to finish going through the items in this envelope. In fact, I'll likely need your help with some other filings. Why don't we get together in the morning first thing, and we'll go over the Irving case and a new matter I just received."

Penny gave her an "okay" sign and left. Hollis went back to the envelope.

Other than a few parking tickets and a couple of minor moving violations, Cantone had no other law enforcement contacts. She was surprised to see that the largest section of information came from a series of newspaper articles about his wife, Constance Cantone, who was the daughter of Matthias Bell's sister Gloria, and her husband, a Silicon Valley guru. She stopped reading.

Constance Cantone was *that* Constance. Hollis replayed her conversation with Gloria Bell Havers.

Gloria's husband had died of a heart attack fifteen years ago. Their daughter Constance was a popular socialite and supported several national and international charities. An article included a photo of her at Lincoln Center, standing in for her father, who had received an award for his support of artists from low-income neighborhoods.

In fact, all the articles were about Constance, except for a small one written eight years earlier announcing the opening of Anthony Cantone's Carmel Valley office.

Hollis checked on his education and employment background. After high school graduation, he'd gone to San Francisco State for a year and then transferred to Stanford University. There he received honors and worked for three years in a Palo Alto office before starting out on his own.

Her direct phone line rang, and she picked it up.

"Hi, I'm on my way out the door."

"Liar," John said. "I thought we were going out for Chinese."

"We are. I got involved in a new case and time slipped away." Noting the silence on the other end, she added, "I'm on my way now, honest."

"Hurry up, I'm hungry," John said, sounding resigned. "But don't drive fast. See you when you get here."

Hollis hurriedly shoved all the materials back into the envelope and turned off her computer. Picking up her purse and keys, she noticed the blinking messages waiting on her phone. They would have to wait. She could tell from her fiancé's tone of voice this was no time to stretch his patience. She locked the door to her office and rapidly made her way to the elevator.

WHEN SHE ARRIVED HOME, JOHN was sitting on the sofa watching CNN with a Corona in his hand. She kissed him and was gratified to be forgiven and kissed back.

She put her things on the dining room table and sat down beside him. "I'm sorry, honey. I know we said we would have an early dinner, but … no excuses. I just blew it."

John Faber was the love of her life. His olive complexion, dark hair, and darker eyes underscored the seriousness of his outlook. But for all that, Hollis was drawn to his quick wit, charming smile, and the fact that he loved her.

He turned to her now, giving her a long look and an impish smile. "As long as you admit you were wrong, I absolve you." He gave her a peck on the forehead. "Now, let's go eat. I'm starving."

Dinner was at their second favorite restaurant, Milly's in San Leandro. It served a Chinese and Mexican fusion cuisine. None of their friends could understand their liking of the odd menu, but Hollis and John had gotten to know Juan and Lily, the owners. The food was a little quirky, but delicious, and the service and atmosphere made it fun and enjoyable.

They placed their order and chatted briefly with the waiter, who without being asked brought Hollis' green tea and John's Tsing-Tao.

"Okay, so tell me about this new case," John said, leaning back on the curve of the booth.

That was another thing she loved about him. He always asked about her work and her day, even though his was much more interesting and dangerous. When they first met, he was a police detective, but his own ambition and sense of justice caused him to seek a career with the Homeland Security Agency. It was a good move; he thrived there.

She recounted the meeting with Odelia and described the contents of Bell's safe. "I'm still trying to figure it out." She took a sip of tea. "I'm executor for an estate whose owner was eccentric and rude. I'm to follow his instructions by locating these designated individuals and returning packets of what initially appears to be miscellaneous but suspicious-looking material. I'm still going through the first envelope." She stopped herself and picked up his hand. "But what about you? How was your day in hush-hush land?"

She kept her voice light, trying to suppress her concern. John loved his work with Homeland Security's Special Projects division. Once he'd pointed to a crime bust on a television news segment where he'd been involved, and she'd suddenly realized what it meant to love someone in law enforcement.

Their food arrived. If John was starving earlier, his appetite was much reduced now. He picked at his favorite egg rolls.

"It's going good. In fact, I'm getting a new project, and if I do well, I'll be in line for a promotion." He cleared his throat. "I'm taking an undercover assignment."

The announcement hung in the air.

Hollis sat up straighter in her seat. "You're going undercover … doing what? How long?"

"It won't be long, babe, two to three weeks, a month at the most."

"A month," she murmured, feeling a twist in her gut.

He lifted her chin so she could see his eyes. "Hey, I've had undercover duty before. It's over before you know it."

"You mean, before *you* know it."

Hollis wasn't a worrier, and she knew John was the finest there was. Still, she would be without her best friend and his wise counsel. She heaved a sigh.

"Without looking too happy, tell me the details."

A grin eased across his face. "I can't tell you a lot about what I'll be doing, but I'll be doing it in Washington State."

For the next minutes, he described the makeup of the insert team and the rough timeline for getting their job done. His appetite picked up, and she heard his excitement through the muffled pillow of her thoughts.

"When do you leave?" she asked in what she hoped was a breezy tone.

"On Thursday," he said. He held up his hand when he saw her protest forming. "The sooner I leave, the sooner I'll be back."

She lightly brushed the back of her hand against his cheek. "Just be back."

CHAPTER FOUR

—∿∿—

Wednesday

IT WAS ALMOST TEN A.M. before Hollis was able to finish work with Penny and turn her attention to the second envelope retrieved from Bell's safe. The name on the outside was Naomi Eaton. The envelope was much lighter than Cantone's and she quickly emptied the contents out onto her desk.

The first was a single page from a 2010 desk-pad calendar for the month of June.

Hollis wrinkled her brow and squinted to read the tiny handwriting that filled various boxes under the days of the week. The entries primarily consisted of names, times, and what appeared to be a four-digit code. Other entries appeared to be appointment reminders. She could see no meaningful information. The only other item in the envelope was a sheet of paper containing Eaton's address and phone number.

Hollis pushed the button for Penny's extension and asked her to come to her office.

"What's up?" Penny asked.

"Take a look at this." Hollis handed over the page. "I'd like you to make a list of the entries by date. While you're at it, see if you can make sense of what it all means. You're faster at deciphering handwriting than I am."

Penny looked curiously at the paper. "Should I bill my hours to the Bell matter?"

Hollis nodded. "Right now, Bell is my priority. I want to finish processing his estate as soon as possible."

After Penny departed, she picked up the next, much larger packet. The name on the outside was Jeremiah Griffin. Hollis was perplexed. What was Bell up to? She kept recalling his disapproval of female professionals, and if this was an attempt to goad her even after his death, he was succeeding.

Once again, she tilted out the envelope's contents. This time she found stapled printouts of approximately a dozen emails. The emails were clamped to an inch-high stack of letters and memos on "Jordan Manufacturing" letterhead.

And, as with the other two envelopes, there was a single sheet of plain paper with Griffin's contact information.

She turned to her keyboard and typed in "Jordan Manufacturing." It was a fabrication company located in Burlingame, not far from the San Francisco Airport. Its website was low profile, offering up only a picture of a two-story building, address, phone number, and email contact. On the "About Us" page, sixteen employees wearing short-sleeved blue-denim shirts stood in a half-circle and grinned into the camera. Hollis wondered if the white-shirted, confident looking man in the center was Griffin.

While she was tempted to read through the correspondence, she placed it back in the envelope. Right now she only wanted to get an idea of what was contained in each, and she had one more to go.

She turned to the fourth and thickest envelope. There were two names across the front: Ian and Millicent Pittman.

The first thing she noticed was that the Pittmans' packet held two passports in the names of Weatherly. The next item she lifted was a gun permit for a Glock, equipped with a laser and issued in Texas five years before.

The bulk of the remaining contents were receipts going back ten years. The most recent was a medical bill for a doctor's visit dated six months ago.

She raised her eyebrows. What was going on?

Hollis took out a pad and made columns: who, what, where, and when. After listing the names, she noted the content of the envelopes and the location of the owners: two in the Bay Area, one in Sacramento, and one in Carmel Valley. She leaned back in her chair. She could see no connection between the individuals.

Her phone buzzed.

"Hollis, if you want to see Gordon, he's free now," Tiffany said. "His next appointment is in thirty minutes."

Hollis gathered up her pad, a pen, and the Cantone envelope and headed for her manager's office. Gordon Barrett had been a partner with Triple D for four years, but she rarely worked with him since his practice was almost exclusively criminal law. George's departure had given her the opportunity to move up, but it also required that her work be overseen by one of the law partners. Barrett had worked with George and now she'd inherited him.

When she poked her head in his office, he was on his phone. He waved her in and then turned to face his window. Taking a calming breath, she gazed out at the view. Gordon had a corner office with uninterrupted floor-to-ceiling glass windows. The grandeur of the Bay and Golden Gate Bridges was on one side and the San Rafael Bridge on the other. It was just as well that the view from her own office was less distracting, showcasing only Angel Island and the Berkeley hills.

Gordon's voice was rising and he swirled around to pick up his cellphone. "Let me check my calendar," he muttered as he scrolled through the screen. "Look, I can't make any promises. You violated parole. The judge doesn't care about your excuses or how philanthropic your family is. He will likely send you back. Uh-huh ... uh-huh .... Okay, I'll talk to the DA and get back to you." He clicked off. He held up his hand when Hollis moved to speak and pushed the intercom button. "Tiffany, give me twenty minutes with Hollis then get Fred on the phone. I need to talk to him before my next appointment."

He looked at Hollis and smiled. "Sorry," he said, "you've got my full attention."

"For," Hollis leaned in to look at the clock on his desk, "nineteen minutes. So I'd better hurry."

She quickly took him through the saga of Bell: his instructions, the dismissal of his staff, and her discovery of the safe's contents. While she spoke, Barrett reached for the Cantone envelope and dumped its contents on his desk. He quickly flipped through it.

"Do the rest of the envelopes have the same kind of stuff?"

Hollis shook her head. "No, they're all different, seemingly all unique to the individual." Hollis noticed he stole a glance at the clock as he shoved the paperwork back into its container.

"What's your plan?"

She could feel her brow creasing in a frown. "Gordon, doesn't this all sound a bit suspicious to you?" She leaned forward. "I mean, even my cursory assessment of what appears to be questionable information is that we're looking at blackmail."

He gave an impatient wave of his hand.

"Okay, let's say our client was a blackmailer. It appears he's returning his victims' dirty laundry and attempting to redeem himself. What's the crime? Our job is to inform these people that they are off what could be a very nasty hook."

Hollis shook her head slightly. "Well, then, I'm going to meet with Cantone first," she said. "That's the one you're looking at. I'll give him the envelope, have him sign an affidavit, and leave. That's my plan."

He nodded. "Look, I agree this is a bit unsavory. But our job is to represent our client, and I'm trusting you know how to do your job because I'm not a close supervisor."

Gordon glanced at the clock and then back at her. "What do you think your billables will be?"

Hollis hoped she'd hidden her surprise. "Er, I don't know. It's going to include local travel, and it may be a while before I can meet with everyone." She paused to think. "Rather than quote a number I can't defend, let me get back to you once I accomplish the first delivery."

"Good answers, but from now on, when you brief me on a new matter, always have an estimate of your billable hours. You'll discover that as one of our senior attorneys, you're expected to keep the firm's profits healthy and ongoing."

"Not a problem." She gave him a slight mock bow.

"In fact, let's set up a time when we can go over how I like to work." As he picked up his smartphone, he gave her an appraising look. "By the way, the color of your suit is very flattering."

George had never questioned how or where she spent her time, but to be fair, he was the one who was accountable to the partners. Gordon Barrett was considered an excellent asset to the firm. His practice centered on keeping the rich out of jail, and they were willing to pay a great deal to ensure that he did.

Hollis ignored his compliment about her attire. Barrett was a good-looking divorcé. Rumor had it he wasn't shy about reaching out to Triple D's female lawyers for companionship.

After agreeing to a meeting time, she left, keeping her expression neutral.

BACK AT HER DESK, SHE punched in Anthony Cantone's contact number. The call went straight to an answering machine.

"Mr. Cantone, my name is Hollis Morgan. I'm calling for Matthias Bell. He—"

"Wait. I'm here," Cantone replied in a high-pitched voice. "Who did you say you were?"

Hollis cleared her throat. "My name is Hollis Morgan and—"

"Hold on. How do you spell your name?"

She spelled it slowly.

"Okay, got it. By the way, I want you to know I'm taping this conversation," he said in a rushed voice. "What does Bell want now?"

"Mr. Cantone, Mr. Bell died last weekend—"

He gasped, "Bell's dead?"

"Yes. I'm responsible for settling his estate. He left—"

"Well, I know he didn't leave me anything, the crook."

She hurried on, cutting off any further interruptions, "Mr. Cantone, it seems like you have a lot of … questions. Would it be possible to meet with you later this week or perhaps next week? I can deliver a package he left for you. It won't require much of your time."

There was silence on the other end.

Then he said, "So you're acting for Bell?"

"I'm the executor of his trust," Hollis said, trying to contain her exasperation. "I don't want to go into any details on the phone because I would prefer to discuss them in person. Are you available this week or next?"

"Er, uh, yeah, let's make it Thursday afternoon, say one o'clock. My office is in Carmel Valley just outside Carmel By the Sea."

"I have your address," she said jotting down the appointment in her calendar. "I'll see you then."

"Fine, fine, so you're sure Bell is dead?"

After the meeting with Gordon and the call with Cantone, Hollis needed a cup of tea to push back her agitation and increasing suspicions. On her return from the break room, she sipped the jasmine brew and passed by the front desk, where she picked up her messages, enough to form a small pile. She had just closed her office door when her direct line rang.

"Hello, Rebecca, it's Rita."

Hollis froze. She hadn't heard her birth name used for some time. She responded, "Hi Ri, I just saw your message that you've been trying to reach me this morning. I was getting ready to call you." She paused. "I'm sorry; it's been a busy morning. Is everything all right? Why didn't you call me at home?"

Rita was Hollis' older sister by two years. Never close, their relationship had been strained ever since Hollis' incarceration and release. It had improved only minimally after she was pardoned. Rebecca Hollis Morgan was her maiden name, but Rita, and the rest of the family, refused to call her by anything but Rebecca. Even though she'd informed them that she was using her middle name as a sign of her fresh start at a new life.

"Rebecca," Rita said, "I don't have time to go over what I didn't do, and I don't have long to talk. I have to get back to Mother." She sighed and then said in a rush, "Yesterday, we heard from Joe's unit's that his return is delayed again."

Hollis couldn't stop her intake of breath. Her younger brother, her *only* brother, was the single person in the family who hadn't judged her after her sentencing, and the only family member who'd kept in contact with her.

"Was he on a mission?" Her voice held a slight tremor.

"Becca, I don't know." Rita paused and gave another deep sigh. "They told us they would get back to us immediately if his status changes. His status … good grief."

"Can I do anything?" Hollis asked, noticing that her sister had used her nickname, a sign she was relaxing.

"This call isn't about Joe. Come home, Becca," Rita said haltingly, and then in a stronger voice, "Mother wants to see you. Come home, Becca."

Hollis sat quietly, gazing out the window in her office at the stretch of traffic leading across the Bay Bridge to San Francisco. Only it wasn't the traffic she was seeing, it was her family that occupied her thoughts.

She had made peace with her status in the family. Rita, the older by two years, was perfect, Joseph, who followed her by four years, was the handsome darling, and she was the black sheep. To be fair, she hadn't carried that label until she married Bill Lynley and had gotten embroiled in his illegal insurance schemes. Up until that time, she was just considered "different." Her parents were not equipped to deal with emotions, good or bad, and Hollis' compulsion to come to the aid of those in need or who had been wronged made her family uncomfortable.

She smiled, remembering her mother's plea: "Rebecca, why do you always have to get involved? It's none of your business."

"Because I can help," she answered, after realizing it was her truth.

But this was long before her family had turned their backs on her in the courtroom when she was sentenced. During her eighteen months in prison, she came to doubt herself and her beliefs.

The eight years since her release, with only minimal contact with her sister, and scattered, brief phone calls with her father and brother, had left her with an emptiness she'd locked away. And other than secondhand inquiries concerning her health, she had not spoken to her mother since her imprisonment.

Now, her mother wanted to see her.

Gordon Barrett was almost dismissive when Hollis told him she would be leaving for a couple of days to take care of a family issue.

"I hope everything is okay," he said, not looking up from his keyboard. "Hey, do what you have to do." He turned to her and flashed a sincere smile. "Good luck. If you need more time, just leave me a message."

Hollis drove to her condo from work in a daze. She had not seen her family since they'd witnessed her insurance fraud conviction and sentence to prison. They'd never been a close family. Actually, if anything, they were more dysfunctional than most. When the judge brought down the gavel on her future, she exchanged looks with her mother, Ava Morgan, and her mother turned her back and walked away.

Hollis' father, Jack, hadn't been well at the time. Tears slipping from his eyes, he had tried to reach out and give her a hug, but the guards blocked his path.

That was the worst day of her life.

Jack Morgan didn't express emotion very well. None of them did. So Hollis could only imagine the pain he must have felt to show those tears. It haunted her still.

Her mother was another story. She and Rita were just alike. Tall and beautiful, judgmental and petty, and neither spared any criticism when it came to Hollis. Her mother didn't hesitate to tell her that the family had only come to the last day of the trial because Hollis' attorney insisted it would arouse the sympathy of the judge and jury.

Replaying Rita's call in her head, Hollis shivered. Why would her mother want to see her now? She hadn't responded to Hollis' calls when she'd been given a pardon, or graduated from law school, or had been sworn in as an attorney. Her mother had maintained stony silence, and to Hollis' dismay, her father had largely followed his wife's lead.

Hollis pulled into her garage. John, already home, had his suitcases out on the bed. He was watching a basketball game as he went back and forth from closet to his dresser with shirts and underwear for his trip.

"You're home early," she said as she offered her lips for a light kiss.

After the kiss, he drew back and gave her a critical glance. "And you're home late. What's the matter? I can tell from your face, there's something going on."

"Don't you ever tire of being a detective?" she said wearily, slumping back on the lounge chair and lifting her feet on the rest.

Regarding her solemnly, John raised the remote to shut off the TV.

"Talk to me," he said, patting the bed for her to come and sit next to him.

"I heard from my sister," Hollis said. As she plumped up a pillow, she recounted Rita's news about Joe.

John tilted her chin up. "But there's something else."

She snuggled next to his chest. "They want the prodigal daughter to come home for a visit."

He gave her a squeeze of understanding.

"Look, I need to finish packing. Let's have a fast meal out and get back home. You can help me finish getting ready and then we can talk."

Hollis nodded.

They dined at a popular neighborhood café. They kept the talk easy, and soon John had Hollis laughing about some of the "characters" on his job.

"You don't have the corner on characters," she chuckled. "Try working at Triple D." They finished dinner on a high note.

Later, when they were back home, Hollis lay on the bed folding John's socks into efficient rolls that would fit neatly in his softcover suitcase. He was chatting away about "the team" and how they felt more like brothers.

"Do you have a team sister?" she teased.

John looked up toward the ceiling. "Now that you mention it—"

She tossed a sock at him. He caught it midair and sat down next to her.

"Okay, let's talk. You've been um … preoccupied since you got home. It's not just the call from your family, is it? There's more to it."

"How can you say that? I've been talking all evening. Besides, this thing with going to see Mother, well, I admit it has me on guard." She sighed, then told him about Bell and the safe full of file folders. She added, "And then with you leaving, I—"

He placed a finger over her lips. "Don't."

Hollis nodded. "Sorry." She patted his hand, and then

brought it to her lips. "I'm used to you being here or at least knowing where you are. This time ... this time, you'll just be out there."

"You're not worried, are you?"

"Who me, worry?"

They exchanged long looks and then kissed deeply. After a moment, they pulled away and Hollis pointed to his suitcase.

"Come on, we need to finish this," she said.

He stood and bowed then returned to his packing, placing a bulky sweater in the bag. "If I understand what you've been saying, thanks to Bell you have a new job assignment as a high-paid delivery girl. Is it true you're giving out free pizzas?"

"Very funny." Hollis shook her head in frustration. "I'm beginning to think that Matthias Bell deliberately set me up."

She told him about her conversation with Cantone.

"It sounds like blackmail to me," she said, tossing a folded t-shirt in his bag. "But when I briefed Gordon, he nonchalantly told me it wasn't my concern if Bell was a blackmailer."

John shrugged. "Let's say he was a blackmailer. Could it be that you're too sensitive to the fact that Bell was a crook, and now that he's dead, can't be punished? On the other hand, he wasn't all bad; he decided to release his victims."

"That's just it, John." She deftly squeezed his favorite pair of Dockers into the suitcase. "Bell was a jerk. I can't see him fearing the afterlife enough to give his victims back their lives."

"So, now what are you saying?"

"I don't know what I'm saying. I just ... ugh."

John pulled her to him again, and their long, liquid kiss rushed through her. He stood, taking his garment bag off the bed to hang on the door.

"Do you think we can put aside Mr. Bell for the evening? I'm going to be gone for almost a month, and it would be real nice if ..." He slid the suitcase to the floor and turned to her. "If, uh, we could make up for anticipated lost time."

"I thought you'd never ask," she murmured and pulled him to her.

CHAPTER FIVE

Thursday

JOHN'S TAXI WAS SCHEDULED TO arrive just before dawn. Hollis scrambled to help him get all his gear together, and finally they stood amid his bags in the front entry.

"Don't forget the phones. I'll try to text you whenever I get a chance," he said, holding her in his arms. He kissed the top of her head. "And don't keep any of the phones; destroy each one as soon as you get my message."

John had come up with an idea to mitigate his absence by purchasing a dozen toss-away phones before he left for his undercover assignment. It was the only way he would contact her, to let her know he was okay and thinking of her. Cautious, he didn't want his calls to be traced. The phone numbers were in the order of his planned calls. So she would always know which phone to bring with her next.

"Yes, sir," she mumbled into his chest. "I double-checked. They're all numbered to match your phones so you can call down the list, and—"

"And I triple-checked," he said. He looked out the window.

"I've got to go. The taxi's here." He gave her a squeeze. "Good luck with your family. I love you."

She tilted her head back for his kiss.

Hollis hated clingy people. Their neediness left her feeling inadequate; she never felt she could be the answer they were seeking. As her eyes followed John's progress down the walkway, she had a momentary insight into how needy people felt. She didn't want to think she needed him, but over the next month, it would be as if a part of her was in Washington.

LATER THAT MORNING AT HER desk, Hollis finished signing correspondence and returned the documents to Penny's inbox. Grabbing her jacket, phones, and purse, she checked one more time to make sure she had everything. She shoved Bell's file and Cantone's envelope into her briefcase.

Hollis left a message for Gordon Barrett re-confirming she was combining work with family business and would be back in the office Thursday afternoon. She left a similar note on Tiffany's desk and asked that her calls be forwarded to Penny. Finally, she headed for the parking garage.

The trip to Palo Alto wasn't as bad as it could have been, since Hollis chose to make the freeway drive early in the morning. Now, cruising down Highway 880, she noted that the vast majority of commuters had passed and the worst of the traffic accidents had cleared. As she crossed the San Mateo Bridge, summer fog clung to the hills of the peninsula side of the bay, and soon she left the bright East Bay Area sun for chilly gray clouds. She grinned. She loved it.

Hollis' childhood home was in Alameda. Her parents had moved to Palo Alto after her brother Joe got accepted to Stanford. She smiled, remembering how disappointed he was that he wouldn't be able to leave Mom and Dad behind. After two years, he'd joined the Marines.

After driving along Palo Alto's Oregon Expressway and turning into one of the city's oldest neighborhoods, she pulled up in front of a small, single-story Craftsman home. Rita's Land Rover was in the driveway, in front was her Dad's '74 Honda.

"Hello," Hollis called out and rapped on the door. Peering through the screen, she couldn't see anyone in the living room. She raised her voice, "Dad, Rita, I'm at the front door."

There were hurried footsteps.

"Rebecca, stop yelling. I can hear you." Rita took the latch off the door. "We're on the sunporch. Don't forget to wipe your shoes and put your coat in the hall closet."

Hollis dropped her arms, raised for an unrealized hug. Her sister dashed behind her to re-lock the screen door and motioned for her to follow. Rather than wiping her shoes, she took them off and put them in hall closet.

"Hi, Ri, it's good to see you, too. What's it been? Gee, only a few years," Hollis said, as she hung up her jacket and closed the door.

"Don't try to guilt-trip me. I've been here, and you haven't," Rita whispered gruffly. She took a breath and looked Hollis in the eyes. "It's good to see you. Come on, Mother and Dad are waiting."

It was Hollis' turn to take a deep breath as they walked down the hall.

"Sunporch" was a grave misnomer. The good-sized room was lined in dark-wood paneling and furnished simply, with an outdated television that took up one whole corner on a stand that resembled a card table. Hollis noted that her mother's habit of having only enough chairs to seat the people in the room still prevailed. There was no other furniture.

Her mother's words came back to her: "Why would we have more chairs in the room than people who could sit on them? Sofas are a waste of space."

Hollis thought it more likely that not having a sofa helped people avoid having to sit next to one another. Rita returned with a stiff-backed chair and set it across from their parents.

Her father lifted his cheek for Hollis to touch with hers. "You're looking well, Rebecca. I've missed you."

Her mother frowned and turned her head away when Hollis bent down to kiss her. "I think I'm catching a cold." She pointed for Hollis to take a seat. "Did your sister tell you why you're here?"

"It wasn't because you missed me?" Hollis said with a crooked smile.

Ava's lips formed a thin line. "Rebecca, please don't make light of our situation; it's unladylike."

Rita broke in, "Mother, I didn't tell her."

Hollis noticed the exchange of looks among the three, and for the first time felt a growing fear in her stomach. She bit her lip to hold back a retort. Her family thrived on drama.

"What situation, Ri?" she asked, turning from one to the other. "Mother, what is it?"

Her sister moistened her lips and motioned with her head. "Mother could die from this."

Hollis spun around toward her father, who was sitting quietly in his chair, searching her eyes with a glistening of tears in his own. Then she took a breath and knelt by her mother.

"I'm so sorry." She patted her mother's clasped hands. "What's the matter?" She wanted to put her arms around her, but her family, and her mother in particular, hated displays of affection.

Her mother leaned back and muttered, "It's my kidney. It's never been the same since you went to prison."

Hollis closed her eyes and felt herself stiffen in preparation for the attack.

Rita cleared her throat. "Mother, that's not true. You didn't get sick until after Rebecca was released. Besides, she was pardoned, and … er, has turned her life around." She looked at Hollis for an affirming nod.

Hollis was ready to bolt—she had been down this road too

many times before—but instead she gave a weak smile, nodded to her sister, got up and went back to sit in her chair.

"What do the doctors say?" she asked no one in particular.

"Well, Mother has been diagnosed with renal failure. The doctor's say it's not genetic but has been a longtime chronic condition. Unless we find a donor …" Rita's voice faded. "Unless we find a kidney donor, she'll have to start dialysis."

The word hung in the air. Her father sheltered his eyes with his fingers. Finally, Hollis looked at her mother and saw her as if for the first time. Ava Morgan was, and always would be, a beauty, but her looks were blurred by deep character lines in her face. Rigidity, small-mindedness, and what now appeared to be fear lay on her exquisite features like a shroud. A disease with a cure that required physical contact with another person and a regimen of hospital visits hooked up to a machine must be abhorrent to her.

Hollis grimaced. "Mother, when do you start treat—"

Rita held up her hand. "Don't jump to conclusions. We have a little time. We haven't exhausted the donor possibility." She crossed her arms tightly. "We've been tested—the whole family—but no one is compatible."

Hollis stiffened.

They want me to be tested.

She was surprised to feel her heartbeat strike a nervous staccato, and she knew they were all waiting to see her expression and hear her response. For the first time since her mother turned away from her in that long-ago courtroom, they exchanged stares.

"Of course, I'll test. Tell me what I have to do."

SHE SHOULDN'T HAVE BEEN SURPRISED to find out that Rita had already arranged for her to meet with her mother's doctor later that afternoon. Her family was not one to waste any time.

"Well, if I had to cancel the appointment, it was no big deal," Rita had said in response to Hollis' startled look.

Dr. Lowe was tall and lanky. He wore black, horn-rimmed glasses and a disconcerting but friendly carved pumpkin-like grin. Taking Hollis' hand in his thin-fingered one, he said, "Wonderful to meet you at last," and pumped her arm. "I've met all the other family members."

Hollis grinned back. She liked him immediately because his open and warm demeanor had to be driving her family to distraction. She said, "They saved the best for last."

"Rebecca," Rita said with a warning tone.

Dr. Lowe didn't seem to notice and took the next thirty minutes to explain the procedure.

"First, we test your tissue typing for white blood cells by drawing your blood. This will also give us cross-matching information. If the cross match is positive, then you and your mother are incompatible because your mother's antibodies will immediately react against your cells and cause the immediate loss of the transplant. If the cross-match is negative, then the transplant may proceed. If all goes well, you'll be hospitalized for two to five days, feel discomfort for one to two weeks, and be fully recovered in six weeks."

Hollis nodded, but her mouth was dry, and her hearing seemed to be fading. A dislike of hospitals was one of the few genes she shared with her family. She wished John was by her side.

She moistened her lips. "I can get along with one kidney?"

He smiled. "Oh, yes. I would be concerned if your mother had a genetic kidney condition, because you could be threatened as well. But her kidney is failing due to a misdiagnosed infection she contracted years ago. Plus, at sixty-three, she's an acceptable age for a transplant. Rest assured, we'll make sure that your kidney is viable and put to good use."

Hollis tried to look relieved.

Lowe continued, "There will be an antibody screen, urine test, EKG, and I like to perform an arteriogram by injecting a fluid into the blood vessels to view your kidney." He peered at Hollis' alarmed face. "Of course, this all sounds pretty daunting, but we can do it within a couple of days."

She nodded again, trying to appear normal.

Rita stood next to her sister. "Becca, we need you to do this as soon as possible." She started to put her arm around Hollis' shoulder but stopped midair. "Please."

They exchanged looks. Hollis inhaled a deep breath and blew it out slowly. She turned to the doctor.

"All right, I'll do it. When can we start?"

"Great, we can start right now. I know you live outside the area." Lowe smiled and patted her on her back. "I can take a blood sample and do the first elimination tests today. You can take the urine test and if we're still a 'go,' you can come back tomorrow for the EKG and arteriogram."

"I need to get back to work," Hollis said. "Will I be able to leave tomorrow?"

Dr. Lowe ran his hand over his head. "Yes, it's an outpatient procedure, but we'd like you to stay a few hours afterward and maybe overnight just in case."

Hollis didn't want to hear anything more about the "just in cases." She handed her belongings to her sister. "Fine, then can you schedule me for first thing in the morning? I really need to be on the road by noon. I'm combining this visit with a work assignment."

"Not a problem." Lowe picked up his electronic tablet and tapped. "Go to the laboratory down the hall and have your blood taken. Make sure you get something to eat right after the tests if you haven't eaten already." He looked at the tablet screen and turned to Rita.

Her sister appeared to be her typical stoic self. "When will we know?" Rita asked.

"I'll put a rush on it and call later this evening."

Hollis frowned. "Is there need for a rush?" she asked Lowe. "I mean, is my mother in danger of … of …." She couldn't finish.

"No, no, the rush is just for your family, so they don't have to remain in limbo." Dr. Lowe gave a little wave with his hand. "We caught things relatively early, but her recovery depends on prompt treatment, and of course, a compatible donor."

Hollis pulled out her phone to check the time. "I need to make a few work calls." She turned to Rita. "I'll give blood, and then we can go back to the house."

Hollis wasn't squeamish about giving blood, but the several full vials that were drawn from her arm caught her by surprise.

She must have looked pale, because as she put on her jacket, she caught Rita gazing at her sympathetically. "Let's get a quick bite," her sister said. "I brought a casserole for dinner, but you look like you could use something now."

Hollis didn't argue, and they found a deli about a block away. They spoke little and in less than an hour they were back on the road.

Rita cleared her throat. "Why did you agree to do it?"

"I guess, because she's my mother," Hollis said. "And … and it's what you're supposed to do. No matter our upheavals, she'll always be my mother." She added, "Now her system may reject anything donated from me, but I feel okay about it."

Rita gave a small smile. "She's ready. Dr. Lowe's team interviewed her. They'll want to interview you too, if you're a candidate. They need to make sure you're doing this for all the right reasons and understand the psychological as well as physical implications."

Hollis nodded. "Lowe already scheduled me for an interview with a social worker near where I live."

Rita continued, "Mother knew you could be a donor. She knew what it meant to her … her future."

"Hmm, and she still chose me over death."

Rita looked shocked, and then joined her sister in nervous laughter. But her expression quickly grew somber.

"I hope you don't mind sleeping on the sofa. Mother changed your old room into a storage area. I've got the guest bedroom, but I can't sleep on the sofa because of my back and—"

Hollis held up her hand. "I'll take the sofa. You're here a lot more than I am."

She pulled into their parents' driveway.

Rita cleared her throat again, only this time a little louder. "About that ...." She rubbed the temples of her forehead. "If you are compatible with Mother, would you be planning on staying at the house after the transplant surgery? I mean ... you know Joe might be back from Iraq by then and ... and well he deserves to get his old room, then that leaves the guest bedroom for when I come to visit."

Hollis stared at her sister in amazement. This was all Rita could focus on—the sleeping arrangements? "Look, Rita, you can tell Mother that I wouldn't think of imposing on her hospitality, not even for a minute. If necessary, I can always stay in a nearby hotel."

Rita couldn't hide her relief.

Hollis turned her head to look out the window. The emptiness she thought she'd locked away was falling open to the reality of daylight. She straightened in her seat, and with irritation brushed her fingers over her eyes, which had started to tear.

CHAPTER SIX

Friday

THE PREVIOUS TESTS HAD RUN smoothly, so Dr. Lowe, true to his word, arranged for the remaining tests to take place first thing in the morning. Hollis drove herself to the hospital, and in a few hours, all the tests were completed. Afterward he met with her in his office.

"I've been rushing things a bit," he said. "I didn't want to be waiting for results if your mother's health dictated we go forward quickly." He picked up a sheet of paper. "From the initial donor compatibility tests, it appears you are a clear match. Once we review the EKG results and the other lab work, we will know with certainty that your mother will be able to use your kidney."

"Good," Hollis said. "Then I'll wait to hear from you."

BY ELEVEN O'CLOCK, HOLLIS WAS already on the road. She had decided to drive straight from the hospital to Cantone's office in Carmel Valley.

She hadn't slept well on her parents' sofa. She had spent most of the night remembering scenes from her years growing up, along with worrying about her mother's health. Driving the freeway, she wore a grim smile. Resigned, she had decided that for better or worse, this was the family she'd been dealt. If her kidney could save her mother, well, her mother had brought her into this world. Although her mother was probably cursing life's irony: the daughter she wished were dead was the only daughter who could keep her alive.

Anthony Cantone's office was located in an upscale mission-styled shopping strip mall in central Carmel Valley. Carmel Valley, or CV Village as the locals referred to it, was located just east of its more famous cousin, Carmel by the Sea. It boasted the same great food, great wine, and true relaxation, but with a lot fewer tourists.

She pulled into a space directly in front of a door with understated signage that advertised Cantone's occupation as *architect*. Picking up his envelope from the passenger seat, she walked up the paved path and entered a thickly carpeted, unexpectedly small lobby. A young woman with streaked blonde-on-blonde hair busily tapped on a laptop keyboard.

Looking up, she asked, "May I help you?"

Hollis smiled. "Yes, I'm Hollis Morgan. I'm here to see Mr. Cantone."

The woman frowned slightly. "Was he expecting you? He has a full day of meetings."

Hollis checked her response. "I spoke with him day before yesterday. He made the appointment himself."

She stood and Hollis stepped back to look up. The receptionist had to be at least six feet two. Her name plate identified her as Lisa Walker.

"Well then, I'll tell him you're here." She gave Hollis a big, dimpled smile. "I can't tell you how often this happens. Why have an assistant if he doesn't keep me up to date with his schedule? Have a seat. I'll be right back." She headed for a hallway at the rear of the lobby.

Hollis, feeling every inch of her own five-foot-three height, nodded with understanding. She was sure Penny would say the same thing about her. She took a seat on a deep-blue velvet loveseat, one of three that filled the area. She glanced around. The office reeked of money. Oversized color photographs of mini-mansions lined the walls. Framed in black with gold trimmed Lucite, the photos emphasized the lushness of the room's indigo blue and mauve-colored Persian hand-tied area rugs. One byproduct of her paralegal property valuation training: she knew the good stuff when she saw it.

Lisa Walker returned with a middle-aged man on her heels. He came toward her, holding out his hand.

"Miss Morgan, Anthony Cantone," he said in his high-pitched voice. "I must apologize. I neglected to tell Lisa of our meeting. Please, come back to my office."

Hollis shook his hand and smiled. Anthony Cantone was just a little taller than she was. He appeared to be in his late forties, maybe fifties, with thinning gray-streaked dark hair. She didn't know what impressed her more about him, the profuseness of the sweat that streaked down his forehead or the almost cartoonish voice that reminded her of a parakeet. If asked to guess, she would have picked stylish Lisa as the architect and Cantone as the office worker—so much for stereotypes.

In his office, he pointed to a corner that held a small, round conference table and three chairs. Hollis took a seat.

"You said you had a package for me?" His watery blue eyes opened wide with expectation.

Hollis nodded and put the large envelope on the table. "I'll need you to sign an affidavit that you received the contents, and we'll be through." She took out a sheet of paper from her briefcase.

"I'd like to see the material first." He sat and dabbed at his forehead with a tissue from a box on the table.

"Absolutely," she said and dumped the contents in front of him. She wasn't sure if she succeeded in hiding her curiosity, but she tried to look uninterested.

The slips of hotel and airline receipts sat atop the pile, followed by the bundled canceled checks.

Cantone thumbed through the documents, his eyes darting from one item to the next. Finally, he put his arms around the stack, pulled it to him, and gave her a challenging look.

"Okay, it looks like it's all here." He still huddled over the papers. "Why did he do this?"

Hollis shrugged. "Mr. Cantone, I'm just following through with our client's directions. We were told to return these items to you." Hollis paused, and then said in as casual tone as she could muster, "Er, can I assume you're pleased?"

"Pleased?" Cantone gave a harsh, short laugh. "Pleased? Bell has been draining me dry for almost six years because of my fling with Barbara. It cost me five grand a month. It was just one time … one indiscretion." He shook his head. "He knew I couldn't afford to let Constance find out. She'd take me to the cleaners with her divorce settlement …." He suddenly stopped speaking and stared at Hollis. "Are there copies?"

It was her turn to shake her head. "No, I have work papers, but I didn't make copies of the originals."

His look was skeptical.

She tried to assume a bland expression. "Mr. Cantone, this is awkward, but was Mr. Bell, er, blackmailing you?"

His eyes narrowed, and he had stopped sweating. Cantone stood and walked over to sit behind his desk. He shoved all the papers into his top drawer and locked it. He reached into another drawer, pulled out a high ball glass and a decanter marked *brandy*.

Without looking at Hollis, he poured himself a drink. "No, he was holding me hostage."

Taking a seat across from Hollis, he spent the next few minutes—helped by two shots of liquor in his system—celebrating his freedom with tales of being under Bell's choke hold. He was interrupted by Lisa, who reminded him his next appointment was scheduled to arrive shortly.

Hollis was grateful that her undeserved role of confidante was coming to an end. It was clear that Cantone had been waiting to unload his burden to anyone who would listen.

"Constance was Bell's niece," he squeaked. "He couldn't stand that she married me, but he didn't see her like I did. She was just like him. She wanted my money ... and my name." He took a sip. "We've been divorcing for almost two years. She can't decide how much of a settlement she should pry out of me." He gave a short, harsh laugh and took another sip. "He knew that if she found out about my ... outside relationship, she would ruin me."

It was hard for Hollis to imagine anyone with Cantone's lack of sexual appeal having an affair, but hey, who knew?

Still, she was puzzled. "But your wife was his niece. Why didn't he give her the information she needed to, well, break you?"

"One time he told me it was because he loved money more than he loved family. I had no reason to doubt him. The man had no scruples." He ran his hand over his head. "I only know that I don't have to write another five-thousand dollar check again. I can finally breathe freely. Where's that paper you want me to sign?"

Hollis passed it to him and watched him carefully read its contents and then scribble his name. She believed his distress and relief.

"Good luck, Mr. Cantone," she said with sincerity.

They said their final goodbyes, and Hollis left him in the lobby greeting a young couple who wanted their 1950 ranch-style home remodeled into a Chinese pagoda.

THE RIDE BACK WAS UNEVENTFUL. Hollis drove Highway 101 against commuter traffic and made it to the Bay Area in just a few hours. A call came through her Bluetooth—Kip Lyles. He'd called to re-confirm their appointment for that afternoon and asked if she had seen his piece on the front page.

"I was able to find a picture of Bell taken last year," he said. "I added cliffhangers so that our readers would clamor for next week's follow-up."

"I'll make sure to take a look," Hollis replied. She couldn't imagine anyone in San Lucian clamoring to read the *Daily*. "You're still on my calendar for four o'clock," she reassured him.

As she strode to the firm's administrative office, she noticed that the sign-out board indicated Gordon Barrett was in court until midday. She was glad. Her mind was swirling with the implications that she was assisting a blackmailer. Dropping her jacket and purse on top of her office credenza, she headed for the paralegal offices.

"Don't ask," Penny said. "I'm still working on it." Penny raised her head from hovering above an oversized magnifying glass suspended over the 2010 calendar page.

Hollis smiled. "I wasn't going to interrupt. I'm just checking in."

"Humph." Penny was not impressed. Head bent to the page, she penned something on a pad.

Hollis sat in the metal chair in front of the desk. "Bell was a blackmailer."

Penny glanced up and then returned to her project. "I know." She pointed to the calendar. "This is Naomi Eaton's personal calendar. There's a note at the bottom."

"Let me see." Hollis leaned over the desk.

Penny shook her head. "You can't read it; it's in code, but a simple one." She pulled over her pad. "It took me quite a while to figure out it wasn't the weather she was tracking. It was her withdrawals from client accounts." She tapped a square. "The page is actually a summary monthly ledger for her private fraudulent banking system. It covers twelve months."

Hollis sat up in her chair. "What does she do?"

"I looked her up online. Ms. Eaton used to be a stock trader with an office in San Francisco. She got her license in 2005." Penny flipped to early pages in her pad. "On paper she looked great, seemed successful. But when I figured out her coding system, that's when I had her. She took a few thousand from one client's account, probably kept some for herself, and then partially repaid another account. She'd rotate transactions every couple of weeks."

"Let me guess. She was doing pretty well until she tapped into Bell's account."

"You got it." Penny said. "It looks like she only skimmed from commercial clients. I can't tell based on what I have here, but Bell's company is one of the entries. It's likely that the recession hit, and her monetary musical chairs left more than one client short. Since she's not in jail, I assume she somehow got everyone caught up."

Hollis furrowed her forehead in thought. She looked at the paralegal. "I'm curious, what's the note at the bottom?"

"The handwriting is different from the rest of the entries, but it's in the same code, so Bell must have discovered the key." Penny turned the paper around so Hollis could see. "The note reads: 'The goose is dead, long live the goose.' "

HOLLIS LEFT PENNY'S OFFICE TO return to her own. She had the information she needed to make contact with Eaton, and she asked Penny to start on Jeremiah Griffin's file. Gordon should be back in his office and she wanted to pause a moment before she brought him up to date on what had turned out to be an incredible day.

She made herself a mug of green jasmine tea, and its aroma gradually brought the desired calm to her nerves and clarity to her thinking. If Bell was a blackmailer—and she had no doubt that he was—what had caused him to release his victims? Why have his estate incur the cost of a law firm to return his ill-gotten goods?

A cough from her doorway caught her attention.

"Tiffany, come on in. What's up?" Hollis put her cup down and motioned to a chair.

This afternoon Tiffany was wearing a smoke-gray pantsuit with a pastel-green blouse. She looked quite professional.

"I came to apologize for my behavior earlier this week. I … I was upset about something and I took it out on you." She looked down at her hands.

"Do you want to talk about it now?"

"It's not work-related. And … and it's not really appropriate."

Hollis' mind searched for a correct response but it eluded her. She was not used to the role of counselor and her personality skill set for compassion was limited. But then Tiffany had never confided in her before.

She faltered, "Er, I'm willing to listen. I have to see Gordon before he leaves for the day, but I have a few minutes now."

Without a word, Tiffany gave her a grateful smile. She quickly rose to shut the door before returning to her seat.

"There's this guy …. I think he likes me, but he's not my type. Well, he's not the type I want for me anyway." She leaned over Hollis' desk. "I mean he's nice and good-looking, but he's younger and I want someone who … who can be better than me. You know what I mean?"

"Uh—"

"It's not that he's immature or anything, or doesn't have goals. It's just that he's … he's …." Her voice wavered.

Hollis licked her lips. She was definitely feeling out of her depth. "Is he asking for something from you?"

Tiffany shook her head. "No, just the opposite, he's not pushy at all. But I just know it's going to come to a point when … when I'll have to respond, and I don't know how to tell him. It's making me crazy."

Hollis tried to glance discreetly at the clock, but Tiffany caught her anyway.

"I'm going. Like I said, this is really inappropriate. I'm sorry to bother you."

Hollis raised her hand in objection. "No, no, please it's fine. I'm glad you feel you can come to me." She paused, and tucked her hair behind her ear. "I think … I think your worry is premature. You're anticipating a time when you'll have to let him know how you feel. I think you should wait and see how you'll feel then, not how you feel now. It sounds to me like you're struggling within yourself, not with him."

Tiffany stared at her for a moment, and then nodded. "Of course, you're right." She squeezed Hollis' hand across the desk. "Thank you for listening."

She left, and Hollis exhaled, raising her eyes to the ceiling in relief. Maybe her ability to relate to others was improving.

She wasn't sure she liked it. It was a lot tidier to limit her social exposure.

HOLLIS HURRIED ACROSS THE LOBBY to the partner offices and tapped on Gordon's door. He pointed her to the seat in front of his desk.

Gordon spoke without looking up from his keyboard. "I saw your note that you wanted to see me. I came by but your door was closed, and I could hear you had someone with you."

"Ah, yes." She put her pad on his desk. "I want to catch you up on my meeting with Anthony Cantone. It was very interesting."

She briefly took him through the highlights of the conversation.

He was tapping out a text message on his phone. "Hmmm, so it's blackmail, huh? Still, since the victims haven't complained, and you are acting in accordance with your client's directives, I don't see any legal issues with your participation. Do you?"

"No. I just can't figure out why Bell decided to inform them they're off the hook, especially the way he directed it to be carried out."

Gordon shrugged. "I wouldn't dwell on it. All you have to do is complete the disbursements and file his Certification of

Trust." He went back to his phone. "Sounds like we might have substantial billables generated from this matter after all."

Hollis assured him that she would make sure that every possible expense was recorded and submitted to Accounting for invoicing.

She returned to her office, where the blinking light on her phone indicated a voicemail message. It was from Dr. Lowe.

"Good news, Ms. Morgan, you're a perfect donor match for your mother."

Of course, thought Hollis.

HER SISTER RITA WAS CLEARLY relieved when Hollis called her with the news from Lowe. But she wanted to be the one to break the news to their mother.

"You know how she gets, Becca. She's been under a lot of stress, and she doesn't find it easy to say … to say …."

"Thank you?" Hollis offered.

Rita was silent.

Hollis was too tired to push the point. "Yes, I agree that you should be the one to tell her, but I'll be with you. I want her to know I'm aware of what this means and that I'll be there for her."

That I didn't abandon her, not like she did me.

She continued, "Lowe said he would be setting things up and that it may be a little while before the operation. He'll get back to me when he and Mother have settled on a date. Mother's insurance will cover my general costs, and my firm's coverage will provide for anything else."

She realized how glad she was to have work that was all-consuming. With John gone, and this thing with her mother, it was a relief to have Bell's illicit dealings to unravel and give her plenty to occupy her days.

I CAN'T LOCATE NAOMI EATON," Penny said. "Bell's contact information for her is incorrect."

"Maybe not," Hollis said, tossing a San Francisco morning paper across her desk. "Look at the article below the fold: Bell's death has been reported. We're going to have a hard time finding the remainder of his victims."

"Why? They would think they wouldn't have to worry about him anymore."

"Think about it," Hollis said. "If I were them, I'd lay low for a while. They don't know if someone else might pick up where he left off."

"Good point." Penny grimaced. "But Eaton didn't have enough time to move. She probably still lives in San Francisco. Do you want me to get one of the investigators to follow up?"

"Hmm, that's not a bad idea," Hollis said. "You'll need to have them do it today. Let me know if that's going to be impossible and I'll get someone else. While Gordon will have no problem with billing the estate, let's keep costs to a minimum. I have an issue with padding charges."

Penny nodded. "I'll put in the investigative request to locate Eaton and then get started on Jeremiah Griffin's folder. He's the one with all the emails and Jordan Manufacturing memos. Hopefully, he hasn't gone into hiding."

"I remember the paperwork. While you work on Griffin, I'll tackle the Pittmans." She held up the thick package. "I can't wait to hear their story about the multiple passports and the gun-with-a-laser permit. Let me know as soon as you hear back about tracking Eaton."

After Penny left, Hollis dumped the contents of the Pittman envelope on her desk. She picked up the Weatherly passports: one for a male named Ian and the other for a woman named Millicent. Without knowing what Ian and Millicent Pittman looked like, she couldn't tell if the innocent-looking faces staring back at her were theirs.

According to Bell's contact sheet, they lived in trendy Orinda, on the other side of the Caldecott Tunnel. Hollis picked up the phone and punched in their number; she wasn't surprised to hear the "no longer in service" message. The Pittmans must read the papers, too.

A minute later, Tiffany was back. "Hollis, Kip Lyles is here from the *Daily*. He's early so I left him in the lobby.

Hollis shrugged. "Put him in the small conference room. I'd rather meet with him now."

A few minutes later, she entered the conference room and closed the door behind her. Kip was dressed in slacks and a tee shirt under a linen jacket. He looked very journalistic.

"Thanks for seeing me. I won't be long." He shook her hand. "I had a chance to speak with Odelia Larson, and she gave me most of what I needed for the story." He accepted the bottle of water Hollis offered.

Great.

"I would take what Odelia said with caution," Hollis said. "She wasn't particularly happy with her bequest from Mr. Bell."

Kip laughed. "Not 'happy'—no kidding. It was all she could talk about. She said that a lot of people hated him, but she thought he would have treated her better ... because of her loyalty. But she found out that he didn't think much of her either." His face turned grim. "He wasn't a very nice man."

She didn't respond and crossed her arms over her chest. "So, now what is it you want?"

"Can you give me the names of his friends or partners?" He sat up straighter in his chair. "Odelia didn't know of any. But I need a couple of personal quotes."

"He didn't have any friends that I'm aware of, and if Odelia doesn't know, there aren't any. You can try his sister, or her daughter. They're all that's left of his family."

"Good. Can you give me their contact information?"

"Let me call them first and see if they are willing to speak with you."

"That's fair." He got up. "Odelia Larson said that the living room was pretty disheveled when she found it. Did you find anything that would go to his state of mind?" He picked up his notepad. "I guess you'll be hiring a company to clear out the house?"

"Odelia must still be upset. She usually doesn't talk so much. But no, there wasn't anything out of the ordinary left behind. And yes, Matthias Bell's estate will go through routine processing. I'll be making arrangements with an auction house."

He put his pad and pen away. "Well, thank you for speaking with me. You'll let me know about contacting his family?"

Hollis peered at him. "I'll let you know."

She glanced at the time. If she hurried, she could drive out to the Pittman address and just maybe catch one or both at home. It wasn't likely they would have had time to move. Taking the next half hour to clear her appointment calendar, she was ready to leave when Penny appeared in her doorway again, this time with the Eaton envelope.

"I can't get Reese to go out today or tomorrow," she blurted out.

Hollis put her briefcase back on her desk. "Why not?"

Reese Investigations was the firm's go-to company for tracking down even the most secretive matters. They were very good, and very expensive.

"They're all tied up with other clients." Penny said. "However, they can commit to having someone on her doorstep day after tomorrow morning by seven. Will that work?"

"No, she'll have too much time to run, and I don't want to spend a lot more effort trying to track her down." Hollis paused. "Give me her envelope. I have a backup plan. Keep working on Griffin."

Penny looked skeptical but left the envelope and hurried back down the hall.

Hollis grabbed her coat and briefcase and headed for the elevators. She pushed the basement button. The mailroom was familiar to her for a number of reasons; it had almost been the site of her death. But she was here now because she had an idea that bordered on brilliant, if she said so herself. She saw the figure she was looking for huddling over a bin of mail.

"Vince, I need you," she said in a rush.

The young man turned around and smiled. "Hey, Hollis, it's been a while. How are things going? Looking for a particular package?"

Vince Colton had come into her life soon after she passed the bar. He'd been a young adult then, getting over drug addiction and dealing with a drug-addicted mother he doted on. He insisted that Hollis had given him a second chance at life, and she knew he had given her back her humanity. Her own time in prison had jaded her. It was only thanks to the intercession of a dedicated parole officer who believed in her that she had received a pardon, and thus a second chance. Similarly, she wanted to be there for Vince.

She'd convinced George months ago to hire him for the mailroom. The job was just what Vince needed to get back on his feet, obtain an apartment for him and his mother, and return to school.

"No, Vince, I'm looking for a person this time. I need you to use your wits. Drive over to San Francisco—you can take a firm car—and find a Naomi Eaton. And please do it now. You'll earn extra pay."

"Who's Naomi Eaton? And who's going to sort the mail?" He moved to a coat rack and pulled his bomber jacket off the hanger.

He followed behind Hollis as she headed back for the elevators, talking over her shoulder. "She's involved with one of our clients. Here's an address." She handed him a slip of paper. "It's on Portreo Hill. Go there and stake it out. Call me if she's home. Don't approach her, but if she leaves, follow the best you can and call or text me every half hour with what's going on. I'll have Tiffany get someone to cover for you in the mailroom."

He grinned "Wow, this is great! Don't worry I won't mess up. I can do this."

There was something about his eagerness that made Hollis question her sanity in letting Vince loose on the assignment. But her gut told her he could do it. They returned to the firm's lobby, where Hollis asked Tiffany to assign Vince a car.

"He'll need the credit card, too. Oh, and Tiffany, give him one of the extra smartphones to take with him."

Vince stood straighter and smiled at the receptionist. "I'm going on a special assignment. You'll have to arrange for someone to cover me in the mailroom."

Tiffany frowned. "But, Hollis—"

Vince shifted self-consciously from foot to foot.

Hollis ignored Tiffany's obvious discomfort. "Tiffany, I don't have time to justify to you why Vince has to go. Once you get him set up, Penny should be able to explain a little better, but right now, I'm out of here."

Hollis headed once more for the elevators, motioning Vince to join her.

She spoke in a hushed tone. "Okay, this is your shot at another opportunity. Don't blow it."

He nodded. "You can count on me."

It was toward the end of the day and the drive to Orinda was an easy one. Hollis parked on the street next to the start of the Pittmans' long, circular driveway. From her viewpoint, she could see a slate-gray Bentley parked under a wide, ornate porte-cochère.

Someone was home.

She felt her phone vibrate. It was a text from Vince:

Checking in. I think she's here. Lights are on. I'll get back to you.

Hollis made herself count to twenty and hoped Vince remembered her direction to not approach Naomi Eaton. Meanwhile she was feeling pressure of her own to get her meeting with the Pittmans over with. She drove her car behind and to the side of the Bentley. Getting out, she caught the movement of a drape near the front door.

The door opened.

"May I help you?" An older woman, her tone sounding anything but helpful, stood at the top of the marble steps.

Hollis grabbed her briefcase and purse and met the woman halfway. "Yes. My name is Hollis Morgan. I'm with the law firm of Dodson Dodson & Doyle. I'd like to see either Ian or Millicent Pittman."

"Why?"

"I'm sorry, it's a private matter. Are they at home?"

The woman crossed her arms over her chest. "Are you expected?"

Hollis peered at the woman. She could be Millicent, but she doubted it. The gray-haired stout woman had the air of a proprietor, not an owner.

"Unfortunately, the number I had for them has been disconnected." Hollis took a few steps closer. "Perhaps if you'd let them know that I think I have good news for them, they'd be willing to see me."

The woman took a step back toward the door. "Wait here. Do you have a business card?"

Hollis put her card in the woman's outstretched hand. She reentered the house, shutting the door firmly behind her. Hollis took the time to glance at her surroundings. Even from her limited vantage point on the steps, she could see the house was massive, with an expansive yard. Her eyes also caught sight of the luggage stacked in the backseat of the Bentley.

Taking a quick glance at the door, she bent slightly to see the rear of the automobile and memorized the license plate.

The door opened and a statuesque woman appeared. Her jet-black hair was pulled back into a roll at the base of her neck. Small tendrils of hair had escaped, softening the otherwise stern, pale face. Her age was not immediately apparent, but Hollis guessed somewhere in her mid-forties.

"Ms. Morgan, I'm Millicent Pittman. Would you like to come in?"

"Thank you." Hollis smiled and followed the woman into the house. They paused in the silver-gray marble foyer.

"It's rather late in the day. What did you want to see me about?"

Mrs. Pittman spoke with a foreign accent, but Hollis couldn't determine the country of origin.

"I'd like to speak with Mr. Pittman as well. Is he available?" Hollis glanced up the winding, wrought-iron staircase adjacent to floor-to-ceiling windows.

"No, he's not available." Her lips formed a thin line. "I'll ask again, what is this about?"

"I represent the estate of Matthias Bell and—"

"What!" Pittman's eyes bulged. "What does that man want now?"

Hollis held up a hand, palm out. "Mrs. Pittman, if Mr. Pittman isn't available, could you and I sit somewhere so I can explain why I'm here?"

"Milly, let's meet with her in the solarium."

Hollis whirled about and faced Ian Pittman, who had obviously been listening to their conversation from what appeared to be the doorway to the den. He was as tall, pale, and thin as his wife, over six feet with silver-gray hair and hazel-gray eyes that seemed to see right through her. He looked like an alien from outer space.

"Thank you, Mr. Pittman. My name is Hollis Morgan." She held out her hand, and he shook it as if he wanted to grab for the Purell next.

Millicent pointed toward a wide hallway. "This way, Ms. Morgan."

The solarium, located off the family room, was sunny and tastefully decorated in shades of blue and white. It was a large space with wide plank oak floors, and divided up into conversation areas.

"Let's sit here." Ian Pittman sat on an overstuffed loveseat made of a heavy canvas material. Millicent sat next to him, leaving the white upholstered chair across from them for Hollis.

"Now, what does Bell want?" Ian growled.

"Mr. Bell died last week, and I am the executor of his estate."

They exchanged looks of what appeared to be relief, followed immediately by suspicion.

"What was it? Did someone finally get rid of him? Did he suffer?" Millicent smiled with apparent glee.

Her husband put his hand on his wife's. "You can tell we're not able to mourn. So, that brings us to why are *you* here, Ms. Morgan?"

Hollis opened her briefcase and took out the bulky envelope. "Mr. Bell died of a heart attack. In his final instructions, he directed that this envelope be delivered to you." She held on to it. "As a 'ward' of the court, I can't be a party to a criminal action. The items in this envelope raise a lot of questions. Can I assume that Mr. Bell was blackmailing you?"

From the way he fidgeted, Ian seemed to be considering snatching the envelope from her hands and making a run for it. Millicent's forehead glistened with sweat as she leaned into her husband's arm.

Ian's shoulders dropped and he resettled himself in the sofa. "Yes, we are, *were*, his victims. He's been draining us for years." His eyes narrowed. "Wait. Are you here to take his place?"

Hollis protested, "No, not at all, but as I said, I can't participate in a crime. Answer me this: why the two passports? At first, I didn't know if they were yours, but looking at you now, I see you don't match the photos."

Millicent squeezed her husband's shoulders.

"They are friends of ours we were trying to help get out of Croatia," Ian responded. "We had these dummy passports made for them so they could cross the border. Bell got a hold of them somehow and threatened to turn us in."

"Where are they now?"

"Gone and dead," Millicent spat out.

Hollis peered at them with mild surprise.

They're both lying through their teeth.

She'd discovered her skill in detecting lies, and in telling them, as a child and honed it to an art over the years, especially in prison. The benefit in knowing when she was being lied to far outweighed any guilt she might have at needing to tell a lie.

"I'll need to see your ID." Hollis pulled out a pad and pretended to take a note. She looked up. "And the Glock purchase?"

Ian dropped Millicent's hand. Clearly annoyed, he said, "This is America. Last time I looked it was legal to own a gun." He reached into his back pocket, pulled out his wallet, and flashed his driver's license.

"Ms. Morgan, we have things to do," Millicent interjected. "Could you just fulfill your assignment and give us that envelope?" She rose and retrieved her purse from a marble table near the door. She brought out her driver's license.

Hollis looked quickly at the pictures and pursed her lips.

"Thank you, but actually what I have here are just copies." She gave them a sheepish smile and patted the package. "I didn't want to carry around the real documents until I knew I had located you. I can return with the originals and give both the copies and the originals to you then." She gripped the envelope.

They exchanged looks.

"Let's see those copies," Ian demanded.

Hollis nodded, reached into her briefcase, and pulled out a slim manila envelope. She handed it to Ian, who grabbed it. Millicent looked over his shoulder and blanched as he scanned the pages. She put a hand on her forehead.

"Ah, Bell was a hateful man. He held this over us for so long." She accepted the papers from her husband and flipped quickly through the documents.

Ian pointed. "And these are the only copies?"

"Yes, you may keep those," Hollis insisted. "Now that I've met you, I'll rush back to the office and have the originals messengered over." She hurriedly returned her pad and bulky envelope to her briefcase, blessing her compulsive and suspicious nature for compelling her to make a copy of the Pittman documents. The second envelope with the originals lay snug in her case.

"What's in that other envelope you have in your briefcase?" Millicent said.

"It's attorney-client privileged material for another matter I'm working on and has nothing to do with you," Hollis lied, looking her directly in the face. She stood. "I must get back to the office."

Ian shook his head. "Unfortunately, Ms. Morgan, I don't believe you." He stood next to her. "I think those are our original documents in that envelope and I have to ask you to hand it over … now."

He didn't wait for her response, but stooped and yanked the case out of her hands. Hollis was pushed off balance but held on to the handle and pulled the case back. Pittman wrenched it up and out of her reach. He walked over to the top of a chest and popped open the case. Lifting out both envelopes, he slipped them under his arm. He shut the case and held it out to Hollis.

She clenched her teeth. "How dare you!"

"Uh-huh." He went through the papers, lifting out the passports. He air-kissed them and handed them to Millicent.

Millicent's face was flushed and she gave Ian a wide grin. "You're brilliant, darling."

She joined him, and they became absorbed with sorting through the sheets of paper.

Hollis eyed the distance to the door. "Well, my job here is done." She edged toward the doorway. "I think you'll understand if I don't say 'Have a nice day.' " She was almost to the entry.

Ian turned to look at her with narrowed eyes. "I don't know what you have in mind, but we won't be here if you ever come back."

"Now *that's* something you don't have to worry about," Hollis assured him.

CHAPTER SEVEN

~~

Monday

MONDAY MORNING, HOLLIS WAS STILL tense as she glanced at the personnel directory posted on the wall. The San Lucian Police Department had a total of five personnel. Headed by Chief Donald Brennan, the department was comprised of Detective Laura Scott, two patrol officers, an office manager, and the receptionist Joyce Pope. It was now Pope who gave her an appraising look as she spoke with the detective on a phone mouthpiece.

Joyce gave her a broad smile. "Detective Scott will be right out. Can I get you some coffee?"

Hollis smiled back. "No thanks. I'm a tea drinker."

"Oh." Joyce looked confused, as if Hollis had asked for prune juice. "Er, we have a hot water spigot on the water cooler." She opened a drawer. "Here's a tea bag." She held out a slightly battered Lipton bag.

Hollis raised her eyebrows. "That's okay. I'm fine."

The only door leading off the lobby finally opened.

"Ms. Morgan, I'm Detective Scott."

The woman was tall. Dressed in black slacks, a crisp white blouse, and a navy-blue blazer, Laura Scott wore her gold detective badge on her lapel. She was a light-haired brunette with dark brown eyes framed by heavy eyebrows and black-framed glasses.

"Thank you for taking a few minutes to see me." Hollis followed behind Scott as she led her through the door and to the first office on the right.

Scott motioned for her to sit in one of the chairs around the small table. "You caught me at a good time. How can I help you?"

"Last Friday, I went to the Orinda home of Ian and Millicent Pittman. I thought about it all weekend and I decided to err on the side of caution and report the episode to the police."

Hollis proceeded to give her a summary briefing of the afternoon's happenings, including her conversation with Anthony Cantone.

Scott made a few notations on a pad of paper. She looked up when Hollis stopped speaking. "Did you make copies of the documents Mr. Bell had on Cantone and the Pittmans?"

Hollis sighed. "Yes and no. I didn't make copies of Cantone's documents, and it wasn't until I went through the Pittmans' papers that I thought they looked suspicious and made a copy. But … but now they've got them."

Laura Scott glanced at the wall clock. "So, what do you want the San Lucian police to do? The Pittmans live outside our jurisdiction. While your now-dead client may have been a blackmailer, you are tasked with returning the goods he had on them." She held out her hands, palm up. "From the sound of it, other than being embarrassing and perhaps compromising, those papers do not constitute a crime. Certainly not if you're returning them to their rightful owners."

"What about the passports?"

Scott shrugged. "How do you know that Pittman is their name? Their real names may be in those passports."

"Well, I guess that's a possibility," Hollis said, though that didn't explain the photos, which looked nothing like them.

"You said the one other guy you spoke with—Cantone," she tapped her pad with the pen, "Cantone's papers and Cantone himself seemed harmless. You don't know anything about your other deliveries." Scott stood. "Monday is a busy community public relations day for us. I've got to get going. You know, I think your client was a jerk who maybe knew his end was near and didn't want to die with dirty deeds on his conscience."

Hollis gathered her purse and briefcase. "I'm sure you're right. I'm sorry to have taken up your time." She went out into the lobby.

She stopped to check for messages on her cellphone. Scott scurried past with a wave of her hand.

Hollis plastered on a smile and gave a fluttering-fingers wave.

Back in her car, she hit the steering wheel with her fist. The visit had been a total waste of time.

HOLLIS HAD GOTTEN INTO THE office about midmorning and was about to refresh her cup of tea in Triple D's break room when her phone vibrated.

Vince.

She clicked the phone on. "Vince, what's been going on? What happened to texting me every half hour until you saw Eaton? Where are you?"

"Aw, Hollis, I knew that would be the first thing out of your mouth. Sometimes you make me feel like a baby. You got my text on Saturday, didn't you? I didn't see Eaton on Friday night and I had to do my cleaning job on Saturday. I went to her house on Sunday, but she never showed. So I went back to her house first thing this morning and I saw her leaving."

"I didn't want you to work over the weekend," Hollis scolded. "Why didn't you answer my texts? I could've come with you. And where are you now?"

"In the car, across the street from her next-door neighbor's house."

"Okay, fine. That's all I need to know." She reached for a piece of paper and pen from her desk. She took a breath. "All right, describe her for me."

"About your height, blonde, kinda old, maybe in her thirties, but a nice shape. She was dressed in all black and wearing sunglasses, so I couldn't see her face."

Hollis ignored the age slam and frowned. "How do you know it was her?"

"First, she used a key to unlock the front door, and then I heard her say 'Eaton' when her cell rang while she went to get her paper from the sidewalk."

"Well, that *is* a clue," Hollis agreed. "You're done. Go home, take the day off, and get some rest. I'll see you tomorrow."

"Wait. Don't you want me to go back and follow her?"

"No, I just wanted to know where to find her. You're done with the assignment and you did a great job. Take the car back to the lot and we'll talk tomorrow."

Vince grudgingly agreed and clicked off.

Hollis leaned back in her chair, hugging a mug of steaming-hot lavender tea. Detective Scott might not have been impressed with Hollis' concerns, but there was something wrong with the way the whole Bell matter was playing out—something very wrong.

GLAD SHE'D FINALLY CONNECTED WITH Vince, Hollis returned a half-dozen of the calls noted on pink message slips Tiffany had put on her desk the week before. That morning, she'd received a non-urgent call from Dr. Lowe, but she put it aside when she noticed the Post-it from Penny asking her to come by when she got a chance.

Hollis grabbed her cup and headed for Penny's office. She found her on the computer.

"Hollis, good you're back. It looks like it's going to be a busy week."

"Then let's get ready for it," Hollis said. Penny did not expect morning niceties, so Hollis held up the note. "I got your message. What's the matter?"

"Nothing critical." Penny pulled out a file from the bottom of a stack. "I just wanted you to know that Mr. Griffin—Jeremiah Griffin—seems to be on the up and up. I can't find anything among all those emails and memos that would incriminate him."

"If it's not obvious, maybe it only makes a difference to Mr. Griffin." Hollis flipped through the pages. "I've got to clear my desk of client work, and then I'll take a look at them. Meantime, Vince was able to locate Naomi Eaton and we'll be making her delivery next. I hope she's less combative than the Pittmans."

Penny gave her a questioning look and Hollis recounted her visit to Orinda and her morning visit to the police department.

"Better let Gordon know," she warned.

Hollis sighed. "He's my next stop."

That was her intention, only Gordon wasn't in his office and had signed out until the afternoon. She taped a note on his monitor that she needed to see him.

Back at her own desk, she punched in Dr. Lowe's number.

"Hollis, thanks for getting back to me," Lowe said. "Uh … the family asked me to tell you that your mother prefers to wait until September to schedule the transplant. She doesn't want to have to recuperate during the summer."

So much for her sister's promise to wait until Hollis was present to give her mother the news. Hollis smiled. The delay was probably because her mother was afraid of sweating.

"That's almost two months away. Can she afford to wait that long?"

Lowe hesitated. "Well, ideally we would do the surgery immediately, but your mother is a strong-minded woman and it's important that the patient be in a positive frame of mind."

"Is there any more testing, or anything else I need to do?"

"Just stay healthy," Lowe said. "My nurse practitioner will be contacting you in about four weeks. I want to put you on a restricted diet up until the operation. But other than that, all systems are go, unless your mother's condition worsens and we have to move faster."

"I'll be ready. That's one of the benefits of being a probate attorney; there are very few matters that must be dealt with immediately." She added, "How's my mother handling things?"

"Considering the seriousness of her condition, quite well and," he paused, "I'm sure they'll be getting touch with you personally."

Hollis said, "Don't be too sure."

HOLLIS WORKED THROUGH LUNCH, CLEARING her inbox and drafting briefs for Penny to research and proofread. She got up to make copies and bumped into Vince, who was just entering her office.

"Vince, what are you doing here?" she said. "I thought you weren't going to come in until tomorrow. Do you have trouble following directions?"

He just grinned. "Ah, Hollis, don't be pissed. I feel fine, really. I can't sleep now. I'm too hyped up."

She sighed. "I give up. Come on in and tell me about your stakeout." She sat back down behind her desk.

He took a chair. "That's why I was comin' to see you. I figured you'd want more details."

"So, you spotted Eaton. What more details are there?" She clasped her hands, and then realization crossed her face. "You followed her, didn't you?"

He looked sheepish. "Penny told me that she had her nailed for a crook. I wondered if she might make a run for it. I wanted to be able to help you, so … so, yeah, I followed her."

"Okay, Vince that's it. You're assigned to the mailroom, period." Hollis didn't try to hide her anger. "You could have gotten hurt. We don't know who these people are. I told you that I have to be able to rely on you to do exactly as you're told. I just wanted you to verify she lived at that address, and—"

"Hollis, before you bust a brain cell, I verified that she doesn't live at the address you gave me."

"What?"

"Naomi Eaton doesn't live there." He leaned his elbows on the desk. "When I saw her get into her car, she had a suitcase with her. I knew I had to follow her. You'd already gotten off the phone, and I'm sure you wouldn't want me to talk on a cellphone while I was driving." He gave her a devilish grin. "So, I took a risk and tailed her." He looked to see if she was relenting.

"Go ahead. Then what happened?" Hollis was determined to keep a straight face.

"She came over the Bay Bridge and drove to the other side of San Lucian. She used a key to enter a townhome in a neighborhood with all new construction and took the suitcase in with her."

Hollis spun in her chair to look out the window. Her forehead was furrowed and her thoughts raced. Finally, she turned back to Vince who was sitting quietly, waiting for her response.

She couldn't help smiling. "You'll live to see another day, Mr. Colton. It was good you followed her. I'm sorry I didn't give you credit for thinking on your feet. But I'm not sorry for getting on you about not following directions." She took a breath. "Now, let's see the new address."

Vince grinned and handed her a folded paper from his wallet. "It's not nearly as nice a neighborhood as her first place. The back faces a warehouse area."

She nodded. She knew the working-class community from the address and could easily imagine why Eaton would choose to hide out in it. Her phone rang and Vince motioned that he was leaving to go back to work. She gave him a thumbs-up sign.

"Ms. Morgan, my name is Jerry Griffin. I understand you've been trying to get in touch with me. Your message said it was urgent."

Hollis quickly grabbed a pad of paper and pen. "Yes, Mr. Griffin, I am an executor for the estate of Matthias Bell. Mr. Bell left directions that certain documents and materials be returned to you and I'd like to set up a time to meet."

She listened to the silence.

"Mr. Griffin?" she prodded.

"How much are you going to want?" he asked in a defeated tone.

Hollis suddenly realized how Bell's victims felt when they got her call. They had been tormented for so long, they couldn't see the end. She swiftly disabused him of the notion.

She cleared her throat. "Mr. Griffin, my job is to return documents affecting you that Mr. Bell was … was holding … nothing more."

"I don't understand. What do you want?"

The weight of her task was gradually hitting her. Hollis pushed aside her inclination to impatience and spoke slowly. "Mr. Griffin, if you allow me to meet with you, as I said, I have documents and papers that belong to you and need to be returned. Once you accept them, I can assure you, without any monetary exchange, I will be out of your life forever."

She could hear him gasp and stifle what sounded like a sob.

"Yes, yes, please. I'm sorry. I believe you. It's just that it's been so long." He swallowed. "I can see you this evening, but not here. We can meet at a Chinese restaurant I know in Emeryville. We'll have privacy."

Hollis didn't know where "here" was, but she knew the location in Emeryville and they settled on six thirty. She clicked off the phone.

Up until now, she had seen her assignment as ticking off a to-do list for her client in order to close out a case. She hadn't paid attention to the recipients of her news and the angst they would feel. She'd assumed that if they were being blackmailed, they'd done something to deserve that anxiety.

She picked up Jeremiah Griffin's papers and glanced through them. They seemed innocent enough, and she couldn't tell what secrets they held. If Penny hadn't been able to search them out, then it was likely nothing obvious. Hollis shoved everything back into its envelope. She would be glad when this was over.

When Hollis went to see her boss, she found Gordon with a cellphone propped up on one ear, at the same time texting on another phone. Still, amid his multitasking frenzy, he was able to wave for Hollis to sit down. A smile played on her lips as she realized he had a client on the phone and was sending another client a message. She wondered if he would bill them both for the same minutes. She saw him hit "send" and a couple of minutes later end the call.

"Thanks for waiting," he said. "That was an overseas call. One of our clients fled to Ecuador and I'm trying to get his family to coax him back here." Gordon shook his head. "Then my fiancée wants to buy a vacation condo in Vancouver." He caught Hollis' expression of growing impatience and ran his hand through his short-cropped hair. "Sorry. Why did you need to see me?"

Hollis placed a sheet of paper in front of him. "These are my notes." She paused to let him scan the page. "As you can see, I think we're representing the estate of a felon. It's clear he was blackmailing these people over a period of years. And to top it off, some of them are crooks, too. While I made copies of all the files Bell left behind, I inadvertently made it known to the Pittmans. Now they have the originals and the copy of their file."

She went over the details of her meeting with the Pittmans. Gordon raised his eyebrows and his eyes grew wide.

"Hollis, you know you're developing a reputation at Triple

D for being a lightning rod for trouble. Probate Law is not supposed to be this … this *dangerous*."

She muttered, "I couldn't agree with you more."

"How do you think it will go with Griffin?"

"I'm not anticipating any issues." She didn't want to point out that she hadn't anticipated any issues with the Pittmans either. "But I'm being a bit more cautious. I may have to make two trips."

He leaned forward over his desk and clasped his hands. "You know, Hollis, your other cases have started to slip."

He held up his hand when he saw her open her mouth to protest.

"I didn't say you've missed any deadlines, but you've spoiled me with your habit of getting things done in advance. Additionally, you used to do a weekly summary briefing, which you missed this week."

"You're right," she said. "The Bell matter has taken over my desk. Penny's a big help, but she can only get so far on her own, and I have her assisting on Bell as well."

"I understand you're also recruiting team members from the mailroom."

Hollis flushed. "I take it Tiffany told you."

"No, Tiffany told Martha, who told her boss, who told Ed Simmons, who told me." He was clearly annoyed. "What was this guy doing? We can't bill out a mail clerk's time."

She stared at her manager. He wasn't concerned about Vince, or a top partner in the firm, or the fact she hadn't sought his approval first. He was unhappy about losing billable hours.

"You know, Gordon, I needed to track down an elusive Bell recipient. If I'd had to do it on my own, it would have cost the firm hundreds, perhaps thousands of dollars." Hollis leaned forward, her hands clasped. "I think our section got away cheap."

His raised a skeptical eyebrow and said, "The size of your

bonus and mine depends on us ranking first in the firm. We're not going to make it unless we step up our game."

"Got it." She saluted and left.

HOLLIS RETURNED TO HER OFFICE, miffed but grudgingly agreeing with Gordon. Her other work had taken a backseat to the Bell assignment. The sooner she put his "clients" out of their misery, the better. She crossed the lobby and noticed Tiffany staring blankly at her computer monitor.

"You okay, Tiffany?" Hollis asked, curious.

"Huh? Oh yeah, I'm fine. Er, Penny's looking for you." She busied herself with shuffling files.

Not sure she was ready for another counseling session, Hollis dropped her notepad and mug off at her desk and made her way to Penny's.

"Tiffany said you needed to see me."

"I would have come to your office," Penny said, clearly flustered. "I just wanted you to know that you heard back from Naomi Eaton. She returned your call."

Hollis sank in the chair. "Finally. I'll call her when I get back to my desk." She closed her eyes a moment. "Were you able to get to those cases Gordon was grousing about?"

"You probably didn't notice when you dumped your coat on them," Penny said in a dry but friendly tone. "They're on top of your conference table."

"Great." She stood. "I'll go through them, then I'll call Eaton back. I'm headed out to Emeryville for dinner with Griffin. I'll be back in the office first thing tomorrow."

It took less than a half hour for Hollis to review the files Penny had left for her. Sticking notes with directions on each, she stacked them in her outbox. With a hurried glance at the clock, she decided to make a hasty initial contact with Eaton then leave to meet Jeremiah Griffin.

"Yes?" a woman's voice answered in a crisp tone.

"My name is Hollis Morgan. I would like to speak with Naomi Eaton. Is she available?"

After a moment's hesitation, she said, "I'm Naomi Eaton. I understand you're trying to reach me. Why?"

"I represent the estate of Matthias Bell. He died recently and left directions for certain items to be returned to you. I'm calling to set up that transfer." Hollis spoke quickly, trying not to feel defensive.

"I see." Eaton paused. "I can only meet with you tomorrow. I'm going out of town and ... well, it's the only time I have. Can you make it work?"

Hollis looked at her desk calendar. "That should be fine. I'll make it work. What time did you have in mind, and where?"

"Knowland Park, in the parking lot, tomorrow at three o'clock."

Knowland Park.

"Er, you're welcome to come to our offices downtown," Hollis offered. "We can speak privately."

"That's what I don't want. Can you meet there or not?"

"Sure, of course. I'll be there."

"Good." She clicked off.

Hollis leaned back in her chair. Knowland Park was one of the oldest parks in Oakland. It had once been a vibrant family space, but over the years, its lush patina had dulled and it had suffered from a lack of funding, which had caused its popularity to drop. In an age of video games and virtual everything, it was hard for Mother Nature to compete. Why would Naomi Eaton choose such a place for a meeting?

GLANCING AT THE TIME, HOLLIS stuffed Griffin's envelope into her briefcase and dashed out to the elevators. Fortunately, the Silver Dragon was not far, and she arrived ten minutes early. She thought she'd have a cup of green tea and catch her breath.

During the week, the restaurant catered more to the local lunch crowd than the dinner customers, who came mostly on the weekends. Since it was late afternoon, it wasn't busy, and she noticed a man sitting in the corner nervously fidgeting with a menu. He had arrived even earlier.

She walked over. "Mr. Griffin?"

"Yes." He jumped up and almost tipped over his chair.

Jeremiah Griffin looked nothing like his name sounded. Of average height, with thick blond hair, a cleft chin, and sea-green eyes, he was quite handsome. Unfortunately, he either had no fashion sense or was colorblind. He wore a cotton short-sleeved red-plaid shirt and tiny checked deep-purple pants. Jeremiah Griffin was a nerd.

"Sorry if I startled you," Hollis said and extended her hand. "I'm Hollis Morgan."

"Oh, yes, yes, nice to, er, meet you. But I guess we're not really meeting because … well because—"

"Right," Hollis interrupted. "This shouldn't take long. I have your documents here. If you could show me some ID?"

"ID, ah, sure. Will my driver's license do?"

Hollis smiled and nodded.

A waitress came to the table to take their orders. Griffin pointed to the house special and Hollis ordered won ton soup and green tea.

He took out his driver's license. Fortunately Griffin looked exactly like his photo and Hollis let out a slow, relieved breath.

She handed back the license. "Why was Matthias Bell blackmailing you?"

He jerked his head as if she'd slapped him. His cheeks flushed. "What makes you say that?"

"Because he had other victims."

Griffin's brow wrinkled. "There were others from the company who were gambling?"

"What? No." Hollis waved her hand. "I meant other … never mind." She realized Griffin wasn't as bright as he looked. "Are you a gambler?"

He had been sitting on the edge of his seat, and now he slammed into the back of the chair. "I'm okay now. I go to Gamblers Anonymous. But for a while there, I had it pretty bad. I don't like to think about what it's like to win … or lose anymore." He gazed past her.

"So, you stole from your own company?"

Griffin nodded. "That's what all those memos are about. They're orders I collected on but delayed filling—until I had the money, I mean. The customer never suffered. I mean, I could never steal."

Hollis played with her napkin. "You *borrowed* the money?"

"Yes," Griffin said in a rush. "Yes, I just borrowed it. But then … but then …."

Their food came and they started to eat.

Hollis asked, "How did Bell find out?"

Griffin picked at his food. "I don't know." He looked confused. "Bell said we had a mutual friend who saw me drop a bundle on the tables. This friend said that I must have inherited it, because I didn't make that much. But golly, I don't have any friends who gamble, for sure not anymore."

Golly?

He continued, "Anyway, Bell was suspicious and somehow got his hands on some memos and phone messages."

Hollis opened her briefcase and lifted out the envelope. "Are these the memos?"

Griffin reached for the pages and his eyes glistened. "Yeah, yeah … but these are just copies. Did he give you the originals?"

"Yes, I have the originals. I had to make sure you were who you said you were. I've had a bad experience trying to follow through with my deliveries." She watched him closely as he scanned the pages. "How much did you have to pay Bell?"

"Twenty-five hundred a month," he mumbled and then looked her in the eyes. "You're not going to blackmail me too, are you?"

"No, Mr. Griffin, like I told you over the phone. Once you

sign the release, you can go back to your life with one less debtor."

He took a deep breath. "Where do I sign?"

CHAPTER EIGHT

Tuesday

HOLLIS GOT TO THE FIRM just after dawn the next day. Gordon's jibe about her productivity had really irked her, and before she took the time to deliver Bell's last envelope to Eaton, she was determined to get back into her stride. When Tiffany came in a couple of hours later, she was halfway through her inbox, mostly done with the weekly summary report, and had a jump on the following week's assignments.

"I'm on my way to make coffee," Tiffany said. "Can I bring you back some more hot water for your tea?"

Hollis looked up at the listless tone in her voice. "No, no thanks. I'm going to get through this box before the day is done." She was turning back to her work when she noticed Tiffany's hesitation.

"Is there something else, Tiffany? Are you still having … issues with your friend?"

"What? Er, no." And she was gone.

Hollis frowned. She was going to have to sit Tiffany down and find out what was going on.

She finished writing case notes on Bell's victims. When she looked up from her work, it was almost noon. She hadn't eaten a thing all morning, and now she was hungry. She signed out and went to her car.

Before turning on the ignition, she picked up her phone and called her friend.

"Stephanie, I just finished a boatload of work, and I've got to wrap up a client's directive that's making me nuts. I need a break. Can you do lunch?"

Stephanie Ross was one of her best friends. Smart, attractive, and relentless, she was a forensic tech for the county. Thank goodness for her relentlessness; it had gotten Hollis out of a few tight spots in the past.

"Uh, yeah, sure," Stephanie said brusquely. "It'll have to be a quick one. I got called in to look at an exhumed body for a possible murder victim. Where do you want to meet?

"I'm parked outside the rear door of your building."

"I'm looking out the window, but I don't see your car."

Hollis chuckled. "How are you going to see my car out the window?"

"Hollis, wait a minute, I'm not in my lab in Oakland. I'm at the county lab in San Lucian."

"What?" Hollis said, disappointed. Then she realized what her friend had said. "Hold on, the San Lucian police exhumed a body?"

"Look, I don't have time to explain," Stephanie said. "I've got to get back to work. It's going to take you a little while to get here from downtown. But if you want to do a late lunch, I can be ready by one o'clock. I'll be able to talk then."

Hollis didn't usually follow crime cases, nor did she particularly like the criminal justice reality shows on television, but an exhumed body in San Lucian was not an everyday occurrence. Her curiosity was definitely engaged.

She hadn't counted on the Oakland A's playing an afternoon game, and traffic was sluggish until she passed the Coliseum.

She was a few minutes late for her meeting with Stephanie, but she need not have worried. Stephanie was just coming out of the county coroner's double doors as Hollis pulled into a parking space.

Stephanie opened the passenger door and leaned over to give Hollis an awkward hug. "Hi, I'm sorry for being so late, but this body has me slammed."

Hollis smiled. "Don't worry about it. I just got here myself. Let's go eat. When do you have to be back?"

"I have a good hour, but let's eat somewhere close. I don't like rushing my favorite pastime—eating," said Stephanie, donning a pair of sunglasses.

They settled on a sandwich shop a few blocks away. Their orders taken at the counter, they were given numbers and told that the servers would deliver the food to their table.

"Well, what has you all wired up?" Hollis asked.

Her friend rolled her eyes and motioned with her hand. "I'll start from the beginning, and you'll see why I'm so crazed." She took a sip of water. "Last week a San Lucian detective got a call from this woman who thought her uncle had been murdered. So, the detective tells the lady to come in so they can take her story. Turns out the woman was pretty disgruntled, not so much about her uncle but about the money he was going to give her. Still, she had enough facts that couldn't be brushed away. The guy's fairly important in the community, so the chief asked the DA to get a court order, and yesterday the grave of Matthias Bell was opened."

Hollis froze with her fork midair.

"What?" Stephanie asked, seeing her friend's reaction.

"Stephanie," she said, pointing at herself, "I'm the executor for Matthias Bell's estate. It's his directive that's got me counting backwards."

"You're kidding."

"Not even a little bit," Hollis said.

They stared at each other for the long moment it took for the server to bring their food. Even then they were both silent for the next couple of minutes, deep in their own thoughts.

Hollis took a sip of her iced tea and said carefully, "I don't suppose you can tell me why his body was exhumed?"

"No, not yet. There's an informal gag order," Stephanie said in a lowered voice. "And no, I can't tell you what I've found because I'm not finished. I don't make guesses, hypotheses, conjectures, or wishes. You'll have to wait like everyone else."

Hollis didn't persist. She knew Stephanie could never be enticed to be the source of a leak.

"You should come with me to the station and talk with Detective Scott," Stephanie said. "She's handling the case until the chief comes back from vacation."

"I can't. I've got an important client meeting right after I leave here," Hollis replied. "I'll meet you there when I'm finished. It shouldn't take long."

Stephanie nodded. "Good idea. I'll be done by then, and it will give me a chance to write up my notes and make a report." She dabbed at her lips and rose to her feet. "I've got to get back to the lab. I won't say anything to Scott until you join us. She tends to overreact."

Hollis looked doubtful. "Hmm, that's not been my experience with her; when I came in with my suspicions, I couldn't get her to react at all. But I agree, wait until I get back. I shouldn't be any later than four o'clock."

Stephanie wrapped her uneaten sandwich in the paper napkin and slid it into her purse. Hollis did the same, and they both headed out the door.

Hollis turned to face her. "Can you just tell me—?"

"See you at four o'clock, Hollis."

THE MAJORITY OF KNOWLAND PARK'S extensive lands were pristine and undeveloped. The area included the Oakland Zoo and numerous walking paths that weaved around its many oak trees and lush grounds. While its popularity had declined over the years, it still attracted a decent number of families, school children, and fans of its birds and wildlife.

Hollis pulled into a parking spot near the rear of the lot so she could see Eaton when she arrived. Almost a half hour early, she scanned her messages to make sure the meeting was still on.

There was a tap on her window.

She started slightly and pushed the button to roll the window down.

"Ms. Morgan?" a woman asked in a deep voice.

"Yes." Hollis began to open the car door. "Naomi Eaton, I presume. Where can we talk?"

Eaton stopped her progress and pointed to the rear. "Is there a problem with me sitting in the backseat?" She opened the passenger door without waiting for an answer and slid in.

Hollis returned to the driver's seat, annoyed and more than a little frustrated. Naomi Eaton sat behind her and stretched her legs across the small hump. Hollis was forced to view her awkwardly over her shoulder.

The woman was wearing black aviator sunglasses. She appeared to be of average size with a round face. Her thick black eyebrows contrasted boldly with her blonde hair, pulled back into a short ponytail. She looked nothing like Hollis' idea of a Wall Street trader, more like a suburban housewife. Certainly nothing like a criminal capable of the activities Penny had described.

"So, let's see what you have," Eaton demanded.

Hollis frowned. "First, I'll need to see some ID."

With a slight snort, Eaton took a wallet out of her jacket pocket and flashed a card with a picture. Hollis held her wrist and peered at the photo.

She squinted. "This is a gym ID, and it doesn't look like you. Can I see your driver's license?"

Eaton pursed her lips. "It was stolen. Wait, here's my passport." She pulled a U.S. passport out of the same pocket.

"Do you always walk around with a passport?"

Eaton gave her a disparaging look. "Like I said, I don't have my driver's license. Some people, like you, want something more official."

Hollis inclined her head in agreement. The passport was for Naomi Eaton all right, and the woman behind her matched the photo. She handed back the passport.

"I'll need you to sign a release." Hollis pulled out a sheet of paper and pen and passed both back.

She could see Eaton reading the page.

"Miss Eaton, how long had Bell been blackmailing you?" she asked casually.

Eaton dropped the pen on the car floor and a profanity escaped her lips. She frantically patted the mat until it was retrieved.

"I didn't mean to startle you," Hollis said.

There was silence.

"About three years," Eaton said, her voice wearier than ever. "He was an asshole."

It was all Hollis could do to stop a disbelieving snort from escaping. Talk about the kettle calling the pot black, or was it the other way around?

"Well, my job is just to make deliveries." Hollis reached into her briefcase for the packet. "Here's your envelope."

Eaton opened it, lifting out the calendar page. She sighed with satisfaction and then leaned over the seat to look Hollis in the eye.

"Did you look inside?"

Hollis nodded. "Yes, I did. But I didn't get the purpose of the calendar page. I figured it meant something to you ... and Bell."

Eaton searched Hollis' face for the lie; then, satisfied she was telling the truth, she leaned back in the seat and tapped her mouth with her fist.

"Yep, he was slime." She looked at Hollis in the rearview

mirror. "I thought someone would find his files eventually. I'd have thought he would hide them better." She again sought out Hollis' eyes in the mirror.

She's lying about something.

"He left me directions where to look, and your envelope was there," said Hollis, wondering where this conversation was going.

"Do you think he had other copies?" She paused. "I mean, should I expect to be hounded again?"

Hollis looked at her. "No, not as far as I know, and I have no reason to think otherwise. This is the only copy."

Eaton nodded. "Are you going to tell the police?"

The question seemed to be offhand. Eaton had opened the car door and was halfway out.

Hollis didn't want to tell her that she had tried to tell the police without success. "Bell's dead. You're his victim, and I'm his attorney. What's to tell?"

"Yeah, right." Eaton slammed the door and bent down next to Hollis' window. "Uh ... thank you."

Hollis took her time pulling out of the parking space, and it appeared that Eaton wasn't going to move toward her own car until she left. She smiled as she pulled onto the MacArthur Freeway. Hollis didn't want Eaton to know that Vince, sitting on a bench near a clump of trees, had already taken down her license plate number.

That's one for me.

LATE IN THE AFTERNOON, THE San Lucian Police Department was still bustling. Hollis wondered why such a small city could have so much activity. There was very little crime, but the community involvement went on forever.

She gave her name to the receptionist and waited for Stephanie. She didn't have to wait long.

"Hollis, I thought you'd never get here," Stephanie said as she half guided, half pushed Hollis through the lobby's double doors. "Detective Scott wants to see you as soon as you arrive."

"Why?"

"I already briefed her." Stephanie stopped and gave her a pointed look. "Matthias Bell was murdered."

Hollis stared at her in disbelief. "How can that be?"

"Look, you and I can talk later, but Scott is waiting. I told her you were coming," Stephanie said quickly. "And, Hollis, no cute stuff. This is serious."

Hollis frowned. "Hey, I know how to act. But I can tell you now, I don't think Scott likes me."

There were outside Scott's door. Stephanie did an across-the-throat motion with the side of her hand. Hollis mouthed *okay*.

Detective Laura Scott reached across her cluttered desk to shake Hollis' hand. "Well, Ms. Morgan, I guess I'm going to have to eat my words. It seems your instincts were right. Now we're going to need your help."

With Scott's apology, Hollis felt she could afford to be gracious. She smiled.

"Not a problem, Detective. I can't get over the fact that Matthias Bell was murdered. How was he killed?"

Laura Scott stood and began to pace, her long legs crossing the room in a few steps. "We have Stephanie to thank for gleaning the details." She motioned for Stephanie to speak.

Her friend took a breath. "Bell was killed by an overdose of insulin. But because he was an elderly man, the hospital staff assumed it was a heart attack. He was an insulin-dependent diabetic; his doctor recognized the multiple injection sites and thought nothing of it. I conducted the autopsy and found his insulin levels to be outrageously high. I checked his pancreas for tumors that could possibly account for the insulin increase, and he had none. No tumors meant someone had administered a deadly dose. Even though he was rushed to the hospital, it was already too late."

Hollis raised her eyebrows and said, "I didn't know he was a diabetic. So it was two weeks ago Saturday when he died?"

"Yes," Stephanie assured her. "The injection could not have been given much more than a couple of hours before it took effect. It was a massive dose."

Hollis nodded slowly.

Scott tilted her head and asked, "Can you tell me if Odelia Larson said anything to you about the strangeness of Bell's death?"

"No." Hollis peered at her. "She wasn't very happy with her last paycheck, and she got pretty vocal about that, but nothing about his death."

Scott sat back down and looked at her. "I'm going to turn on the tape." She pushed a button on a small, dark machine at the edge of her desk. "So we come to you now, Ms. Morgan. Tell me what you know of the circumstances surrounding the weekend Bell died and your contact with Odelia Larson."

Hollis flinched. Her initial reaction to being taped was a flashback to her time as a suspect and later her incarceration. Even though her pardon had given her back her life, it wasn't just soldiers who suffered from post-traumatic stress.

"Sure," Hollis said and recounted Odelia's calls, Bell's letter, and her own entry into his safe. "When I initially went through the envelopes, I didn't know what the material meant. It looked highly suspicious because of its randomness. His note directed me not to make copies, but I'm an attorney, so I recorded the contents and made arrangements to return the envelopes to the owners."

Scott said, "Give me the names on the envelopes, and we're going to want that list of recorded items as soon as you can get it to us. Go on …. When did you suspect something was wrong?"

"The conversation I had with Anthony Cantone." She paused. "Then, when I met the Pittmans, I knew something was up. That's why I came to see you."

Scott shot her a look of irritation. "Right, so where are the envelopes now?"

"They've all been delivered," Hollis said ruefully. "I delivered the last one just before I came to see you."

"How efficient of you," Scott said in a mocking voice.

She leaned back in her chair with a little bounce and stared past the women. Stephanie had remained silent the entire time, and Hollis wondered where this was going. Hollis wasn't sure she liked Scott, so she didn't volunteer any more than she was asked. The chief would be back the next day, and while he wasn't wild about her either, he wasn't as condescending.

Scott turned off the machine. "It's getting late. Will there be a problem getting that victim list to me first thing in the morning? Include the contact information you have for each."

"You'll have it in the morning," Hollis said.

Hollis and Stephanie gathered their belongings.

"But why would his victims want to kill him?" Stephanie blurted at the door. "He was giving back the information he had on them."

Scott and Hollis exchanged looks.

Hollis answered, "Because one of them didn't know he'd already planned to release his hold."

Chapter Nine

—~~~—

Wednesday Morning

FOR ONCE HOLLIS DIDN'T TAKE the time to gaze at the splash of color in the sky as the sun rose over the East Bay Hills. She was dashing to her office, in a hurry to get the Bell list ready for the police. Fortunately, Penny had taken the initiative to compile a contact spreadsheet, and Hollis merged it with the contents list from the envelopes.

It took Hollis only an hour to finish, but she didn't think that Scott or the chief would appreciate her speed.

There was a tap at her door, and Tiffany gave her a forlorn look. "I don't feel well. I'm going home. I just came in to get a couple of things. You should forward your calls to Penny."

"Okay, not a problem," Hollis said. "Sorry to hear you're not feeling well, but I'm glad you have the sense to go home."

"Yeah," said Tiffany. "I should be back tomorrow."

Hollis watched her retreating back. She was letting this relationship thing get the best of her. Was it also making her sick?

There was another tap at her door and Hollis looked up into Penny's solemn face.

"What?"

"I think you've got a new client," Penny said, sitting down across from her desk, uninvited. "A Kiki Turner."

Hollis smiled. "Kiki? She sounds like a stripper."

Penny expressed cautious amusement with a reluctant half-smile. "I think she is. She found you through Martindale-Hubbell, so she's not a complete lightweight."

Martindale-Hubbell was a website for persons seeking lawyers or law firms by their area of practice. There was rating system and basic attorney background information. While not totally comprehensive, it was a respected site for lawyer references.

"Well, a new client will make Gordon happy by helping my 'billables,'" she said, using air quotes. Taking the slip of paper from Penny, she said, "I'll call her before I go to the San Lucian Police Department."

"I listened to the message you left on my phone." Penny folded her arms across her chest. "Murdered ... I had a bad feeling about Bell."

Hollis was disinclined to lapse into a chatting session, even if such occasions were rare with the normally unsociable paralegal.

"Let me get back to work," she said. "I'd like you to start summarizing the last of George Ravel's files. I know it seems like busy work, but it's got to be done." Hollis scanned her phone calendar. "I should be in and out of the office the rest of the week, if you need me."

Seemingly happy with her assignment, Penny left with renewed purpose.

Hollis punched in the number for Kiki Turner.

"Mrs. Turner, this is Hollis Morgan with Dodson Dodson & Doyle. You wanted to set up an appointment to see me?"

The voice that answered was soft and warm. "Oh, yes, Ms. Morgan, I'd like to see you about setting up a will or trust or something. I'd like to do it sooner rather than later. When is a good time for you?"

Hollis had already looked at her calendar. "I could see you tomorrow, midmorning, or next Monday afternoon."

"Tomorrow will be fine. What time?"

"I can give you an hour at ten o'clock, and because this is just a consultation to see if I can help you, there will be no charge."

She gave a small chuckle. "All right, and I'm not concerned about the money."

Hollis raised her eyebrows. "I'll see you tomorrow then."

She was about to return to her work for a third time, when she felt the phone vibrate in her purse. She snatched it up and looked at the screen:

San Francisco 49ers by 10.

She smiled. It was John using his safe texting greeting. The San Francisco 49ers were his favorite football team. She exhaled a breath she didn't know she had been holding.

She placed the phone on the floor and gave it a sharp stomp with her foot.

Her head jerked up when she heard a small cough. Penny was standing in the doorway. It was clear she'd seen Hollis crush the phone.

Hollis gave her a sheepish smile. "Don't ask." She tossed the phone in her wastebasket and walked back around to sit at her desk. "What's up?"

"Er, Chief Brennan wants to see you right away. He told me to just give you the message. He didn't have time for details."

Hollis was mildly irritated. She wasn't being paid to be on call with the San Lucian Police Department. However, the chief was a no-nonsense kind of guy, so this must be important. Fortunately his list was ready, and she would kill two birds.

THERE WAS ONLY ONE OTHER person in the police lobby, and

he was reading the screen on his iPad. Hollis walked up to the front desk.

"Joyce, I'm here to see the chief. I think he's expecting me."

"Sure, Hollis." She motioned with her head to the man sitting engrossed. She whispered, "I think he'll be more than glad to see you, so he can pass his meeting with the gentleman from the chamber of commerce off on Scott. They want the chief to make a speech."

It had been less than two minutes, and she was still standing by the counter, when Joyce tapped her headphone and said, "Go on in. He's in his office."

Chief Donald Brennan looked every bit the suburban police chief. There had been a turnover in the department over the past six months. Either through retirements, or transfers, the top three positions were held by a new cast of characters. Brennan was a little over six feet, with brown eyes and lighter brown hair. In his fifties, he was more stocky than fat and carried any extra weight well. His face appeared stern but Hollis had seen him at city fundraisers when his smile transformed him into a large teddy bear.

Unfortunately, he didn't smile often and the first impression of sternness was more accurate with regard to his overall personality.

He came from behind his desk to shake her hand.

"Ms. Morgan, good to see you again. Take a seat and tell me what you know about the Bell murder." He pointed to an office chair in front of his desk.

"First, I don't know much about the murder at all. Nothing, actually." She wondered if he had chosen a particularly stiff chair for his guests, because she couldn't get comfortable. She shifted in her seat. "Detective Scott taped my statement. My only involvement is in carrying out Matthias Bell's estate instructions upon hearing of his death."

Brennan gave her a hard look.

"We haven't spoken much since I started here, but I've gone

through some of the recent felony cases in San Lucian, and you seem to have been drawn into a lot criminal activity over the years, Ms. Morgan. Why is that?"

"Just lucky, I guess." Hollis wished she could swallow her remark. She had a feeling that flippant comments would not endear her to Brennan.

They didn't.

He bristled and his eyes narrowed. He picked up a file and took out a sheet of paper. "Where were you on Saturday, July eleventh?"

"What?" she asked in disbelief, and shifted in her seat. "You can't think I had anything to do with Bell's murder?"

"I don't know, Ms. Morgan. That's why I'm asking the question."

Her jaw clenched. "At home, and I have an alibi. Can you answer a question for me? Who tipped you off that Bell was murdered?"

"His niece." He looked down at his pad. "A Constance Cantone. She had her doubts and evidently good contacts in the mayor's office. She insisted his body be exhumed. Guess she was right to be suspicious. Do you know an Odelia Larson?"

Hollis wondered where this was going. "Yes, I know her."

Brennan leaned back in his swivel chair. "Do you know her to be honest and trustworthy?"

"Odelia is a lot of things, but I would say she was also honest and trustworthy. Why?"

"That's interesting, because Odelia Larson has given a statement saying that you didn't like Matthias Bell and that you resented having him for a client."

Hollis counted to five and took a breath.

"I don't like most people, but I don't think they deserve killing."

He gave her a half-smile. "I see." He rocked back and forth. "So who do you think killed Bell?"

She shrugged. "Matthias Bell was a disagreeable person. I'm

98

a probate attorney and I knew him only in relation to his estate creation and distribution. Other than that, I rarely talked to the man. A firm in San Francisco handled his business matters."

"What's the name of the firm?"

"I don't know the name off the top of my head, but once I get back to my office, I can call you with their contact information."

Brennan stopped rocking. The sound of young voices and footsteps paused and then passed by his door. He started rocking again.

"Third grade tour." He motioned toward the door with his head. "Who inherited his estate?"

"It's good-sized. The bulk—including real estate, stocks, bonds, and cash—goes to a sister in the Midwest. A modest sum will go to Mrs. Cantone, and there is a monetary gift to a church in Daly City. Lesser amounts went to his staff."

He rubbed his chin. "Yes, his staff. We're checking into everyone's background. Do they know of the amounts?"

"The staff do. He had checks ready for them. I also formally notified his sister and niece of his estate and their inheritance. His sister made the arrangements for his funeral, but she said she wouldn't be able to attend and would send a wreath."

Brennan raised his eyebrows.

Hollis recounted the almost uncaring conversation with Gloria Bell Haver for the chief. It hadn't lasted ten minutes. Like brother, like sister. She had seemed irritated that her brother had died without considering her calendar.

The chief had apparently been absorbed in his own thoughts. Standing abruptly, he said, "I've got to ask this question. Was Bell blackmailing you?"

The question startled Hollis, and she jumped slightly in her seat. "What? No, he wasn't." Her cheeks flushed and when she spoke her voice was raised, "Why would you ask that?"

He waved his palms downward. "Now, Ms. Morgan, see it from my viewpoint. I know your background, so it doesn't matter to me. But from what you told us, Bell wasn't beyond tormenting his victims with … well, with exposure. Scott tells me you've got a steady clientele who might not know of your prison record."

"My record is public," Hollis snapped.

He nodded, his voice calm. "Yes, but how many people run a background check on their probate attorney? It's a field of law which brings you in contact with a lot of money, and your client is dead. Who's the wiser? A blackmailer could threaten to bring your past to the forefront, particularly a past that involved fraud."

Hollis was about to react angrily when instead she paused and spoke with resignation. "Yes. I see, as you say, 'your viewpoint,' but, no, I wasn't being blackmailed."

Brennan took a moment longer to look into her eyes before reaching out to shake her hand. "I want to thank you for coming over and briefing me." His lips formed a thin line. "Nothing you've told me has changed my decision. I've sent Detective Scott to Odelia Larson's house to arrest her for the murder of Matthias Bell."

"What?"

The Chief shuffled a stack of papers. "It's classic. She had motive, means, and opportunity. She felt Bell had shorted her, and felt insulted by the small bequest after all those years of loyal service. She had round-the-clock access to him. And," he sat back in his chair, his broad arms folded across his chest, "with her nursing background, she was capable of injecting a syringe full of insulin."

"That's ridiculous," Hollis protested. "Odelia is an elderly woman. She couldn't overcome Matthias Bell."

"Yeah, well, Matthias Bell was an elderly man. I can tell you that angry men or women don't always run on all cylinders. Murderers have a distinctive frame of mind. Adrenaline takes over and they aren't themselves, in fact—"

Hollis raised her hand, cutting him off. "Chief, please, not now. How much longer before they get here?"

He turned and looked at the wall clock. "Humph, they should be here in about ten minutes. I called you because Odelia Larson wanted you here. She wants you to represent her."

CHAPTER TEN

Wednesday Afternoon

HOLLIS WAS BACK IN THE police department waiting room, waiting for the arrival of Detective Scott and Odelia Larson. The chief had asked for privacy to make a few calls. She took a seat in the far corner away from the Chamber representative, who was clearly getting restless and had put all his electronic devices away except for his phone's time-of-day screen.

She debated calling Stephanie for more details about the insulin injection that killed Bell, but instead she punched the number for Penny, who answered with palpable excitement.

"I'm so glad you called." Penny said. "Gordon has been looking for you. He won't tell me why, but you're to see him as soon as you get back."

"Transfer me to him, now."

"I can't. He's on the other line, and I've got an errand to run during my lunch, so—"

"Fine." Hollis sighed. "Just slip him a note that I got his message and tell him I need to talk to him too."

"All right."

She clicked off.

Hollis had just put down her phone when Scott came through the hallway door and walked over to her.

"Your client is being processed in the back. You can see her in a few minutes."

She's not my client.

Scott pointed to the corridor. "You can meet with her in one of the empty private offices."

Hollis picked up her briefcase and followed her to a sterile-looking office with a desk and two chairs. She put her belongings on the floor.

"Detective Scott, do you really think that old lady killed Matthias Bell?" Hollis said.

Scott shrugged. "It doesn't matter what I think. It's what the evidence shows. She was hiding evidence of the hypodermic needle in her room. And the fact is she's all but admitted she was the only one who could've done it."

A buzz went off on her communicator.

"They're bringing her in," Scott said.

Hollis folded her arms across her chest.

The "they" were the department's two patrol officers, who looked about sixteen. A hint of mustache growth appeared above the lip of one and the other kept his right hand on his gun as he led the elderly woman into the room. She almost laughed out loud, until she saw the look of fright on Odelia Larson's face. The young patrolmen closed the door behind them.

"We'll be right outside," Trigger-finger said.

Hollis raised her eyes heavenward in exasperation.

Odelia took a chair and Hollis sat next to her, already looking in her purse for tissues.

"I can't believe any of this," Odelia murmured, her eyes clear. "I don't … I mean I didn't like Mr. Bell, but not enough to kill him. I … I've done some things but—"

"Odelia, stop. Don't tell me anything about your activities," Hollis said. "I can't represent you. You can't be my client. I don't practice criminal law."

Odelia gave her a weak smile. "I don't mind."

Hollis opened her mouth to speak.

"I don't care what you say." Odelia wagged her finger back and forth. "I know you, Ms. Morgan. I've seen how you think and act over the years. While we may have had our differences, I trust you. I want you to represent me."

"But, Odelia, I wouldn't be your best advocate. I don't know the procedures and process for putting your case forward I—"

She reached over and patted Hollis' hand. "You'll figure it out."

Odelia refused to listen to Hollis' objections, and after a few minutes she stood. "Like I said, you'll figure it out." She knocked on the door, and one of the officers poked his head in and escorted her out.

A frustrated Hollis stared after her.

Chief Brennan joined Hollis in the hallway, watching Odelia make her way back to the holding cells.

"I've seen all types, Ms. Morgan. Believe me, that woman could kill if she had a mind to." He turned to look at her. "So, are you going to take her on? I didn't think you handled criminal cases, but I guess it's all the same."

Hollis leaned against the wall. "No, it's not all the same. I've never been in front of a jury." She ran her hand over her face. "She could be sentenced to prison because I don't know what I'm doing with criminal law."

She turned to face the chief.

"That said," she continued, "I don't think she did it. And *even I* could get her off with the flimsy case you have against her. Have you talked with the DA?"

"You can't have it both ways, Ms. Morgan. I don't have to share anything with you if you're not representing Mrs. Larson. But I will tell you this. Odelia Larson admitted to Detective

Scott that she knew Bell had cheated her out of her expected pay *before* you gave her the check."

Hollis stared at him, the impact of his words slowly sinking in.

An hour later when Hollis pulled into her parking spot in Triple D's garage, she was still ruffled from her meeting with Odelia Larson and the chief's revelation about what the elderly woman knew and when she knew it.

Gordon's door was open but he was on the phone. He glanced up and waved her in. He said a quick, "I'll get back to you," to the caller and clicked off.

"Hollis, I understand from your paralegal that you're meeting with a new client tomorrow, Mrs. Kiki Turner."

Hollis formed a "T" with her hands. "Gordon, time out, I have an emergency I need to speak to you about."

It must have been the tone of her voice, because for once he put his phone inside his desk drawer and gave her his full attention.

"Talk."

Hollis was thankful she'd already briefed him about Bell and didn't have to start from the beginning. Instead, she went straight to the chief's call.

She wrapped up her explanation, "Bottom line is I can't talk her out of wanting me as her counsel."

Gordon steepled his fingers in front of his mouth. "Well, I have a solution. I can represent the court case and you can work with me on dealing with the client. She trusts you and you're already familiar with the cast of characters. One of those victims killed Bell." He paused. "Regardless, it doesn't matter to me whether Larson killed Matthias Bell or not. She deserves a defense. But are you sure you want to get involved? Criminal law is not as … as cut and dried as probate."

Hollis' suppressed the urge to argue that she was up to any

case Gordon gave her. But she stopped, as she knew John would want her to, and gave it a moment's thought.

She smiled. "I'm up for the case. As co-counsel, I can be your feet on the ground, and as you said, Odelia already trusts me. That alone would save billable hours."

Gordon slapped the top of this desk.

"Ah, that's what I wanted to talk to you about," he said, pulling out a notepad. "Your paralegal tells me that you're meeting with a Mrs. Kiki Turner."

Gordon was smiling so broadly that she was put on guard.

"Yes," she said tentatively. "I haven't signed her. It's just a consultation."

"But you expect to sign her?"

"Yes, it's likely."

He slapped his hands together.

"This is great news." He got up and sat on the edge of his desk. "From the expression on your face I can tell you don't know who she is."

Hollis wondered what he was leading up to. "Oh, that. I know she's a stripper but—"

"*A* stripper!" Gordon exclaimed. "She's *the* stripper. She's the stripper who married Harold Turner a couple of years ago. She's worth millions."

She unconsciously stiffened. She now knew what was behind Gordon's elation. "Well, I don't think a standard trust will garner an inordinate amount of billable hours."

"Did you hear what I said? She's Kiki Turner. Don't you listen to the news? Don't you watch the entertainment channel?"

Hollis manage to suppress her snort. "Ah, no, I don't."

Network shows depressed her. Except for sporting events, she and John watched cable and public television.

"Good lord. Kiki Turner married ninety-three-year-old Harold Turner when she was thirty-six or thirty-seven. She had one daughter at the time—I can't remember her name—by another, hmm, liaison. The daughter is grown, married and has at least one child of her own. But they're estranged; I don't think the daughter liked what her mother did for a living." He went around his desk and sat back down.

He continued, "Harold died earlier this year. It's time for the big payoff."

"Okay, though I don't see—"

"Kiki Turner is rolling in dough, and there's a rumor she's dying."

Gordon's revelation caused Hollis to wrinkle her brow. Clearly her potential high-profile cases—one a murder and the other, a celebrity estate—were not as simple as they appeared. And either one could keep her busy for a while to come.

Gordon pulled his phone out of the drawer and turned it on. "I'll go to the police department and sign up Mrs. Larson on my way home this evening. I've never dealt with Chief Brennan, but from what you've told me, he's not going to be a challenge."

"I should come with you. Odelia is cranky enough to believe that I'm pulling a bait and switch on her, and not sign with you," Hollis said.

His phone trilled.

She was ready to club him for allowing his incessantly ringing phone to interrupt their meetings. He looked down at the screen, and shrugging, picked up the phone.

She'd had enough.

She raised her voice to say, "Gordon, I've got work to do. I have other clients, too."

He nodded but motioned for her to wait. He finally finished his call.

"Sorry, I'll meet you in San Lucian at four thirty." He scribbled something on his pad of paper. "I just want you to take extra care. The Bell case is high profile. And the Turner estate would mean a lot to the firm ... and your career."

"Got it."

His phone trilled again, and she got up and left.

She returned to her office to make a call to Detective Scott, informing her that she and Gordon Barrett could see Odelia Larson that evening.

"So, you *are* going to represent her," Scott insisted.

"Gordon Barrett will act as her attorney. I will be assisting as co-counsel," Hollis said. She pulled out her notepad. "Detective Scott, Chief Brennan said that you have proof of Odelia Larson's motive to kill Bell. What did you find?"

"I'm not inclined to hold case interviews over the phone, Ms. Morgan," Scott said, "but you've been a help to us. Miss Larson evidently gained access to the box that held Bell's final checks to his staff. She knew the amount that was coming her way. As you said yourself, she was very unhappy, and we think she was unhappy enough to kill."

Hollis held her tongue and said goodbye. She rubbed her eyes with her fingers. She wished she knew what kind of "proof" the police had against Larson, but guessed she would find out soon enough. Hollis worked well under stress, but things were starting to make her a little crazy. The fact that Bell was murdered was just beginning to sink in. She frowned. Assuming he didn't know he was going to be murdered, why would Bell release his victims and pay off his staff? It didn't make sense.

This last revelation raised a completely different set of questions.

CHAPTER ELEVEN

———— ❧ ————

Wednesday Late Afternoon and Evening

"Excuse me, Hollis," Tiffany said from the doorway, "a Mrs. Turner is here to see you."

Hollis had googled Kiki Turner and was reading her credits. She reeled her thoughts back to the present. "Direct her to the small conference room. It's private and faces the bay. Gordon wants me to give her the royal treatment."

"This ought to be good," Tiffany mumbled, returning to the hallway.

"I heard you," Hollis called out.

Hollis did not shock or surprise easily, but she had to admit she was taken aback by her visitor. Kiki Turner had crystal-blue eyes shielded with a double layer of fake black lashes and a face framed with jet black-hair thickened with a bounty of long, curly, black hair extensions. Her artificially enhanced pouty lips blazed with a bold red lipstick. And yet, despite her heavy makeup, one could detect a smattering of freckles that covered her narrow nose. The overall impression was actually endearing.

"Thank you for seeing me so quickly," Turner said in a clear and steady voice. "As I said on the phone I ... I don't have much time and I want to get my will settled."

She took off her deep maroon Prada jacket and put it on the back of the chair. Underneath, she wore a black cashmere turtleneck and black slacks. Her row of gold bracelets clinked richly as she put her red Kate Spade bag beside her on the table. Hollis hid her knowing smile, grateful that her friends had tutored her in Fashion 101.

Hollis nodded. "Didn't your husband leave the estate in a trust?"

"Yes, but it ended with me." She smiled ruefully. "We both thought that I had many years ahead of me." She looked into Hollis' eyes. "One of life's ironies, I guess."

"So you want to use a will instead of a—"

Turner held up her hand. "Wait, before you get started with the legal bit, let me explain my situation." She moistened her lips. "I know what I am ... and what I am not. I am not going to pretend I wasn't on the stage as a stripper, and I'm not going to pretend that Harold's money came with a higher education. I left high school when I was sixteen, but I looked twenty. The next years I worked as ... as a stripper to support myself and my daughter."

She poured a glass of water from the decanter Tiffany had put on the table.

She continued, "I smoothed out my rough edges and by the time I met Harold ...." She chuckled. "We met in the library, can you believe it? I love to read and so did he. He was visiting the main library because they were honoring him for his sponsorship donations. He saw me poring over a book and ... and the rest is history." Her voice faded at the last words.

Hollis cleared her throat. "I understand your husband was a very nice man."

"He was. We didn't love each other—not *that* way, I mean. But we were good friends and we enjoyed each other's company."

Turner stopped. "I don't know if you can understand that."

"I think I can," Hollis responded.

Turner swallowed. "Good. About six months ago … about six … about …." Tears poured from her eyes.

Hollis passed her a box of tissue sitting on a nearby credenza, but said nothing.

"Thank you. I'm okay." Turner dabbed at her eyes and stroked her neck with her hand. "About six months ago, doctors gave me a year to live. I've wasted a lot of time in denial and the rest of the time depressed. This past Monday, I woke up with a new sense of purpose. I want to take care of my estate, and take care of the loved ones I'm leaving behind. And I want you to help me."

"That's why I'm here. Let's get started." Hollis smiled and flipped open a pad of paper. "You mentioned you have a daughter … what's her name?"

"Alicia, Alicia Marie Lynch. That's her married name."

"She's currently married?"

"Yes, why?"

"Nothing." Hollis was doing the age math in her head. "Do you have other relatives you'd like to provide for?"

There was a long pause. "Yes, my granddaughter, Kate."

Hollis placed her pencil on the table. "Mrs. Turner—"

"Please call me Kiki."

"Kiki," Hollis said. "May I ask how old you are?"

Kiki grinned. "I celebrated my fortieth birthday last month." She leaned forward. "You shouldn't believe everything you read on Wikipedia."

"So true." Hollis laughed. "Well, you look great." She took out a sheet of paper. "So that I don't make any more false assumptions, I'd like you to fill out this basic information sheet I ask of all our new probate clients."

She took the sheet. "You have to realize how good your doubt about my age makes me feel." Her voice dropped. "On top of everything, I know my looks will go, too."

Hollis' voice softened. "For me, I find it's best just to deal with today. Tell me about your daughter and what you have in mind for your estate."

Turner sighed and squared her shoulders. "I was seventeen when I had Alicia—seventeen and very irresponsible. My parents were never married and my brother and I lived with my mom who ... who was an alcoholic. She died when Alicia was two, and fortunately by that time I had grown up and realized that it was all on me. No one was going to save me."

Kiki Turner paused for a breath. She reached into her purse and took out her phone to look at the time.

"I'm sorry, Ms. Morgan, but I have an appointment. Your assistant said I would only have an hour of your time, and it's been a half hour over that already."

"Call me Hollis." She shrugged. "Don't worry about it. If you want to have me draft your estate documents, I have a retainer agreement you can sign. We can set up another appointment when it's more convenient for you."

"Yes, I would like to retain you." Turner smiled. "I like you. You don't seem like the usual attorney."

"I take that as a compliment. How long before you have to leave to make your appointment? I'll need you to sign the agreement and it would help if you could complete that information sheet before you go."

Turner was already penning her signature and filling in her information. "I can give you another fifteen minutes. I'm driving myself today and I have tendency to get lost."

Hollis nodded. "Just to get me started, do you want to leave your estate to your daughter for her lifetime then have the remainder go to your granddaughter?"

Turner looked up from her writing. "Hollis, here's where it gets complicated, and my long story comes in. Alicia is a bona fide, card-carrying bitch who wouldn't give me the time of day."

Kiki's Turner's words didn't faze Hollis, but she concurred that in that case the trust would likely be too complex to plan during the remaining ten minutes.

"If there's a chance it may be contested, there are extra precautions you may want to include in your trust. How about meeting next Tuesday?"

They settled on a time, and Kiki Turner stepped quickly through the lobby and out the doors.

Tiffany stood by Hollis as she watched Turner take the elevator. "Is she a new client?"

"Yes, she is."

"She's a little odd," Tiffany mused. "I can't put my finger on it. I can tell she's got money, but her manner … I don't know."

Hollis turned abruptly to face her. "You know, I think you've been talking to Penny too long. Let's give our client a break."

Tiffany blushed. "I'm sorry, you're right. I'm the last one to point fingers." She turned to go back to her desk.

Hollis sighed. "No, it's me. I'm taking on this crazy Bell case with Gordon."

"Is that the one with the safe we opened? The one Vince was working on?"

"Yeah, 'was,' but now it's taken a left turn and it's more complicated." Hollis leaned over the reception counter. "I understand you told Ed's secretary about Vince's assignment. Your remarks were made within the firm, so no big deal. But you'll be privy to client matters a lot, and all the attorneys have got to know that you are not another set of ears or a possible leak. Besides, what I'm telling you is not new. It's not like you to be indiscreet."

Tiffany looked miserable. "I know, I know. I knew it was wrong for me to say anything as soon as the words left my lips. I'm sorry." Her eyes glistened. "It won't happen again. I … I …. Never mind."

Hollis was hungry, and she wanted to get ready for the meeting with the chief and Scott in the afternoon. She would have to consider having another talk with Tiffany to address what had been bothering the receptionist for the last couple of weeks.

She was thoughtful as she reviewed the final write-up of the timeline of events. The taped statement she gave Scott was fine, except knowing that Chief Brennan would want to verify that she hadn't changed her story.

Her story.

She flinched. Even all these years later, her conviction and prison time still haunted her—though each year a little less. Her ex-husband's death, her eventual pardon, and her swearing in as an attorney had not completely erased the nightmare of those long years. How easy it was to be at the wrong place at the wrong time or with the wrong person at the wrong time …. Well, lessons learned.

Hollis finished typing the timeline and then pulled out her pad and titled a page: "Bell: If I knew Then What I Know Now: Things That Don't Fit." She promptly made a list of questions.

First, Bell was not a generous man—just the opposite. Why would he return the blackmail documents to his victims? It was more likely he would, even from the grave, take delight in having the material discovered by someone else and his victims exposed, or even exploited again.

Second, he left the remainder of his estate to a church in Daly City just outside San Francisco. Bell hated religion. Why, then, this church?

Finally, she hadn't given his victims a lot of thought, but it was clear they still felt threatened. It wasn't easy to pack up and disappear with a few days' notice. Granted, if exposed, some had more to worry about than others. But they knew they were off the hook, so why leave town now?

If she were asking these questions, Brennan likely asking his own "what doesn't fit" questions. Still, Hollis knew Bell, and the police didn't. She didn't think the chief seriously considered her a suspect, but her distrust radar was in full operation and she wasn't about to experience being a suspect all over again.

*

Gordon was in his car in the police parking lot talking animatedly on the phone when Hollis pulled in next to him. Catching his eye, she motioned that she was going in. He nodded and held up five fingers.

For once, the police station lobby was silent and empty. Joyce tapped away on her computer. She glanced up to smile at Hollis.

"I'm sorry, Hollis," she said. "The chief is on the phone." Her voice dipped to a loud whisper as she added, "It's about that Bell case. He's been grumpy ever since he came back from vacation. A lot of good it did him. I already told Detective Scott you were here."

The door to the offices swung open, and Detective Scott, wearing a severe navy-blue pantsuit and white blouse, stood motioning for Hollis to come in.

Hollis looked over her shoulder and was relieved to see that Gordon was out of the car and on his way.

"We're sorry to keep you waiting, Ms. Morgan. We've had a hectic morning, and this evening isn't looking much better."

"Detective Scott, I'd like to introduce you to Gordon Barrett," Hollis said.

She held out her hand. "Laura Scott, Detective," she said in her matter-of-fact voice.

Gordon returned her handshake and they followed Scott's low-heeled rubber soles as they quickly padded down the linoleum hallway.

"The chief is waiting," she said.

She scurried in front of them as if they were off to see the king. Hollis' legs weren't as long, and she was glad she'd worn her flats. She wasn't inclined to rush, and both of them had to pause for her to catch up at the chief's door.

Chief Brennan was poring over what appeared to be 8½ by 11, black-and-white photos. He looked up as they entered and pushed the pictures to one side. Gordon walked up to him with one hand outstretched and the other offering a business card.

"Hello, Chief, I'm Gordon Barrett. I'm representing Mrs. Larson. Ms. Morgan is my co-counsel. When can we see our client?"

The chief chuckled. "My, my, *two* attorneys. Larson's very fortunate." Then the smile left his face. "I just got off the phone with the DA. You're fast. I guess your agenda is already in motion. I've been informed the arraignment is tomorrow."

Gordon shrugged. "No hard feelings, Chief, but my client is an innocent elderly woman, and as soon as we can clear her name, the faster you can get back to locating the real killer. Now, if you can show us to a private office, can we see her?"

The chief nodded to Scott, who stood and motioned for them to follow her to a room across the hall.

"Wait in here," she said.

Hollis leaned toward Gordon, who was scanning his phone. "Nice job. You sounded like Perry Mason in there. It was a smart move to contact the DA ahead of time. I won't question your phone calls again."

Gordon snorted. "*All* of my calls are for a good reason. I don't like surprises. Oh, by the way, make sure you have Larson sign a waiver acknowledging that you are the probate attorney for the Bell estate and will be working to defend her."

"I have the waiver here." She pulled out a sheet of paper and savored the look of respect Gordon gave her.

Just then, the door opened and Odelia walked into the room, head held high, trembling only slightly as she pulled the chair closer to the table. Hollis didn't detect any negative effects from her short stint in jail.

"Odelia, are you all right? How are things going?" Hollis asked.

"How do you think, Ms. Morgan? I'm in jail for the first time in my life." But she gave a shaky smile. "Now, who is this young man?"

"Gordon Barrett, Miss Larson," he said. "I'm your lawyer." He held out his hand for her to shake and handed her a business card. "Ms. Morgan is going to be your day-to-day contact, but I'll be presenting your case—if it goes that far."

Odelia swallowed hard. "Do I have to stay in jail?"

"Not at all. I'm going to ask the chief that you be released into my custody tonight, and then tomorrow morning I'll have you out on bail." He stood. "In fact, I'm going to leave you in Hollis' good hands, and I'll go see Brennan, now."

He motioned for Hollis to take over and left the room.

"Odelia, everything is going to be fine," Hollis said firmly. "Ah … I understand from the chief that you knew about the amount of your paycheck before I gave it to you. Is that true?"

Odelia sniffed in disgust. "I didn't know I could expect to be harassed by my own legal team."

Hollis said nothing, but waited for Odelia to answer.

"Yes, all right, I knew what that man was planning to do." Odelia stifled a sob. "I thought he cared about us. I thought he would take care of us. A hundred thousand dollars was insulting. I have friends who work for far less affluent individuals who got three times that amount and a house or a car, too."

"So, your curiosity got the best of you, and you opened his letter to me. Did you also have to break into the box in his desk?"

Odelia wrinkled her brow and nodded.

"How did Scott find out that you knew the contents?"

"I don't know," Odelia wailed. "I thought I put everything back the way it was."

Hollis made a note on her pad. *Fingerprints.*

Gordon returned to the room with the phone to his ear. He put it against his chest to block out his words to Hollis and Odelia.

"Hollis, she's free to go," Gordon said. "Take her home and get her settled in." He turned to Odelia. "Your hearing is at eight thirty in Department Seven. I know I can count on you to be on time. No, make that eight fifteen. The clerk in that court is impressed by defendants arriving early."

Gordon Barrett went into the hallway and asked an officer to take Odelia away to collect her things. He returned to the room and motioned to Hollis.

"This should be a slam-dunk," he said. "Tomorrow, I'll ask for a much-reduced bail then head out to the DA's office and see what they have on her."

His phone buzzed, but to Hollis' relief, he glanced down and didn't answer. "I'll meet you in court at eight."

Hollis put her hand on his arm. "I think I should pick up Odelia. She probably won't be in any state of mind to drive. You and I can talk while she's waiting for the hearing to start."

Gordon nodded in agreement. "Sounds like a plan."

CHAPTER TWELVE

Thursday

HOLLIS WAS QUICKLY DEVELOPING A new respect for Gordon Barrett. He had arranged for Odelia Larson's case to be heard first on the docket that morning, and it was clear that he and the judge knew each other. After the court clerk specified the case particulars, Judge Melanie Brown peered at them over the rim of her glasses.

"Mr. Barrett, how does your client plead?"

Gordon stood. "Not guilty, your honor, and since Mrs. Larson is an elderly woman with many years of community ties, she poses no flight risk. We ask that she be released on her own recognizance."

Judge Brown turned to the prosecutor. "Mr. Pugh?"

"Your honor, Mr. Bell was a prominent figure in the community. Mrs. Larson's crime has done away with one of its most valuable citizens."

The judge looked down at the file. "I shouldn't have to remind you, Mr. Pugh, that it is an alleged crime and that we don't apply justice based on the prominence of the victim." She glanced up. "The defendant is free on her own recognizance. Bail is set at two hundred thousand."

Gordon Barrett rose in protest.

"Your honor, my client is an unemployed senior citizen. She—"

"Don't push it, Mr. Barrett. Your client can walk out of this courtroom."

Gordon tilted his head in acknowledgment. "That is true, your honor."

"Fine then, I'll set a preliminary hearing to consider any motions thirty days from today." She hit the gavel. "Next case."

Odelia pulled on Hollis' sleeve. "What does it mean? Am I free to go?"

Gordon and Hollis hustled Odelia to the back of the courtroom as the next case came forward. They had already consulted with her about putting her house up as collateral in the event bail was required.

"You're free for now." Hollis looked her in the eyes. "But it means we have one month to prove you didn't kill Matthias Bell."

IN THE COURT PARKING LOT, with Odelia gazing forlornly out the car window, Gordon told Hollis he had another case and would meet her back in the office that afternoon.

"Keep our client quiet. Tell her not to talk to any reporters. Interview her in depth tomorrow, after she's rested." He tossed his briefcase in the front seat of his BMW. "Since you've already had contact with Bell's victims, you'll go back to each of them and try to find out who had the means and opportunity to kill him. We don't have to prove anything. We just need reasonable doubt."

Hollis was ahead of him. "I'll need Vince Colton to help me."

"Vince Col—" Gordon raised his eyebrows. "Oh, yeah, *that* guy." He frowned. "I know I said you could pick who you wanted, but is he really qualified?"

"I know he is, and he'll help me get the job done," she said. "I'll tell Tiffany to bring in a temp. The firm needs two people in the mailroom full-time anyway. You might bring that up at the management meeting, too."

"Two full-time mail clerks might be a tough sell," Gordon mused. "On the other hand, even with overtime, Colton will be less expensive than professional staff."

Hollis was now thoroughly absorbed with looking down at her hands. "I'll probably need to offer him a little more money—not a lot, but this is a special assignment."

Gordon was just about to reply when his phone rang. He glanced down and clicked it on, mouthing, "Okay, but not a lot." He rolled up his window.

Hollis bent over and tapped his window with her knuckles. He rolled it down, his hand over his phone mic, and gave her a questioning look.

She said, "I've got another case, too. Remember Kiki Turner?"

"Congratulations." He grinned. "Yeah, this should be a good month for reporting billables. Text me if you hit any snags. See you in my office tomorrow."

She stepped back as he drove the car out of the lot and pumped her arm in the air. Then she hurried to her car.

It was no trouble for Hollis to get Odelia Larson settled in at her condo. The woman had been more than compliant, and it was clear that the day in court had been traumatic for her. She told Hollis she was going to have a cup of tea then go to bed and stay there.

"Ms. Morgan," she added, "you can tell Mr. Barrett that I will follow his instructions without a complaint and to the letter. I'll expect to see you to go over my story at eleven o'clock tomorrow."

"You take it easy, Odelia," she said, and closed the door behind her.

Hollis practically ran to her car. She was anxious to get back to talk with Chief Brennan. Looking out for the Highway Patrol, she sped to get to the police station. Turning into the driveway, she breathed a sigh of relief to see his car still sitting in the parking lot.

The chief looked up from his computer monitor. "I'm impressed, Ms. Morgan. It's been a pretty busy day and you're still on the job." He took off his glasses. "How can I help you?"

"I want to help *you*," Hollis said. "I can't believe you think Odelia Larson has it in her to inject a stronger man with a hypodermic."

"But Mrs. Larson is a smart, creative lady," he observed. "I honestly believe that if she put her mind to it, she could disable and kill Matthias Bell. She's younger than he was. But I admit, we usually have a lack of suspects. Here we have too many, and that's just as bad. Even so, she's number one."

"Ah, you said *if* she put her mind to it.' " Hollis smiled. "You don't think she *did* put her mind to it."

He shrugged. "Doesn't matter now. The DA thinks she did it, and unless another viable candidate appears, she's our murderer."

Hollis gripped her briefcase; she was ready to get to the point of her visit. "Chief, can I see the police file?" She raised her hand. "Before you object, I know you don't have to show it to me. But I'm betting you tried to convince the DA to wait."

The chief took a sip of coffee. "San Lucian is small, but it's a cross-section for regional social sentiment, and next year is an election year. It's my thinking that since you feel strongly about Larson's innocence you could get to the bottom of things a lot faster with your private resources. Unfortunately, I can't sit around. Bell's murder requires a quick response."

Hollis sighed and leaned back in her seat. "Ah, well, then let us by all means respond." She looked up to see a smile creeping onto the chief's face. "What?"

He pulled a file from under a stack of folders and laid it

emphatically on top. "I've got to go down the hall for a few minutes to make some copies. You're welcome to rest here before you go home." He jutted his chin toward the folders.

"Er, thanks, I would like to rest a bit. It's been a hectic day." Hollis smiled and added, "Thank you, Chief."

He shrugged. "Don't stay too long. I want to go home."

Hollis opened the file as soon as the chief shut the door. It was thin. Scott had reported that the department had been contacted by Constance Cantone, who suspected foul play in the murder of her uncle. Mrs. Cantone had spoken with him only a few days before to ask for his support divorcing her husband.

Hollis looked up from the file. Had Anthony Cantone's mild and sincere manner tricked her into believing his relief was due solely to getting Bell's blackmail material? She tapped her head with the palm of her hand.

Was she slipping? She hadn't picked up on his lie.

But according to Scott, Anthony Cantone had a solid alibi, and that left the police with Hollis' own visit to the department about Odelia's anger over her paycheck to point them in the elderly lady's direction.

Evidently, the coup de grâce occurred when Odelia left a clear set of prints on Bell's black case. Her prints were on file from her past employment as a nurse for Hayward Hospital, and with that, the chief had his viable suspect.

Motive and opportunity.

WHEN SHE GOT HOME, HOLLIS fell into bed, exhausted and exhilarated at the same time. It was clear from the police file that the case against Odelia was not open and shut. Hollis had technically helped them to check off all the boxes but one. *Means.* And while it was theoretically possible Odelia had injected a needle into a grown man without him fighting back, a jury wouldn't think so. Which was why the chief had let her see the file; he didn't think so either. He was counting on Hollis to find the holes.

She sipped from a glass of her favorite Malbec and mused. The only thing missing was being able to share her day with John. She grinned. It was good he was gone, because he wouldn't care for her foray into criminal law. Her scheduled morning interview with Odelia would keep her on top of her caseload going into the following work week. There would be time for Vince to join her in looking up Bell's victims.

Game on.

CHAPTER THIRTEEN

—∾—

Friday

HOLLIS SETTLED INTO THE OVERSTUFFED sofa in Odelia Larson's living room. It was a cozy condo with a few pieces of sturdy oak furniture. Two Queen Anne chairs and a matching loveseat, where Odelia now sat, faced the sofa. It was all upholstered in the same floral print.

Hollis didn't want to get too comfortable and scooted forward. "Odelia, I know this whole experience has been upsetting, but it's critical that you confide completely in me and Gordon, so we can clear you of all charges and you can go on with your life. If you hold anything back, you will make it more difficult for us to get you off the prime suspect list."

Odelia wore white pants with a lime-green top. She looked like a grandmother on her way to meet friends for lunch. She'd prepared tuna sandwiches cut into small triangles and frosty glasses of iced tea.

Her shoulders slumped. "Ms. Morgan, this has got to be the very worst thing that has ever happened to me, and it's all because of that horrible man." She moistened her lips. "I gave him the best service any employer could expect, and he repaid me with peanuts."

"Er, Odelia, I think you need to get over the paycheck Bell left you and focus on how we are going to defend you against murder charges."

She waved a hand in the air. "Well, I didn't do it. That's the main thing." She took a bite of sandwich and chewed thoughtfully. "All right, I won't be difficult. After the ambulance left with Mr. Bell, I ... I knew he didn't look good. So, I made ready to follow them to the hospital. I was halfway out the door when I realized that when his family came—for the first time, I might add—everything would be topsy-turvy." She paused.

"So you—"

"So, I knew about the black case in his desk. He had pointed it out to me a long time ago and told me that it held information for his accountants and other special papers." She took a sip from her glass.

Hollis raised an eyebrow.

She's lying.

Odelia continued, "I was curious. I wanted to know what he planned to give me. I'm ready for retirement. I can't afford any surprises."

"So that's why when I gave you your check, you reacted, but you didn't seem surprised."

"Yes, I suppose so."

"And Bell's letter to me, did you read it too?"

Odelia's stern face paled. "No, of course not. I'm not a bad person."

She's lying again.

Hollis looked at her, and after a moment, Larson broke the gaze. Hollis took out her pad and pen to make a note.

"Did Matthias Bell have any regular visitors? Any friends or business associates who came to see him?"

Odelia nodded. "Certainly. He worked out of the house about half the time. His office at home has a separate side entrance.

Sometimes men and women would come to the front door and I would direct them to go around the side. But usually they knew to go straight there."

"Do you know any names? Would you recognize their faces?"

Odelia scowled and slowly shook her head. "No, they never gave me their names, and I'm not sure if I would recognize them or not. Maybe."

Hollis sighed, and then flipped through her pad to a sheet full of notes. "Chief Brennan tells me that if Bell's niece, Constance Cantone, hadn't called to complain, we'd never know that Bell was murdered. Do you remember when she came to the house?"

"Oh, yes." Odelia nodded eagerly. "She's a real piece of work. She must smell money. She only visited twice: to tell him she was getting married and to tell him she was getting divorced. She wanted money both times."

"How do you know?"

"Ah, what?"

Hollis remained expressionless. "How do you know what they discussed?"

"Er, I heard them. They were in the living room, and their voices were raised."

Hollis said nothing.

They both knew that any conversation in the living room would only be overheard if a person listened closely. Hollis waited for Odelia to say more, and when she didn't, she cleared her throat.

"Did Mr. Bell agree to give her the money for a divorce?"

"Oh, yes. But he thought it was funny. He laughed and laughed and told her that he would take care of things for her. She seemed to be happy, and she departed."

"When was this?"

Odelia closed one eye and thought. "I'd say about three weeks ago."

"So Bell was alive and well when she left?"

"Oh, my goodness, yes. He was in a very good mood." Odelia blinked rapidly. "It was almost scary."

Hollis stood and gave her a long look. "I need to get back to the office. I'll contact you in a day or two." She paused at the door to address a flushed Odelia. "Oh, between now and then, you may want to practice telling the truth."

VINCE SHIFTED EAGERLY ON THE edge of his seat in Hollis' office.

"Before you get all excited, let me explain the assignment," Hollis said.

"I don't care. Do you hear me? I don't care." He laughed. "I get to work with you. I'll learn so much."

Hollis smiled and gave up trying to get him to calm down.

"Okay, okay, but you're going to be functioning as a professional. We need to interrogate Bell's victims properly. This is a capital crime case." She reached for her cup of tea. "I'm sorry. Would you like some coffee, water?"

"Water is great."

Hollis reached into the small refrigerator in her credenza and pulled out a bottle of water.

Handing it to him, she continued, "Like I was saying, our client, Odelia Larson, is out on bail for the murder of Matthias Bell, who was a blackmailer. This is a high-profile case because of who Bell was, and the newspapers are all over it."

"Got it," Vince said, and sat back. "What is it you want me to do?"

"Help me point the finger away from our client," Hollis said. "I need your observational skills and your instincts."

"You got it, my observational skills and my instincts."

"Good." Hollis leaned forward. "Now let's get down to the specifics. Penny and I have already gathered a good bit of information about the victims, but we need to augment that with additional intelligence, descriptions, and any relevant comments that might help determine if any of them could be the killer."

Hollis placed four files on the conference table. "I want to take you through each one, starting with the Pittmans."

Vince scanned the file, reading as he went.

"According to Detective Scott, they've disappeared into the ether," Hollis said, taking out her notepad. "They ran the license plate I gave them. The car is leased to a company that doesn't exist. It was found this morning, parked and stripped in the Oakland Airport long-term parking lot."

"No surprises there." Vince smirked.

"No, there isn't. The police always ask the Oakland and San Francisco airports to check their long-term lots first. It's a favorite dumping ground." She tapped a piece of paper on top of the stack in front of her. "Ian and Millicent Pittman don't exist, but the names on those U.S. passports copies you see in the file do—"

Vince interrupted, "According to your notes, the people associated with those names are wanted by Homeland Security. And they're not U.S. citizens."

Hollis nodded. "Detective Scott provided that tidbit of information. They both spoke with an accent that I'm unfamiliar with. It wasn't from a Latin country. I got the sense it was Eastern Europe or maybe Russian."

"Maybe they're terrorists or international criminals," Vince said with a tinge of excitement.

She frowned in concentration. "I wouldn't think so. Why would they put up with being blackmailed by Bell? They could have disappeared long ago."

Vince frowned. "I see what you mean. So they were just crooks. Or, maybe they were hiding out after committing some crime, and Bell caught them."

"I get the feeling it wasn't that complicated." Hollis tapped the table top with her pen. "Possibly if they were here illegally, and Bell somehow found out. They built a low-key life and just didn't want to be discovered. They might fear being sent back to wherever."

"Hmmm, then they'll be twice as scared knowing that you've seen their papers," Vince said. "You should be careful, Hollis. They know you have their secrets."

Hollis didn't want to admit that Ian Pittman also had her copies of the original documents. "I don't think I have anything to worry about from the Pittmans," she said. "But for now, let's move on to Anthony Cantone. He was my biggest surprise."

"Why?" Vince picked up the thin file.

Hollis furrowed her brow. "Anthony Cantone seemed like an everyday guy who was just glad to get out from under Bell's threat. His wife was Bell's niece, and apparently she was scheming to get her uncle to squeeze more money out of him. There's a good chance Cantone knew she was already planning to take him to the poor house. While he seemed genuinely surprised to learn of Bell's death, I got the sense he was lying to me about something." She bit her lower lip. "I do know this: he was scared of his wife, who with Bell to back her would be a forceful opponent. And I think that would make him a desperate man."

Vince lifted the third file. "And Griffin?"

"He already turned himself in," Hollis said. "Detective Scott told me that he'd seen the article about Bell's death. He knew I'd have to give the police his name. And, he didn't want to wait for someone to come on his job. So, I understand, he went on his own to the police."

"Hmmm, smart move," Vince remarked. He picked up the last file. "What about Eaton?"

She leaned back in her chair. "Now she's the one I would be most inclined to say has the motive and forethought to kill. She's cold and calculating. She stole from clients and the statute of limitations has not run out. Bell could have destroyed her life. But on the other hand, that's just it: her career seems to be everything to her. I don't see her putting it at risk again. Having the ability to kill and the chutzpa to actually to do it are two separate things."

"Ah, you know," Vince tapped the small stack, "from what you've just said, any one of these guys could have killed Bell."

Hollis pointed to the stack. "Yeah, it seems that way, but remember, we only have to point the finger away from our client. There is nothing glamorous about the surveillance I'm asking you to do. It's a lot of sitting and waiting, but it's necessary."

"Don't worry about me. I know you're giving me a chance to show what I can do."

Hollis smiled. "Well, we're both working with Gordon on a case. At least we don't have to solve it. But I haven't told you the best part."

His brows lifted. "What?"

"You can earn more money."

He stared at her in disbelief, and then slowly shook his head. "Naw, it's really good I can earn more money, but the best part is that I get to work with you."

HOLLIS KNEW GORDON WOULD BE happy about her two new clients, but not as ecstatic as he appeared that afternoon when she briefed him in his office. He questioned her in detail about Odelia's interview and then wanted to see the list of Bell's victims.

She pointed to the pile of pages next to his phone.

"Good work," he said, glancing through the pile. He sat back and looked at her. "I'm going have to leave much of the investigation up to you. I've got another matter that goes to trial next week. After that, I can focus on the Larson case." He put on a pair of glasses. "Here, take a look at the accounting report. Look at our billables. Now *that's* what I'm talking about!" He clapped his hands twice. "I guess my little pep talk worked: first Kiki Turner and now you've brought in a client who's the suspect in a high-profile murder. Did you get Larson to sign the waiver?"

Hollis handed over the sheet of paper.

"Bravo, Hollis. I can't wait for next Tuesday's management meeting to brag about our teamwork."

Good grief.

"Gordon," Hollis ventured, "Vince Colton and I are probably going to be out of the office a lot until I get this Bell case turned around." She looked down at her nails. "We're not going to be able to work regular hours, so Vince is going to need some overtime. Remember, he helped me locate one of the key victims. It would be really helpful—and cost effective—if I could make liberal use of him to assist in wrapping this up as soon as possible."

"Vince Colton," Gordon said, puzzled. "Who's Vince Colton?"

Hollis sighed and told him. Again.

ONCE SHE WAS HOME, HOLLIS immediately entered her notes from the day into her laptop. Odelia was hiding something; she was certain. *Could* she have killed Bell? But the list of more likely candidates was growing. And as Gordon had said, they only needed to prove reasonable doubt.

Chapter Fourteen

Saturday/Sunday

The next day was Saturday, and Hollis spent most of it cleaning up the townhouse and running errands. Usually she would have gotten her friend Rena to run around with her, but Rena was out of town. She, her husband, and their son were in France at some fashion convention. A recent postcard pointed out that they were somehow able to have a great time without Hollis and John.

She looked around with satisfaction. At this rate, she'd be able to have all day Sunday to read in bed.

Her phone trilled.

"Come on, let's go out," Stephanie prodded. "It's the weekend. Dan got his hands on some last-minute tickets to the Coliseum to hear the Back Door. This is their last tour to the U.S."

"Ah, I don't know," Hollis hedged. "I know you're being kind, but I don't like being a third wheel."

"Oh, no, you don't," Stephanie said. "What about that time when you and John took me to the art exhibit in San Francisco?

Did you have to ask me twice? And Dan was in town, but I knew he would never want to go."

"Well, that's true. I guess I—"

"Good," Stephanie broke in. "We'll pick you up at five o'clock. We'll have dinner at Kimball's after the show. Got to run, bye."

Hollis smiled to herself. It would be fun. John preferred dinner and a movie to the crowds of an arena. She hadn't been to a concert in years. She had to scamper. She only had a couple of hours to find something to wear and get ready.

She was taking one last look in the mirror when her doorbell rang.

Dan Silva, Stephanie's main man, was a deputy sheriff for the county. He was tall and handsome, with dark hair and a thick moustache. He'd taken her friend's heart by storm. Hollis was impressed with him for another reason: a few months earlier he had believed her when others hadn't, and he had saved the life of a dear friend.

He stood in her doorway now, offering his arm.

"Your chariot awaits, ma'am." He smiled. "We're running a little late. Are you ready?"

Hollis smiled back. "Ready. I assume Lady Stephanie is in the car?"

"Yeah." He dropped his playful accent. "She's the reason we're late. Fortunately, these are good side balcony seats, so they'll seat us even if the concert has started."

Hollis took out her house keys. "Still, we'd better be on our way."

The Oakland Coliseum was showing its age with its dated lighting and slightly worn carpeting. After making minimum renovations, the city of Oakland was asking citizens to vote for a massive new stadium bond. Still, once the Back Door singers took the stage, the arena was transformed into a musical wonderland.

Stephanie sat in the middle. She leaned toward Hollis and whispered, "Everything okay? You look kind of ... kind of, oh, distracted."

"I'm fine. I'm just missing John. I wish he could hear the band … and be here."

Stephanie patted her arm. "Has the doctor scheduled your mother's transplant yet?"

Hollis shook her head. "They're playing it by ear and closely monitoring her condition. My mother will stall as long as she can." She flipped through the program.

Dan and Stephanie exchanged looks.

Stephanie said, "I know you and your mother aren't close. Why did you agree to do this? You could be seriously affected."

Hollis looked down at her hands. "When I was in prison, one of the inmates told me how she dealt with her background." She paused. "She wanted to know how women who were raised with caring parents felt. She wanted to feel like they did. So, to cope, instead of inventing a pretend friend, she invented a supportive family."

There was silence.

"Is that what you did?" Stephanie asked.

Hollis nodded. "Here was my chance to pretend. I … I wanted to feel like the kids who had attentive parents. So I pretended I had them. I showed my enthusiasm regardless of how they responded. I … I acted as if they were proud of me."

"Did it work?" Dan asked.

Hollis responded slowly. "No, but I made it about me, not them." She leaned toward them. "You see, I need to feel like a good daughter. I don't want to be cheated out of not knowing how it *feels* to be a good daughter. And a good daughter donates a kidney to her mother."

Two hours and a great performance later, the three sat in Kimball's, next to a window on San Francisco Bay. There was a musician playing ballads in the bar, and his music drifted out to the restaurant.

They were hungry, so the server took their drink and meal orders at the same time.

"That was a great concert," Hollis said. "Thank you so much for the invitation and getting me out of the house."

"When is John due back?" Dan asked.

Before she could answer, the server brought their drink order. Once Dan gave his nod of approval to the server, Hollis sipped from her wine glass.

"It will be at least another week, maybe two," Hollis said. "The good news is that once he completes this assignment, he won't have to travel for several months."

Stephanie looked at her with concern. "I know you're used to living alone, but it's been a little while. Come stay with me."

Hollis shook off her offer with a little irritation. "I'm fine. Please don't mess up the evening." She tapped her glass with theirs. "To friends." She took a swallow.

Dan cleared his throat. "Er, Hollis, Stephanie told me about the Bell murder. I understand you're moving into criminal law." He half-smiled.

Stephanie gave him a light shove. "Dan, do you have to talk about work now? We're relaxing here." She gave Hollis a pointed look.

"It's okay," Hollis said and turned to Dan. "No, I'm not taking on criminal law, but I am assisting another attorney who's representing Odelia Larson." Hollis gladly moved to a safer subject. "If you knew her, you would be certain she couldn't have done it." She turned to her friend. "Come on, Stephanie, just a few minutes of work talk, I promise."

"Hey, forget I'm here," she said. "Oh, good, our food …. I'll be able to eat mine while it's still hot. You two talk amongst yourselves."

The server deftly delivered the orders and left them alone. True to her word, Stephanie picked up her knife and fork, plucked up some dinner, and regarded them contentedly.

"Dan, you can't believe everything you read in the papers," Hollis said. "Matthias Bell was no saint." She took a bite of food.

He nodded. "I heard about the Bell tolls."

"The what?" Hollis grinned.

"That's what I call his blackmail business," Dan said. "His victims paid a toll for a day's peace of mind."

"True enough. But now the victim net has gathered up an innocent, and that's my client."

"You've got to admit that something must have changed." Stephanie dabbed at her mouth.

"What do you mean?" Dan asked.

"Stephanie's right," Hollis said. "Something must have caused one of his victims to revolt. They'd been paying for months and in some cases, years. Why kill him now? He probably knew their financial breaking points and stayed just underneath them."

Dan tapped his finger on the table. "If you take that route, wouldn't that go against your client?"

"Now what do *you* mean?" Hollis asked.

He continued, "She's *not* a toll payer. She's an angry old lady who feels her employer wronged her. Her motive is retribution. Could she have planned his demise? I wouldn't bet against the idea. Or she got up that morning and something broke inside … she saw red."

Stephanie shook her head. "Larson is elderly and—"

"So was Bell," Dan broke in. "He was much older. She could have caught him off guard. Who knows?"

Both of them turned toward Hollis, who had been sitting there swirling the wine in her glass.

Stephanie nudged her. "So, what do you think?"

"I don't think Odelia Larson killed Matthias Bell. Yes, she might have had motive, means, and opportunity, but there's one thing she didn't have, and that was the *need* to kill him." Hollis raised her hand when she saw Dan start to protest. "What I mean is, while I do not believe she is telling the truth, or at least the whole truth, I think I know her well enough to realize that she would relish defying him much more than killing him."

CHAPTER FIFTEEN

Monday

THE WEEK WAS NOT OFF to a great start. Hollis stood over the reception desk, waiting for Tiffany to finish a call. Although she was pretty sure the receptionist was deliberately extending the conversation so that Hollis would give up and go away, she couldn't prove it. Finally, she clicked off.

"I'm really busy," said Tiffany. "I'm not sure when I can get someone to replace Vince."

Hollis tried to hide her frustration. "Tiffany, I've already got approval from Gordon to hire a temp. I've told admin, so all you have to do is your job: pick up the phone and call the agency." She took a deep breath. "Okay, let's start over. I'm sorry about that last part, but could you *please* just tell me what's going on with you?"

"I'm fine," she said, slamming her notepad down on the desk. "I'll take care of it, okay? When do you want them to start?"

"Immediately," Hollis snapped, but then added in a softer voice, "Today is kind of crazy for me, but let's get together for coffee tomorrow so you can tell me what's bothering you. Are you okay with that?"

Tiffany nodded, her face a picture of woe. "I appreciate you trying to help me, but it's not that kind of thing."

"What kind of *thing* is it?"

Tiffany opened her mouth, then closed it and seemed to get a grip on her emotions. "So, how long do you think you'll need the temp?"

Hollis sighed. "Probably not more than a week, but leave it open. Vince is going to need a permanent backup at any rate." She paused. "I've got to get going, but we'll talk tomorrow. Deal?"

Hollis saw lines of worry on the receptionist's forehead.

"Deal."

HOLLIS WASN'T SURPRISED THAT VINCE was able to finish sorting the mail by midmorning. He was just a little out of breath when he stood in her office doorway.

"We can go anytime. I can do the afternoon delivery when we get back."

She grinned. "You're faster than me. I have to finish this client letter first. I'll meet you out front in a half hour."

Tiffany was away from her desk when Hollis and Vince came through the lobby. Relieved, Hollis signed them both out of the office. They picked up an office car and drove the first few miles in silence. Hollis, behind the wheel, kept sneaking glances at Vince, who appeared to be fascinated by the city streets of Oakland.

"Vince, how's your mother? Is she still in rehab?"

"Yeah, she's still there." He hesitated. "She got out about two weeks ago, and she swore to me that she would stay clean. She would've too, but last week her pusher found out where we lived. He came over when he knew I was at work. I … I told her she'd be on her own, that I wouldn't help her if she didn't check herself right back in." His voice choked.

When they stopped at a light, Hollis turned to look at him. He sat stone-faced, his jaw clenched.

He continued, "I must've scared her, because she did what I said. I gave the center enough money to keep her for another thirty days. By that time, I hope to have us moved someplace else."

She said nothing. She guessed he'd realized by now that he had become the parent.

"Hollis, how old do I look to you?" he asked, gazing out the window.

She wrinkled her brow, recollecting where she'd heard that same question before. "I'm not the best judge of age. Remember, I know you're twenty-one, but I'd say you look maybe twenty-three, twenty-four."

"Oh."

She couldn't tell from his "oh" if he was pleased or disappointed.

"Go over to the left; that's it over there," Vince said, pointing to a row of newly constructed townhomes that bordered on an office park. "Eaton went into the one next to the end on the right."

Hollis took down the address and noted the Prius in the driveway. The plates they'd gotten on the car Eaton used in Knowland Park were for a rental. She drove past the homes to a lot two blocks away then turned and tucked the car among others already there. She had a good vantage point on the unit.

"We need to know if she actually lives there," she said. "You've got to get her to open the door. She knows what I look like."

"I'm a little old to be selling magazines door to door. What do I say?"

"I just need to get a look at her. Say you're just moving in and could she give you the name of the cable provider."

"That's all you got?"

Hollis gave him a warning look and he shrugged an okay. He got out the car and strode over to an industrial Dumpster.

Reaching for a medium-sized paper bag partially full of trash, he gave Hollis a big grin and walked up the four steps to the door.

She slid down a bit in her seat and peered out the window. She could see the door open and hear Vince engaging someone in conversation. After a few minutes, he waved at the person and quickly made his way down the steps. Then he walked in the opposite direction of the car.

With immediate understanding, Hollis pulled out and headed around the corner to meet him.

"Did you see her?" he said, slamming the car door behind him.

"No, I didn't. I thought you were going to get her to stand on the porch?" She was annoyed. They would need a plan B.

Vince clicked on his safety belt. "I couldn't get her to stand on the porch because it would be a problem for her, being in a wheelchair and all." He didn't try to hide his smug smile. "Naomi Eaton doesn't live there."

"I thought you said you saw a woman fitting Eaton's description open the door with a key and walk in with a suitcase."

He ran his fingers through his hair. "Believe me, she wasn't the one I saw. Obviously the old lady wasn't Naomi Eaton, so I asked her if someone named Naomi lived there because a friend found out I was moving nearby and said to look her up."

"And ...?" Hollis prodded.

"And she said she'd lived there for almost five years, and she didn't know anyone by that name." He paused. "But ..."

Vince looked thoughtful.

Hollis nodded. "But something isn't right? This is Oakland. People just don't go opening their doors to a young man carrying a bag of trash." She gave Vince a knowing look. "Especially disabled, elderly people."

"That's it," said Vince triumphantly. "That's what was bothering me. She gave me too much information. Why tell me how long she'd lived there unless she was covering for Eaton?"

She had to agree. They had likely found Eaton, or now that they'd tipped her off, found her most recent residence.

"So, what do we do now?" he asked.

Hollis' brow furrowed in thought. "We have to talk with her. It could be she's paranoid and thinking someone else is trying to blackmail her, or she's a killer covering her crime. Either way, we need to get her to surface."

"Where does she work?"

"According to Penny, she may be a freelancer." Hollis turned to face him. "The police will probably check with the State and find out who's paying her payroll taxes, but then I would have to get him to tell me, and that could take some persuading." She rubbed her hands together. "We do have one small advantage. When I met Ms. Eaton, she showed me her ID before she handed me her passport, and I got a look at her gym card. I didn't catch the name of the gym, but the logo was some kind of bird, and it had a local area code. Whatever, I'll draw it out and get Penny on it. Between the two, we should get some result. I'd like to talk to her before the police do."

A moment later, on her phone, she told Penny what she needed. As Hollis hoped, the paralegal assured Hollis she'd get right on it, albeit in her driest tone.

Vince said, "Hmm, that takes care of Eaton. Now what? Who's next?"

"We're going to split up. I want you to watch Cantone's condo. We need to know if he still lives there. He didn't strike me as a slippery character, but he disconnected his home phone. That had to be for a reason." Hollis paused. "Here's where your value comes in. Stake out his place until you see him. You don't need to make contact. I just want to be sure he hasn't run off. There'll be overtime pay."

He shrugged. "Like I said, Mom's still in rehab." He looked out the window. "There was a slim chance I'd be going out tonight, but I don't think it's going to happen. So, I got Cantone."

Hollis debated hearing more about his chances for "going out" but decided against it. There would be a better time.

"Okay, let's go back to the office. I'll bring Gordon up to date regarding Eaton, then I'll get you Cantone's picture, address, and anything else that might clue you in to where he is and where he could be."

Vince nodded.

"Take some of the business cards from the firm with you."

He gave a short laugh. "Yeah, just in case I get arrested."

Hollis continued, "While you're checking on Cantone, I'll check out the Pittmans. They have the money to leave the country, but Scott sent me an email. She checked with Homeland Security, and they haven't left under real or fake passports, yet."

When they entered the office, they discovered Tiffany had gone home early that afternoon and one of the new law clerks was covering the desk for her. Hollis noted how quickly Vince was able to sign for a car without enduring side comments from a receptionist.

"Check back with me every few hours, so I know what's going on." Hollis handed him car keys and a spare cellphone. "I'm going to be around all weekend. You should be able to get me on my cell. If you can't, and something comes up, leave a message on my work phone."

"Got it." He pocketed the phone and keys. In a robotic voice with gestures to match, he teased, "If I find Cantone, I will call you first. I will not approach."

"Hmmm." She turned to go back to her office.

"Hollis," Vince called out, "thank you!"

She gave him a wave and a half-smile.

At her desk, Hollis picked up Penny's reconstructed Pittman file, including copies of material left by Bell. There was also a typed sheet of notes detailing her research.

Hollis started to read. Ian and Millicent Pittman had no visible means of support. He was forty-four and she forty.

They had lived in the mansion Hollis visited for five years. She glanced at the date on the oldest page of Bell's material. It was dated four years earlier.

She noted the information she remembered from the passports. The travel pages had been empty. There were no date stamps for the couple. She tapped her forehead with the heel of her hand; she could put them through PeopleSearch. She had run PeopleSearch on Cantone but none of the others.

In a few minutes, she was logged on. The search identified eight files on Ian Weatherly, and the bar slid slowly across the screen until the download was complete.

The largest file was a series of address changes. From state to state, city to city, it appeared that over the last ten years the Pittmans—make that the Weatherlys—had moved no fewer than three times a year. No wonder they could pick up and leave on a moment's notice. The remaining files included Ian earning a graduate engineering degree from the California Institute of Technology. But the one piece of identifying information she was unable to glean was his country of origin. There was little left to review; his file cross-referenced his wife, Millicent Weatherly.

Millicent's entries were fewer but had more information. Her maiden name was Goran. She had come to this country from the former Yugoslavia at the age of twenty-seven. She'd graduated from Kepler University in Linz, Austria. A year later she married Ian in Los Angeles and became Millicent Weatherly.

Hollis paused. Still, Bell had used the name Pittman, and yet after running searches on the couple, Hollis had found no public information under that name. She leaned back in her chair, deep in thought. After a few minutes her phone vibrated.

San Francisco 49ers by ten.

She smiled and let out a deep sigh. She missed John. Had he been home, they would have kicked this Bell matter around. He'd help her sort through her thinking.

Hollis placed the phone on the floor and crushed it with her foot.

She faced an evening with a good book and a tall glass of wine. Once, she would have seen these activities as a good way to spend her leisure time. But now, the night seemed empty without her man by her side.

It was time to go home. She packed her briefcase and turned out the lights.

HOLLIS HAD BROUGHT JEREMIAH GRIFFIN's file home from work, and she flipped through the pages, making notes for Penny to prepare in a briefing for Gordon. Griffin appeared to be on the up and up, but if he wasn't and she didn't find out in time, it wouldn't be because she'd neglected to keep him on the view screen.

Her office cellphone vibrated. It was a text from Vince.

I think I found him. Waiting for him to show. Will let you know. I'll get back to you in twenty.

Great. He didn't tell her where he was. She texted him back: *Where are you?*

She waited a few minutes, but there was no response. Knowing Vince, he was not beyond ignoring her until he was able to show her his prize. He could drive her crazy.

SHE'D GOTTEN THE TEXT FROM Vince at nine thirty, and it was now almost eleven. He said he would get back to her in twenty minutes, but there had been no further word.

She sent a text: *Get back to me now, where are you?*

She would have gotten in her car and started to look for him, except she had no idea where to start. Pacing the room, she reached again for her phone when it went off in her hand.

"Vince," she yelled. "Are you okay? Where are you?"

"I found him," he whispered. "He switched cars on me. He's gone inside Gold's Gym. Wait."

He was gone.

"Vince? Vince." She gritted her teeth.

"Hollis, I'm here in the lobby," Vince continued whispering. "He almost tricked me. He came out wearing something different than what he wore going in. I'm going to follow him home."

"Vince, listen to me. It's almost midnight. Go home," Hollis said in what she hoped was a calm and steady voice. "If he's going to the gym late at night, he's probably a regular, and we can catch up to him tomorrow."

"I can do this, Hollis," he said. "I won't show myself. I'll just see where he lives."

She could hear his footsteps as he walked to the car. He clicked off.

"Be careful," she whispered to the silence.

Chapter Sixteen

Tuesday

HOLLIS COULDN'T SLEEP.

When her phone trilled about an hour later, her heart was beating so loudly, she thought it might jump out of her chest.

"Vince? What happened?"

"I got him, Hollis, I got his address." Vince sounded triumphant. "I followed him to an apartment in Berkeley. Do you want the address now?"

"No, I don't want the address now. I want you to go home and to bed. We'll talk tomorrow ... I mean later today, in the office." She'd expected her voice to sound shaky, but she'd managed to keep it surprisingly firm.

"Okay," he agreed. "But did I do good?"

Hollis gave a short laugh. "You did good, kid."

HER SPIRITS WERE HIGH WHEN she got into the office. For the first time in days, she paused and stared at the rising sun's rays breaking through the fading blue of the sky.

Vince was safe.

She returned the Griffin file to the drawer and cleared her desk of its usual stack of papers. Then she pulled out the client sheet Penny had prepared on Kiki Turner to ready herself for the ten o'clock appointment. Much of Penny's write-up was information Hollis had already heard directly from Kiki.

One item she had not seen—Penny had attached a clipping from a monthly fan magazine that had a picture of Turner's daughter, Alicia. Alicia was as fair as her mother was dark, though with the same crystal-blue eyes. Taken about two years earlier, the photo showed Alicia on a beach in a skimpy bikini and in the arms of a very handsome young man—Derek Lynch, her husband. They made a glamorous couple.

Hollis looked up at the tap on her door. Vince stood there with a sheepish grin on his face.

"Hey, Hollis, how you doin' this morning?"

"Come in, you rascal." She pointed for him to sit. "In a partnership, there are no cowboys. You left me hanging, not knowing what to do." She could hear her voice rise, and she took a breath. "Promise me you'll never do that disappearing act again, or this partnership is finished."

The smiled faded from his face, as he realized she was not amused. "I'm sorry. I guess I got carried away." His smile returned. "But it was exciting waiting and watching until I spotted him. I knew I had him. Then I had to follow …." He looked up to see her dour expression and hung his head. "I promise."

"Okay, that's past." Hollis took up her pen. "What's the address?"

He reached into his shirt pocket, pulled out a slip of paper, and handed it over to her.

"It's in a big complex one block off University Avenue near the campus. It would be a good place for him to hide out if he wasn't so old. It has a lot of students coming and going at all hours, and he stands out."

Hollis smothered a snort. Vince clearly had age issues. She could only imagine what he thought of her. Surely there were still adult students in the world.

"I'll need to pay him a visit," said Hollis. "But first, I want to meet Constance Cantone and find out why she knew an autopsy would reveal her uncle's murder. After that, I'm ready to tackle the Pittmans. Let's get back out there this afternoon."

"Sounds good to me."

Tiffany buzzed. "Hollis, can you come out here for a second?"

Hollis went out into the lobby and caught sight of a massive flower arrangement almost too big for the wide counter.

"Whose anniversary?"

"No one's," Tiffany whispered. "Mrs. Turner's chauffeur brought them in when she came for her appointment." She smiled. "They're a little overwhelming, but I like the sentiment. By the way, she's in the small conference room."

"She's early. Let me get my notes and go right in. Is anyone with her?"

"No, just her," Tiffany said. "Is someone else coming?"

"No, just checking." Hollis knew the odds of Turner reconciling with her daughter were small. "Well, I'd better get in there and hear the story." She turned to give Tiffany a grin. "You seem to be in a better mood. Has everything been straightened out? Er, I haven't forgotten your agreement to tell me what's on your mind. Are we still set for your lunch break?"

"You're still willing to talk with me about something personal?"

"Of course. Let's say twelve thirty. It will be a long lunch, and I should be finished with Turner by then." Hollis picked up her pad and headed for the door.

Tiffany nodded, a small smile on her lips.

Hollis entered the room and blinked twice at Kiki's outfit of the day. She was wearing three shades of Versace pink: blouse, sweater, and slacks. Her black hair was coiled into what resembled a loaf of French bread lying heavily on one shoulder.

"Hollis, I can call you Hollis, can't I?" She didn't wait for her to respond. "I have a doctor's appointment this afternoon and … and I want to get everything ready for you to start work on the trust. I … I'm going to be contacting my daughter, and I expect she'll want to talk to you."

Hollis frowned. "Mrs. Tur … Kiki … I won't speak with your daughter unless you want me to. You're my client."

"Oh no, I want you to speak with her. In fact, I told her to speak with you." Kiki smoothed her clothing and settled into the chair. She pointed to Hollis' pad of paper. "Good, you're going to need to take notes when you hear my story."

Hollis took a seat, and Kiki continued, "Like I told you at our last meeting, I was a little wild as a teenager." She clasped and unclasped her hands. "Not bad, but I … I got pregnant when I should have been in high school. I was living in a transition home for teenagers. It's a long story. The home didn't care, and I didn't get hit with a lot of guilt. Still, they had to kick me out. I didn't have any money so … so I had to go to … to work."

Hollis cleared her throat. "Is this when you became a stripper?"

Turner smiled. "No, that was later. I was an escort." She smiled. "A very successful escort."

Hollis said nothing.

"Unfortunately, I wasn't a very good mother …" her voice drifted, "or, maybe not the mother Alicia needed. We never got along. She fought me even when she was a baby. She would eat anything anyone else fed her, but she'd turn her head away from me."

"That must have been a … a challenge for you," Hollis said.

"Yes, it was. Although when she got older, she was more than willing to take my money. I suppose I tried to buy her love." She gave a short laugh. "Well, that was a waste of cash because it didn't work. She went to college, met the loser she married, and in a twist of fate, they had a lovely daughter. She's almost two. Her name is Kate." Turner's eyes filled with tears.

Hollis handed her a box of tissues. Turner dabbed at her eyes and delicately blew her nose.

"From the very beginning, Kate loved me. She came to me immediately, and she cuddles in my arms like a little angel. She is my heart." Turner blew her nose.

"Uh, Kiki, I think I know where this is going," Hollis said. "You want to disinherit your daughter and leave your estate to your granddaughter."

Turner tapped her ringed finger against the walnut conference table. "You see, I knew you would understand. But there's one other thing. I think Alicia's husband, Derek, thinks something is up. He would push for her to contest my will."

"You mean he already thinks you're planning on disinheriting Alicia?"

"Not exactly. They don't know my exact plans and that I'm … I'm dying. But he found out that I gave away some of my jewelry and a couple of art pieces. I told him it was none of his business, but he got Alicia to call me. Her call was short and to the point—one of the few calls I've gotten from her this year. She wanted to know how I was doing. I'm usually the one to call to set up a time to have Kate visit. Or Derek calls to ask me to babysit. So, I knew he had pressured her."

Hollis put down her pen. "You said you encouraged Alicia to contact me. Why?"

"I want you to tell her I'm dying and that my estate will be going to Kate."

Oh no.

"Er, Kiki, I don't think that's a good idea," Hollis said firmly. "As a probate attorney, I have worked many cases, and family disputes can cause unnecessary grief, before and after the individual has passed."

Kiki's voice broke. "You don't understand. My daughter hates me. She thinks I'm an embarrassment. She once told me that I was … that I was trash."

Hollis winced and sighed. "I'm sorry, that must have really

hurt. But I still say that having a stranger tell her about her mother's medical condition won't endear her to you either. She could take it out on you."

"How do you mean?" Turner frowned.

Hollis shrugged. "Well, she could stop you from seeing your granddaughter, because she knows that would hurt you most."

Turner was silent, and then she slowly nodded. "You're right. She would do that."

Hollis frowned. "Tell you what, how about the three of us meet here in our offices? I can do most of talking." Her voice picked up energy. "She wouldn't rant and rave here, and if you and she have something to say, then it will be out in the open."

Turner clapped her hands. "Yes, that's perfect. How soon do you think you could have the papers drawn up?"

Hollis held up her hand. "We need to talk about the details of your trust a bit more. Are you sure you want to disinherit your daughter? How large is your estate?"

"My bankers tell me that as of last month, it's worth fifteen million, including the real estate holdings."

Hollis raised her eyebrows. "Okay, well, that's a good sum. I'm going to need to see all your statements, assets, and deeds so I can get started. Here's a list." She slid a paper across the table then scribbled a note to herself. "But in that regard, even a modest bequest to Alicia could help to end the animosity between you."

"I've already gathered the papers you need, but I'll check your list." Turner folded the paper and put it in her purse. "And as to the bequest … no. She told me she didn't want it. She said she didn't want any part of my 'dirty money.' At least, those were her words before she married the jerk. But now, if it was up to him, I think he would persuade her to take any and all of my money."

"Well, let's take one step at a time," Hollis said. "Give me your daughter's contact information and a few calendar dates that you're available."

Turner wrote quickly on a sheet of paper and passed it to Hollis. "Don't worry about my calendar. I'll make myself available." She stood and extended her hand. "Thank you, Hollis. I'll messenger those documents over to you. You should have them later this afternoon."

"Good. I'll be on the lookout."

Hollis walked her out to the elevators and said goodbye. Tiffany approached as the doors closed.

"Are you still interested in doing lunch?"

Hollis smiled. "Actually, I'm starving. Can you get coverage for the front desk? We can go now."

At Hollis' insistence, Tiffany picked their lunch location. Tribeca's was an Italian restaurant in Downtown Oakland, known for its basic home-style Tuscan cuisine. Off the beaten path to foot traffic, it was not busy, and they were able to get seated quickly. The server came to their table right away to take their orders.

Hollis leaned back on the booth's cushioned seats. "Okay, now tell me what's going on."

"First of all, it's nothing I can't handle. It's actually my fault it's gone on this long. I brought it on myself—"

"And you have no one but yourself to blame," Hollis broke in. "Enough with the platitudes. Tell me, what's wrong? What is *it*?"

Tiffany sighed. "It's about what I told you a few days ago. It's about that guy. He's younger than I am, and although he's a good guy, I wanted someone who could mentor me, someone who could …."

Hollis made a sympathetic face; she'd finally put the pieces together.

She edged closer in her seat and tried to connect with the downcast eyes of the receptionist. "The guy is Vince, isn't it? Are you two, uh, a couple?"

"Yes!" Tiffany almost shouted, causing the couple at the table nearby to look over. She lowered her voice, "Yes, yes, I just want to say it out loud. Vince is a good guy, don't get me wrong. I know you like him, but ... but he's got personal issues and his mother ... well. Have you met her?"

Hollis stiffened. "So, despite who he is as a man, you think you could do a lot better?"

Their food came, and after the server left, Tiffany gave a slight shake of her head.

"That's just it. I love who he is as a man." She twisted a roll of spaghetti onto her fork and held it midair. "It's my head, not my heart, that's saying all the practical, mature and ... and whatever things. I want to go to college, maybe to law school." She paused then continued, "I've been saving almost every paycheck. My family's not rich; my Dad works in construction. My mom has worked in the Macy's business office for the past twenty-three years. I'm their only child. They always say they put all their hopes and dreams in me."

"And if you bring home an ex-drug addict who has a mother in drug rehab," Hollis said, "it will hurt them immeasurably."

Tiffany nodded. "But I can't tell Vince that. I can't hurt him because of something he can't change ... or help."

Hollis put her elbows on the table and her chin in her hand. She knew Vince probably cared for Tiffany, which was why his behavior had been equally bizarre.

"He's trying to impress you, isn't he? That's why you got irritated with him over the detective assignment. He wanted to show you he had more potential than the mailroom."

Tiffany nodded. "And then there's the age thing. I'm almost four years older than he is. I want an older man."

"Wow," said Hollis, not knowing what would be expected of an older man. "Vince always seemed more mature and older than his age to me. Is that why you asked me how old you looked?"

"Yes, and I didn't want friends to think I could only attract a ... a child."

There was momentary quiet as they ate their lunch. Hollis took a last forkful and tried not to roll her eyes.

"You know, Tiffany, someone once said that the heart wants what the heart wants. I'm hearing what's in your heart and I'm hearing what's in your head. Life is short; you don't get a replay. Vince is a good person. You're a good person. Trying to make him into a bad guy so you can stop caring about him doesn't sound honest to me. If you don't feel good about him or being with him, just tell him so."

And stop taking it out on the office.

Tiffany said nothing, but Hollis could tell she was thinking about what she'd said. Their conversation drifted to the weather and the condition of the office's law library. With unspoken agreement, they began to gather their things to leave.

Tiffany pulled on her jacket. "I did hear what you said, Hollis. Thank you for the good advice. I need to think. I do want to apologize for my behavior these past weeks. I guess I didn't know it showed."

Hollis patted her on the shoulder. "No worries." She was feeling pretty good about her role as a sage advisor. "Er ... can I forward my calls to you for the next few days? Penny is out of the office in training and—"

"Sure." Tiffany laughed.

DETECTIVE SCOTT HAD NO PROBLEM providing Constance Cantone's contact information.

She chuckled on the phone with Hollis. "You're on the case now. You're entitled."

Mrs. Cantone lived in a luxurious, single-story home near Skyline Boulevard in the Piedmont hills. Hollis announced herself at the entrance and the decorative wrought-iron gates swung open slowly. She drove around a landscaped circular lawn framed by weeping willows partially shading a large bed of colorful annuals.

Hollis waited patiently at the front door, wondering why it

was taking so long for her to answer the door. Constance had already buzzed her in.

It finally opened.

"I'm sorry, my decorator called just after I let you in the gate." She stood to the side.

Initially, in the muted light of the entry, Constance Cantone looked to be in her twenties, until Hollis glimpsed the faint white scars in front of her ears that marked a facelift. Her white-blonde hair was worn in a long ponytail held back with a black scrunchie. She was a tiny woman, slightly shorter than Hollis, but with a curvy figure set off by a white, embroidered crop top and beige slacks.

"Not a problem. I'm grateful you had time for me." Hollis followed her into the living room.

Constance took a seat in a wide, tan-suede chair and pointed to the matching one opposite. Hollis sank into its comfortable cushions.

"I know you're representing the woman who killed my uncle. Why do you want to talk to me?"

Hollis sat forward. "She didn't kill your uncle. And I wanted to know what made you suspect that your uncle's death was anything but a heart attack."

Constance closed her eyes, and she was quiet for such a long moment that Hollis was tempted to clear her throat. But then Constance's eyes flashed open.

"Of course you'd say that." She ran her finger over her eyebrows. "I just knew … I just knew, that's all. My uncle and I had a special relationship. I'd been to visit him the week before, and he promised me that he'd help pay for my divorce attorney."

Hollis said nothing.

She sniffed. "I know you've met Tony. Need I say more?"

"But what made you—"

"My mother—my uncle's sister—and he were estranged. I don't get along that well with my mother, either. But he was good to me. I knew she was his primary heir but it would be a cold day in hell before she remembered to give me my share. And then I heard he was giving some of his money away to some church .... Oh no, that was not Uncle Matthias."

Hollis nodded. "That was a red flag for me, too."

Constance stood and started pacing the room. "I knew something was wrong, that's all."

Hollis drove thoughtfully back to the office. Her instincts told her that Constance Cantone was telling the truth. There was no reason for her to lie, and she readily admitted that she had a better chance of getting more money from her mother if she showed an active interest in her uncle's death.

Still ....

Chapter Seventeen

———⁓———

Wednesday

HOLLIS ARRIVED AT WORK BEFORE the sun rose and immediately set about clearing her desk. Between the Larson defense matter and the new Turner case, her office time was being eroded, and she didn't want to neglect her other clients who counted on her full attention to get their issues settled.

A few hours later it was midmorning, and she was satisfied that she'd caught up on her paperwork. She picked up the phone and punched in Alicia Lynch's number. Her call was snatched up before she could get a full ring in.

"Yes?" a male voice boomed.

"Er … I'm sorry, I was trying to reach Alicia Lynch. I was told this was her number," she said, on guard.

"It is. I was in the other room when I heard it ringing. I'm her husband, Derek. Can I help you?"

Hollis smiled. His white lie was unnecessary.

"My name is Hollis Morgan. I'm an attorney with Dodson

Dodson & Doyle. I represent her mother. May I speak with her?"

"Of course, Mrs. Turner told us you would be calling. Well, she told me, actually. She knows that Alicia tells me everything. We're anxious to have this … all settled. Alicia and I have been working hard to keep up and—"

"Yes," Hollis interrupted him. "If I could speak with her, then we could get things started."

He felt the nudge. "I'll go get her. She's with the baby."

Hollis could hear muffled conversation in the background as Derek appeared to be explaining her call, and why his wife should take it.

Finally, he returned to the phone.

"She told me to handle you," he said, with just a hint of *I told you so*.

"Fine then," Hollis said, hoping her irritation registered. "Do you think you and she could meet with me and your mother-in-law this afternoon at one o'clock?"

"Today at one is perfect. We'll be there," said Lynch.

"Hollis, you've got a call on the main line—Kip Lyles. I'm ready to transfer," Tiffany said crisply.

Hollis sniffed and picked up the phone.

"Ms. Morgan, good morning. Well, it appears there's a bigger Bell story for the *Daily* after all," Kip Lyles said. "I was hoping you could make time for me later today." Sensing her hesitation, he added, "I won't take long."

"Mr. Lyles, I can't imagine what sort of news you expect to hear from a probate attorney. I didn't find the body and I don't have any insights."

"Ah, now you're being coy. I know that you're working with Gordon Barrett to defend Odelia Larson. You were at the house. My angle is to report what it's like to move from being a probate attorney to a criminal lawyer. I'm using that serial approach you suggested. Besides, the chief said you would be doing him a favor."

The chief was calling in a chit.

"Why aren't you after Gordon Barrett? It's his case," Hollis said. "I'm not a criminal lawyer."

"All the other media outlets are talking to Barrett. He's been around and they all know him, but … but *I* know *you*. Have you found any clues? Or, have—"

"Mr. Lyles … Kip," Hollis muttered, looking down at her calendar, "I can give you fifteen minutes at five thirty this afternoon. It's all I have."

"I'll take it." He clicked off.

HOLLIS CONCLUDED A SUMMARY BRIEFING for Gordon. It was easier to catch him up in writing than in person. She checked the time once more. She'd had a piece of fruit for lunch. The meeting with Kiki Turner and her daughter Alicia was in another hour, but she wanted to make sure she was ready. She'd had confrontational family interactions before. Nothing brought out the worst in people like a disappointing probate. Kiki had sent over her past "celebrity" clippings and her tax returns, so Hollis could get to know her better and follow her evolution over the years.

She was certainly an interesting lady.

Hollis finished making side notations on a draft Turner trust. When Tiffany announced the arrival of Alicia and Derek Lynch, she was prepared.

They shook hands in the lobby and Hollis directed them into the conference room.

At the doorway, she motioned to Tiffany. "I'm expecting Mrs. Kiki Turner as well. When she gets here, just direct her in," Hollis said.

Tiffany waved her forward to the reception desk. She whispered, "Mrs. Turner just called and said she wasn't feeling well, and for you to go ahead with the meeting as you and she discussed. She'd like you to visit her at home or give her a call after the meeting."

Hollis frowned. She'd been set up.

Alicia Lynch was every bit as beautiful as in her photos. She was the mirror image of her dark-haired mother, only with blonde hair. Taller than Hollis by at least three inches, she wore minimal makeup with her hair in a single long French braid. Her only jewelry was a pair of small, simple, intertwining gold hoop earrings. Same eyes, same features, but different.

Derek Lynch, on the other hand, could grace the cover of *GQ*. He too was blond—out of a bottle. His hair was attractively streaked, reminiscent of surfing days. He was six inches taller than his wife and wore jeans, a maroon polo shirt, and a black linen sports jacket. Sockless in his boat shoes, he looked good, and he knew it.

Hollis shook their hands and turned to Alicia. "I just found out that your mother won't be joining us."

A look of panic crossed her eyes and she swirled to face her husband. "You told me Kiki wasn't going to be here."

He held up his hand to calm her and shot Hollis a glance to catch her reaction. "She isn't, is she?" he asked. "I knew she wouldn't show up."

"Well, *I* didn't know," Hollis said, tossing her pad of paper on the table. "I would have preferred her to be here, because these types of matters are not only personal but can really impact a family's future relations."

Alicia tapped a finger on the table. "Well, I don't know what 'type' of matter this is," she said with her fingers in air quotes, "but we have no family relations. I want nothing to do with my mother. I … I … I don't wish her ill. I just wish she'd go away."

"Baby, we talked about this." Derek gave her shoulder a squeeze. "We're just here to listen."

Hollis assessed the interchange between the two and decided that Derek didn't have the upper hand he thought he did, or wanted. His tone was placating, not commanding.

"Ahem, perhaps if I shared … I mean spoke to you about your mother's … er … situation …" Hollis stammered.

They looked at her with expectation.

Hollis took a deep breath. "This is difficult, and your mother wanted to be here to tell you herself." She paused. "She's dying."

Their faces didn't change. Then Alicia's hand went to her mouth to stifle a gasp. Derek flushed to his dark roots and his eyes went back and forth as if reading a book.

Hollis continued slowly, "She's been given six months. Right now she's not in any pain and her state of mind is good. She told me that she feels—"

"Excuse me," Derek interrupted her. "You're her probate attorney, right? So, has she already written her will?"

"Derek!" Alicia called out.

Hollis was gratified to see that Kiki's daughter still appeared to have some modicum of caring. "Your mother explained your relationship to me—"

"There is none," Derek blurted out.

Hollis gave him a look that caused him to sit back in his chair.

"And …" she continued pointedly, "and it sorrows her, but she respects your position about her … her background. Therefore, in her trust she has decided to leave, except for a few bequests, her entire estate to your daughter Kate. She is to receive half upon her twenty-first birthday, and the remainder on her thirtieth birthday. Upon your mother's death, you will receive five hundred thousand dollars."

Derek Lynch couldn't hold back. "How are we to live until then?"

Hollis didn't know if he meant until Kate turned twenty-one, or until Kiki died. She had a feeling it was the latter.

"Mr. Lynch, your mother-in-law is dying. She is making a distribution to her daughter and she wants to make a distribution to her granddaughter. It is her money to do with as she pleases."

Hollis was glad that she had convinced Kiki to make her daughter a direct bequest; a completely disinherited family member could have more basis to sue. This way a reasonable person would say the allocation was based on the quality of the relationship.

"Ah, no, you're not going to get rid of us that fast," Lynch growled, and raised his voice. "How much are your fees? Are you getting a percentage?"

Hollis pursed her lips and narrowed her eyes. She was about to speak again when Alicia stood.

"Tell Kiki that if she thinks she's going to manipulate me into recognizing her as my mother, she's *so* wrong," she yelled and pointed her finger at Hollis. "And tell her that if she thinks she's going to continue to see *my* daughter after this power play of hers, well, she's wrong there, too."

Alicia Lynch reached for her coat and purse. Derek stood and patted his hair in place. They headed for the lobby.

He stopped, blocking Hollis from reaching the hallway. In a low voice, he said, "Besides, how do you know she's not lying to you? How do you know she's dying?"

Hollis chewed the inside of her lip. "Mr. Lynch, you mean other than the fact that it makes no sense for her to lie? What does she have to gain? Mrs. Turner is reconciled to the relationship with your wife. And by the way, I get paid either way."

She moved past him.

Alicia was already pushing the elevator button. She motioned to her husband, who glared at Hollis.

"You'll be hearing from us," he spat.

Hollis gave him a small smile. "I'm sure I will."

She turned to go back to her office.

"Well, I can tell that went well," Tiffany said, looking at the Lynches' stiff, retreating backs.

Hollis gazed around Kiki Turner's large living room with

its white furniture on a snow-white carpet. If it weren't for the overlarge tiger rug in front of the white marble fireplace, she'd be looking over her shoulder for the men in white jackets. She hadn't wanted to talk to Kiki on the phone. She wanted to speak to her in person.

"Do you like it?" Kiki entered the room from what appeared to be a study.

"I'm afraid to touch anything. Everything is so … pristine," Hollis dodged.

"Hmmm, interesting answer. Come on and sit with me in the kitchen. I think you'll feel more relaxed there."

Hollis followed her and agreed. The kitchen, huge as it was, was homey, and Kiki pointed to a barstool next to the granite slab island. Hollis took the seat and gave her a quick rundown of the meeting.

Kiki wasn't surprised by her daughter's reaction, nor did Derek Lynch's response seem to bother her. But it did raise the question in Hollis' mind of why Kiki would choose to knowingly antagonize her daughter.

"I take it you want to slap my wrists about missing the meeting." Kiki smiled as if reading her mind. She pushed a basket of bread rolls toward her. "Try these. They're cheese puffs stuffed with a sausage mixture."

"You're the client. I just want to make sure I give you my best work." Hollis bit into a light flaky dough with a tangy, savory meat center. "Hmm, not bad. Actually, very good."

Kiki smiled. "I put learning to make hors d'oeuvres on my bucket list. I couldn't cook at all before, and I didn't want to attempt anything that would … would take a lifetime to learn. Appetizers seemed simple enough."

"They really are good," Hollis repeated without taking another bite, a little thrown by Kiki's conciliatory manner.

"Good enough so that you'll forgive me for missing the meeting?"

Hollis dabbed her mouth with a paper napkin.

"Yes, they're that good," Hollis said, "but I have to tell you that in some respects, I'm glad you weren't at the meeting. Alicia did not take the news well."

Kiki closed her eyes and then opened them. They were clear and knowing.

"So, go over again what happened."

Hollis detailed the conversation and tried to downplay Derek's obvious greed. It would only throw more fuel onto the fire of Kiki's negative assessment of her son-in-law. But Kiki wasn't fooled.

"I assume that Derek was unable to hide his joy at the prospect of my early departure?"

"He was as you described him, but I think Alicia was more concerned about the problems with your relationship than the money."

Kiki started to pace around the kitchen. "She actually said she would keep Kate from me?"

"She was upset, Kiki. I got the feeling, despite what she said, that down deep she still cares for you and the fact that you seem to have more consideration for her daughter than her ... I think that hurt her, plus the shock of hearing you're dying."

"But you said she might take Kate from me, and I thought ..." her voice drifted. She sat back down. "How do I fix it?"

Hollis raised her eyebrows and shrugged. "Right now, their anger is coming from surprise and disappointment. I think you need to have a one-on-one with your daughter and talk ... just the two of you."

The look of fear on Turner's face piqued Hollis' curiosity; she was convinced there was more to this relationship than Kiki Turner had let on.

"Tell you what," Hollis said. "I'll meet with Alicia to set the stage for your talk. If I can get her alone, I might be able to find out what's really bugging her. But you still need to meet with her too."

Kiki grabbed Hollis' arm. "I'm not a monster. The only

reason I didn't want my money going to Alicia is because Derek would have it spent in a few years. And I think he'd leave her after it was gone."

"Well, I don't think I would tell her all that. She's probably not ready to hear anything against her husband. But talk to her from your heart ... not your pocketbook. I think she might come around."

Kiki nodded. "That's a good idea. You talk to her first, and then I'll talk to her alone."

Her face seemed flushed. She was wearing a gold lamé top with white slacks. The shaking in her left hand was noticeable, and Hollis wondered if it was a symptom of her condition.

Hollis picked up her purse and briefcase and headed for the front door.

"I'll call you after we've talked," Hollis said over her shoulder.

In the doorway, Kiki put the back of her hand to her own cheek as if feeling the rush of heat. "You know I've been late all my life. My friends would always complain. But now the doctors tell me that I'm going to die on time." Kiki put a hand on Hollis' arm. "Please convince her, and try to make our meeting happen soon."

Hollis patted Kiki's hand. "I'll try."

HOLLIS SETTLED INTO HER OFFICE. She still had the meeting with Kip Lyles. She was grateful that Gordon was not a publicity hound. He loved having the media's attention and seeing his name in print. But he made it clear he had no interest whatsoever in giving time to the *Daily* for an interview.

"Lyles is all yours. Don't antagonize him," Gordon said, waiting on phone hold. "I've seen the way you handle the press. We need to have all of them on our client's side."

Hollis frowned. "I handle the press okay. I treat them the way I would anybody."

"I know, that's the problem." He fluttered his fingers at her to signal that his call had come through.

She turned into the hallway and bumped into Tiffany.

"Excuse me .... Hollis, Mr. Lyles is here to see you," Tiffany spoke in a rush. "I put him in the small conference room. Do you want me to offer him water?"

"Of course," she said. "Why would you ask?"

"I don't like him." Tiffany wrinkled her nose as if recalling a bad smell emanating from the reporter. "His articles are poorly written. I'm embarrassed for him. Besides, everybody knows he makes up half the stories he writes."

Hollis was puzzled by her attitude. "Give him some water."

Hollis entered the lobby with her hand outstretched.

"Mr. Lyles, I've got another meeting after this. So, how can I best help you?"

"I appreciate your seeing me. I won't waste your time. But the chief told me that it was information that you passed on that helped with the arrest of Odelia Larson." He moved his chair closer to the table. "I know Bell was a blackmailer, and that it's likely one of his victims killed him. Your reputation for digging up the truth is well established. Is it true Bell's niece called for the autopsy because she had suspicions?"

"You'll have to ask the chief. I didn't take the call."

Lyles make a quick note on his pad. "I don't expect you to tell me their names, but do you know anything about any of the victims that would lead you to believe he or she is the strongest suspect?"

Hollis wished that the chief was in the room so she could throw her chair at his head. It was clear he had planted the possibility of a story in Kip's mind, so she would swallow his obvious flattery and could verify the "rumor." The chief's hands would be clean by not talking to the media.

Well, two can play at that game.

"Mr. Lyles, you probably know more than I do. You're the reason the *Daily* is still San Lucian's most popular local paper." Hollis smiled. "What were you doing at Matthias Bell's home on the day he died?"

Lyles started to answer, then checked himself and chuckled. "Ah, Ms. Morgan, can I call you Hollis?" he asked and then continued, "You're good, but the chief said you owed him a favor and he wanted you to help me with my story."

"That's true." Hollis nodded. "Okay, even though my client is dead, I feel ethically bound by attorney-client privilege. But I can tell you that Matthias Bell's estate is not out of the ordinary and will be processed as routine. As far as our client is concerned, I have no comment."

"Do you think he knew the person who killed him?"

"Mr. Lyles, Kip, how would I know that?" she shot back and looked at the time. "I'm sorry, but I've got to get ready for my next meeting." She smiled. "Thank you for your understanding."

STEPHANIE HAD ASKED HOLLIS TO meet her at Crogan's after work.

"We both need a girls' night out, even if the night out only lasts an hour," Stephanie had said on the phone. "I could use a break from the norm."

"So could I," Hollis agreed. "See you at six. Whoever gets there first orders the Sauvignon Blanc."

Crogan's was in the Montclair District in the Oakland Hills. The neighborhood bar had great food, a congenial atmosphere, and drew a cadre of locals, as well as used-to-be locals, like Hollis. Soft jazz played in the background and the constant hum of conversation was never loud enough to be obnoxious.

The friends clicked glasses and each took a long sip of wine.

"Ugh, I've been working on this lab case file for what seems like years," Stephanie groaned. "But it's only been a week. It's frustrating because usually I average three days, max, and now I'm a week into it and I don't see the end. It's making me crazy."

Hollis chuckled. "So you love what you're doing?"

"Yes," laughed her friend. "It's a forensic puzzle, which doesn't come along often, at least not around here." She rubbed her hands together. "How's your client's case coming?"

Hollis shrugged. "You would think that a probate attorney would have a pretty tame practice. I mean, most of my work takes place *after* my client has passed. But for some reason I also attract clients like Bell, whose cases have complicated and criminal overtones that give me the feeling they're reaching out to me from beyond the grave. Odelia Larson doesn't seem to realize how much trouble she's in. She expects Gordon and me to pull her out."

"Umm, so you love it, too?"

They both laughed.

Hollis' phone vibrated and she pulled it out of her pocket.

San Fran

She frowned.

"What's the matter?" Stephanie asked.

"It's John. We have a secret code he sends to let me know he's okay and thinking about me," Hollis said, holding the phone and staring at the screen.

"And …?"

"This is a disposable phone. John bought a dozen of them, six for him and six for me. He numbered them in pairs. I'm supposed to destroy the phone after I get his message so it can't be traced." Hollis didn't lift her eyes from the phone. "This started out as his usual message, but it's only partial. It broke off, and I'm not sure …. Maybe he'll send another."

Stephanie looked over Hollis' arm at the black screen and pursed her lips. "When is he due back?"

"It could be as early as the end of this week or early next week. Remember, he's on assignment." Hollis placed the phone in front of her on the table so she could see the screen.

"He probably got interrupted sending the message," Stephanie said. "He'll play it safe, use the next phone, and text later."

She reached across the table and put her hand on Hollis' arm. "Destroy the phone."

Hollis gave her friend a long look and nodded. She put the phone on the floor, stood, and crushed it under her heel.

CHAPTER EIGHTEEN

Thursday

W HEN HOLLIS WOKE UP THE next morning, she fumbled for her phone. The screen was blank. No message from John had come through. She double-checked to make sure the phone was on and turned up the vibration volume. Brushing aside concern, she was ready for work in an hour, and though she got to the firm early, she found Penny sitting in her office.

Putting her briefcase down next to her desk, Hollis stared at the paper Penny handed her.

"How did you get this information?"

Penny sat primly in the chair in front of Hollis' desk. Her usually expressionless face wore a smug grin.

"I kept my work papers. You gave the Pittmans your last copy—"

"I didn't *give* it to them. They *took* my copy," Hollis protested.

"Yes, they did," Penny said, obviously discounting any extenuating circumstances. "Well, I still had my work papers, and I think they might be useful in tracking down where the mister and missus have disappeared to." She handed over a sheaf of pages.

Hollis flipped through the papers and grinned. "Penny, I want you to take the weekend off."

Penny frowned. "Were you going to need me to work this weekend?"

"I was just joking," Hollis said with a smile. "I meant you did well by retaining your work papers. You probably saved the day."

"Oh," Penny said. A small twitch of her lips gave the hint of a genuine smile. "Then I'll get back to my real work."

Hollis watched her leave with a shake of her head. Penny was a treasure—a quirky treasure, but a treasure. And since she had done well by preserving the Pittmans' information, Hollis was not about to criticize her. She clicked on the phone.

"Mrs. Pittman?" Hollis asked. "This is Hollis Morgan."

There was a gasp on the other end.

"How did you find us?" Millicent Pittman muttered.

"It was a fluke. The number in your file wasn't the number you called me from to confirm our earlier meeting. I scrolled through my recent contacts on my phone, and there you were."

Hollis didn't want to tell her that she'd called at least a dozen other numbers before reaching the correct one.

"My husband will not be happy. What do you want now?"

"To meet you and your husband at some mutually agreed upon location. I don't know where you currently live, but I was thinking of Scott's Seafood in Jack London Square."

"Why do we need to meet? Haven't you satisfied your client's wishes?"

"Yes, but unfortunately something has come up involving law enforcement, and it's necessary to eliminate you as viable suspects."

There was a slight scuffle on the other end.

"Suspects!" Ian Pittman yelled into the phone. "What the hell are you talking about?"

Hollis sighed. Was the couple on a tether?

"Mr. Pittman, you must have overheard my conversation with your wife. I would like to sit down and speak with you in a public place. There have been new developments and I think it would benefit you both to listen to what I have to say."

"Okay, then let's do it now."

"Now?" Hollis answered. "I have other appointments and—"

"*Now*, Ms. Morgan. Any ducks you have to line up will have to wait. We're not going to walk into an ambush. Isn't your office right up the street in downtown Oakland? We'll meet you at Scott's in Jack London Square at eleven sharp. That gives you ten minutes to get there, plenty of time."

Hollis rolled her eyes. What choice did she have?

"See you at eleven."

HOLLIS SAT WAITING IN THE entry for the Pittmans' arrival. After directing Penny to look out for the copies of discovery being delivered from the DA's office, she rushed to Jack London Square. She was on time, but they were late. It was now ten past eleven, and she kept peering out the restaurant's windows to spot the Pittmans. She jumped slightly when she felt a tap on her shoulder. She swirled around.

"Mr. Pittman, I take it you've been watching me to see if I came alone." Hollis glared. "Well, I did."

He had changed his appearance. He was sporting a deep tan—obviously from a bottle—and had brown eyes and hair.

"Oh, only for the past twenty minutes." Ian led her to a table overlooking the dock. "Not that we think you would betray us, but this is a wretched world, and well, we thought … you know you can't trust anyone these days."

Hollis nodded to Millicent, who was wearing large dark glasses. Her hair was colored a subdued dark brown.

Hollis caught her breath.

"Mrs. Pittman, Mr. Pittman," Hollis said. "I hardly recognize you both, but then that's probably the idea."

"Millicent and I sometimes find it necessary in our line of business to … to alter our appearances." Ian gave her a half-smile.

"What is your line of business?" Hollis asked.

Ian chortled and Millicent gave him a warning look.

"Some of this and some of that," he said. "But more to the point, what did you want to see us about? We have an appointment, too."

"You read the papers," Hollis said. "Matthias Bell was murdered. The police are looking for you."

Millicent almost dropped the glass she'd lifted to her lips and Ian frowned.

"What do you mean?" Ian said.

Millicent took off her glasses. "We read about it in the paper. Why are they looking for us? We had nothing to do with his killing."

Hollis almost gasped; Millicent looked much more like the woman in the passport.

Her eyes narrowed, assessing them both. Either they were Academy Award contenders, or they had nothing to do with Bell's murder. On the other hand, any couple who could change their appearance as easily as chameleons wouldn't necessarily have trouble pretending to be surprised.

"There was an autopsy, and it appears Mr. Bell was given a drug."

They both looked at each other, then at Hollis.

Ian spoke first. "So this little reunion is to—"

"My client used to work for Matthias Bell and she's been arrested for his murder. She didn't do it, so I'm working on finding out who did."

"Ah, and did you think we would confess to this murder?" Millicent taunted.

Hollis smiled. "What I think is whatever Bell was holding over your heads is still a viable threat. Don't bother lying. I wouldn't believe you anyway. Maybe you two got tired of being at risk for exposure." She pulled out a file and flipped it open. "I'd like to know about the visit you paid to Bell on the Saturday he was killed."

Ian's jaw tightened, and then he frowned, looking at the file. "Speaking of lying, I see you did make more copies of Bell's material."

Hollis didn't respond but smiled. "Odelia Larson doesn't remember many of Bell's visitors because they entered through his side door. But she does remember seeing a Bentley parked across the street."

Millicent and Ian exchanged looks.

"We did not kill Matthias Bell," Millicent practically growled.

Hollis looked past her. "I'd like to believe you, but will she?"

Hollis nodded toward the restaurant entrance at Detective Scott, who was making her way toward them, followed by a uniformed officer.

"Ms. Morgan," the detective acknowledged as she flashed her badge to the Pittmans. "Mr. and Mrs. Pittman, I'd like you to come with me to San Lucian Police Headquarters. Chief Brennan and I have a few questions for you."

"You haven't been following me, have you, Detective Scott?" Hollis said with mounting irritation. "I'm sure that you wouldn't want to put your case against my client at risk."

Detective Scott frowned. "This isn't my first rodeo, Counselor. Thanks to your assistance, we were able to put out an alert for their car. It was spotted about a half hour ago and called in. I didn't expect to see you here."

Hollis turned to a red-faced Ian. "You really need to drive lower profile cars."

She stood as Scott came around to where the Pittmans sat. Both husband and wife sank down in their seats with expressions of resignation.

"Ms. Morgan, there is nothing here for you to see," Scott said brusquely. "Mr. and Mrs. Pittman or Weatherly, I would appreciate you accompanying me in my car to our station. Do I have your cooperation?"

Millicent leaned into her husband. "Do we have to go with her?"

"Only if you don't want to be arrested," Scott answered for him. "If you cooperate, you'll be on your way within a couple of hours. If not …." She shrugged.

Ian stood, and with a downturned mouth, offered his arm to his wife to stand next to him.

"We'll come with you. We have nothing to do with the Bell murder." He turned to Hollis. "Ms. Morgan, this will definitely be the last time we meet, because I will do everything in my power to avoid being in your presence again."

Hollis pretended to wince. "It was nice knowing the two of you as well."

IT WAS AFTER ONE WHEN she returned to the office. She'd remained at the restaurant to have a bowl of their famous New England clam chowder. It also gave her the opportunity to gather her thoughts and allow the adrenaline surging through her body to return to its normal level. She wasn't surprised that the chief and Scott were already working their way down her list. She would have to brief Gordon and tell him that the element of surprise would no longer be theirs. Still, it was interesting that the Pittmans had already started to alter their appearance. Soon even Hollis wouldn't be able to recognize them in a crowd. According to Penny's research, the doctor's receipt in their envelope from Bell was for cosmetic surgery and pointed to their modus operandi.

Hollis added a quick summary of the Pittman encounter in her briefing for Gordon. She guessed they were international criminals. Clearly not the snatch and grab type, but ones able to move easily in high society circles. Whether or not they were guilty of murder, they weren't likely to be given their freedom.

Not her problem. The chief and Detective Scott would take it from here. She took the phone out of her pocket and activated the screen. It was blank.

Where is John?

Tiffany tapped on her door. "Is your phone on? Mrs. Turner is trying to reach you. She says it's urgent." She walked in and handed Hollis a small stack of message slips.

"No, it's on," Hollis said. "She's been calling my office cell as well. I had to get my thoughts from my Pittman meeting down on paper before I forgot any details. I'll get right to back her."

Kiki Turner picked up the phone on the half-ring, her voice frantic.

"They won't let me see Kate," she sobbed. "Derek said that Alicia is too upset and that she didn't want to talk to me."

"Kiki, calm down," Hollis said. "We had talked about you two meeting at the end of the week. I thought I was supposed to talk with Alicia first. Why did you approach her?"

Kiki sighed. "My intuition told me that Derek would try to turn Alicia against me, and the best way to do that would keep me from seeing Kate. I ... I guess my worrying worked me up into a panic and I called to try and talk with her."

Hollis was glad Kiki Turner couldn't see her look of annoyance. She took a breath. "I'll talk with Alicia and set up a meeting for the two of you to talk, hopefully, tomorrow. Before you ask, yes, I will be there too. I'll make arrangements for us to meet in an office here. But no more phone calls. You two have got to face each other. These arms-length, third-hand conversations are not helping matters. Can you make a meeting in the afternoon?" She pulled up her calendar.

"Of course I can!" Kiki screamed, and then she caught herself. "I'm sorry. All right, no more phone calls, but I don't have much time. What am I going to do?" And she broke into sobs.

Hollis bit her bottom lip. "I will call you to confirm as soon as I connect with Alicia."

The phone clicked off.

*

THE LYNCH HOUSE WAS IN a quiet neighborhood, not too far from Chabot Park. Hollis sat in her car under a lush linden tree, one of many that shaded the curving street. She knew she would have little luck speaking alone with Alicia if Derek was around, and his car was still in the driveway. Penny had been unable to find out his place of employment, but Hollis was betting that either he or Alicia had to leave the house sometime during the day. She was willing to sit there doing paperwork until one of them did.

She'd thought of using Vince, and she might still have to if it got too late, but she wanted to talk with Alicia alone, and Vince would be no help there. Hollis flipped through her emails and wrote directions for Penny to prepare her response. She'd been gainfully occupied for twenty minutes when Derek appeared on the porch. He spoke through the partly opened wrought-iron screen door to someone inside. A moment later, she could see that the someone was Alicia, who gave him a quick kiss on the lips and a wave.

Hollis was beginning to think there might be something to having patience, and she slid down a few inches in her seat. Derek Lynch drove past, looking straight ahead. She put her paperwork back in her briefcase and got out of the car. There appeared to be no one on the street, but Hollis sensed that there were eyes behind a few of the drawn drapes. She stepped quickly up the paved walkway and rang the doorbell.

"What are you doing here?" Alicia glared through the screen door. "You already gave us Kiki's message. There is nothing more to say."

Hollis judged how much it was going to take to get inside the house. She did not want to hold a conversation on the porch. "Alicia, I'm asking for fifteen minutes, and if after fifteen minutes you still want me to go away, you won't have to ask twice. I will go immediately."

The baby must have been in the living room. Her cries were loud and clear.

Hollis put her hand on the door handle. "Please."

Alicia looked at Hollis and then at Kate. "You have fourteen minutes to go."

She unlatched the door and moved aside for Hollis to enter. Once in, she closed the screen but left the door open as she went to tend to her daughter. Hollis took a seat on the sofa.

The house was tastefully decorated in southwest chic. The furnishings, while not showroom expensive, were high-end and comfortable. Hollis noticed the Lynch family pictures lining the fireplace mantle.

Alicia cuddled her daughter. "She's fighting sleep. I'll start your fourteen minutes when I get back."

Hollis acknowledged her time constraint with a nod. She didn't have to wait long. Alicia returned within a few minutes.

She sat down on a loveseat across from Hollis. "Go ahead."

"Alicia, your mother is dying. She wants her wealth to go to her family, and because the two of you have … have a lot between you, she respects your feelings about wanting nothing from her. But she wants to give her money to her granddaughter." Hollis paused. "It's really as simple as that."

Alicia stared up at the ceiling then she met Hollis' eyes. "Is that all?"

Hollis sighed. "She wants to continue to be able to see Kate, maybe even more often … particularly now because of her health. I think if just the two of you could meet—maybe sit in my office and talk—some of the bad feeling could lessen."

Alicia glared at her. "Is that all?"

"Yes, Mrs. Lynch, that's all."

"Good. Now it's my turn." Alicia leaned over and crossed her arms. "Ms. Morgan, you have no idea what it was like growing up with Kiki as your mother. The drugs, the men, the flesh …" Alicia's voice kept rising then she seemed to catch herself. "Kiki didn't and doesn't love me, and frankly I don't love her. I'm her mirror, and she can't stand to look at herself and remember what she was before she caught a rich husband."

Hollis waited a couple of minutes until she was sure that Alicia had finished.

"I don't have the best relationship with my mother either, and no, I don't have anything close to the history you must have lived through. But, when I first told you your mother was dying, you reacted. So maybe down deep, there is still a small part of you that seeks closure."

Alicia's face flushed. "She doesn't want me. She just wants Kate."

Hollis rubbed her forehead. "She's *dying*. She wants to have someone to love and who can love her in her last months. It's not a matter of years; it's a matter of a few months, maybe weeks. She knows she's lost you. Kate is as close to you as she can get. The two of you need to talk. I can make arrangements for a meeting tomorrow if you let me."

"I'll think about it," the young woman said slowly.

Alicia walked to the foyer. Hollis followed her and walked out onto the walkway.

"Kiki stretches the truth a lot," Alicia said, looking down at her feet. "Is she really dying?"

Hollis nodded, turned, and walked to her car. She heard Alicia close the door.

The meeting with Alicia had gone better than she thought it would, but it left her drained and low-spirited. Before starting the car, she closed her eyes and took a few slow, deep breaths. Finally, she reached for the phone to check for John's message, but the screen remained blank. She shoved it back into her purse and drove back to her office.

SHE HADN'T BEEN BACK AT her desk for an hour when she looked up to see Vince standing in her doorway with his usual sheepish grin.

"Hey Hollis, I don't mean to bother you but you said it was

already authorized. I was wondering if you need me to do some overtime work. I … I really enjoy working with you and … and I could use the money."

She motioned for him to take the chair in front of her desk, and she came around to sit in the chair next to his.

"There might be something you could do. Is everything okay?" she asked gently. His eyes looked clear and he seemed calm. She couldn't help but glance at his bare arms, but no fresh track marks were evident. The conversation with Tiffany came back to her, and she wasn't sure if Vince could ever measure up.

"Oh, yeah. Like I told you, I made my mom go back into rehab, but she still didn't like the place and she left it. But she promised me she would go to AA every day, and she does, sometimes twice. She's got a good sponsor. Maybe this time she'll make it." He looked down at his hands. "Her sponsor says I have to get on with my life and not treat her like I'm the parent and she's the child."

Hollis completely agreed with the sponsor but said nothing.

Vince ran his hand over his head. "I need the money to buy this thing."

"Oh," Hollis said wondering what the "thing" was. "Well, the only Bell victim we haven't been able to locate is Naomi Eaton. Penny is getting some background on her and hopes to have some real location information by the end of the day."

"I can find her, Hollis." He moved to sit on the edge of the chair. "I found her once, and I can find her again."

Hollis nodded. "Let's see what Penny comes up with. Check back with me around four thirty."

Vince stood. "All right. I'll check back with you before I leave for the day."

He was headed for the door when Tiffany appeared. They avoided looking at each other but were unable to hide the flush that crept up their necks to their faces. Mumbling something polite, they moved away from each other like reversed magnets.

Hollis watched them both, amused. If *she* noticed their peculiar behavior, then the entire office must be aware of their relationship. She headed for the staff offices. Penny's head was bent over a map, which she was viewing with a magnifying glass.

Hollis leaned against the doorway. "Penny, are you close to coming up with background on Naomi Eaton? Vince would like to do a little detective work, and I want to get Odelia Larson off the alleged murderer list."

"I don't like to admit this, but I can't find her." Penny threw her pencil down on the desk. "She doesn't exist. I tried calling a couple of her old clients, ones that she defrauded, but they stonewalled me. It's almost like they're protecting her."

"That doesn't make sense." Hollis reviewed the worksheet Penny handed her. "Did you follow up on her work address?"

"That was the first thing I did," Penny replied. "I got her employer information from Detective Scott; we know each other from golf lessons. But she let me know that Eaton quit abruptly. She told her boss she was going into business on her own and intended to work from her home. The address they had is the one we already checked off."

Hollis looked over the typed pages. "What about the townhomes where Vince and I tracked her?"

"The townhomes are owned by a church. I remembered Bell's letter, but it's not the church he left money to. This is an Oakland church. One houses their minister and the other they keep for congregation members who are down on their luck and need temporary housing."

"Well, since that's the last place we saw her, Vince has to start there," Hollis muttered.

CHAPTER NINETEEN

———

Friday

HER DESK PHONE BUZZED.
"Hollis, it's Derek Lynch on line five," Tiffany said. "He sounds mad. Do you want me to take a message?"

"No, I was expecting his call." Hollis waited a moment for the connection. "Hello, Mr. Lynch, how can I help you?"

"Don't play innocent with me, Ms. Morgan," Lynch growled. "How dare you come between me and my wife?"

"Mr. Lynch, I don't represent you, and I don't represent your wife. My client is your mother-in-law, and she has a right to speak with her daughter without your influence."

"You talk smart, but you don't act smart. Alicia and I are a team and Kate is my child too, so you can tell Kiki that there is nothing—do you hear me?—*nothing* she can do about it. If she tries, she'll be sorry."

He clicked off.

Hollis was grateful for the interval Penny had left her to approve Bell's paperwork. It would give her time to check her temper after Derek Lynch's not-so-subtle threat. Besides, she was developing an appreciation for criminal investigation. Even after reviewing Penny's documents, she procrastinated before returning to her more straightforward probate client cases. But the next two hours passed quickly, and when the phone beeped again, she was immersed in navigating the narrow pathways of a client's routine revocable trust.

It was Alicia Lynch.

"Er, Ms. Morgan, I'm ready to meet with Kiki." Her voice sounded strained. "I got a babysitter for today, and I can come to your office at three o'clock. Will that be okay?"

Hollis didn't even look at her calendar. "Yes, that can work. I'll check with your … with Kiki, and I won't get back in touch with you unless she can't make it. I look forward to seeing you this afternoon."

"Fine." She hesitated. "Er, I know Derek called you. He … he can get emotional, but he only wants what's best for us."

"I'm not concerned, Mrs. Lynch. I'll see you at three."

This time, as Hollis gazed out the window, her thoughts drifted to Kiki Turner and her daughter. There was a slight chance that healing might take place if everyone could just let go of their guilt and self-righteousness.

Penny came into her office. "Hollis, do you want me to package up all the envelopes you found in Bell's safe, along with his other papers? They're in a box. I handled closing all his bank and investment accounts, and I phoned his sister to go over her options for proceeding with liquidation." She lowered her voice. "I didn't know if she still wanted us to handle her side of the transactions—you know, because we're representing Mrs. Larson—but she said she didn't care, and we could take care of everything."

Hollis wasn't surprised. She glanced at the itemized list Penny handed her.

"Ugh, I need to go through all his papers one last time before we file the trust." The list covered two pages. "And there might be something in here that could help Odelia."

"We still have time," Penny assured her. "The hearing is still three weeks away."

"I've been focusing on the envelopes," Hollis said, "but now is a good time for me to go through all his personal papers and documents. Thank goodness he had another firm handling his business affairs."

"Oh, well, there's still quite a bit, but I'll make it easy for you," Penny offered. "I can put the papers in order by date, or subject matter, or type, or—"

"Penny, I want to do it myself," Hollis insisted. "Just bring me the box."

This time Penny seemed to notice Hollis' effort at restraint. "All right, I'll put it on your meeting table. That will make it easier for you to sift through."

A QUICK LOOK AT THE clock told her that she had only a few minutes to steel herself for the Turner meeting, though she had little to do but act as referee.

Tiffany stood in Hollis's doorway. "Kiki Turner is here," she announced. "I'm putting your meeting in the blue conference room. It's at the end of the hallway, in case there's more yelling and screaming."

"Very funny," Hollis said, trying not to laugh.

When she entered the conference room, Kiki sat facing the door, with her back to the expanse of windows. Hollis thought the choice was deliberate; the glare blocked her facial expressions. She came around the table to shake the woman's hand. Kiki was heavily made up as usual and wearing a navy suit with a lime-green blouse. Her long, curly black hair was down and restrained on one side with a large rhinestone comb.

"This may well be difficult for you," Hollis said, "but I think it's best for your estate. If you and Alicia can reach an agreement, then any contested action will be eliminated."

Kiki gave a small shrug. "I've thought about it, and this

meeting is long overdue. I thank you for making it happen no matter how … distasteful it might end up being."

As if on cue, the door opened, and Tiffany ushered in Alicia Lynch. She took a seat directly facing her mother. The air in the room immediately filled with tension.

"Mrs. Lynch, thank you for coming." Hollis got up and pulled shut the vertical blinds behind Kiki, who looked startled by her action. "That's better. Now we can all see each other."

"Hello, Alicia," Kiki said coolly.

Her daughter gave a slight nod but said nothing.

Hollis opened the file in front of her. "Let's get started. Mrs. Lynch, the terms—"

Kiki chuckled. "I'm sorry, but it is so hard for me to hear my daughter being called Mrs. Lynch." She covered her mouth with her hand.

"What do you mean by that?" Alicia shot back.

Hollis put down her pen.

Uh-oh, here we go.

"Nothing, darling," Kiki soothed. "Just that I've always pictured you as my little girl, not a grown woman with her own little girl."

"Well, that's silly, since you're trying to use *my* little girl for your own purposes," Alicia snarled. "And by the way, I was never your *little girl*. I was just a piece of luggage you had to lug around."

"That's not true. I—"

Alicia batted her hand in the air. "I don't want to hear it. Let's get on with this."

"Good," Hollis said, "because I agree that this … conversation is going nowhere." She faced Alicia. "Today, we want to explain the terms of your mother's estate and her wishes as they relate to her granddaughter. She has—"

"I know I've lost you, Alicia." Kiki bit her bottom lip, twisting the ring on her wedding finger. "But I want Kate to know that I loved her. My money is the only way I have to show her. I'll be gone soon, and after a few months, she won't remember me. But maybe when she's able to go to college, or buy a house, or travel, she'll think of me kindly."

"Are you really dying, or is this another of your lies?" Alicia's eyes darted toward Hollis. "Did you verify that she's dying? Did you talk with her doctor?"

Kiki turned pale and swayed in her chair.

"Mrs. Lynch," Hollis said, "I'm not a family counselor, but if you could put aside your animosity for just a short while, you can be out of here and on your way. Now, to answer your questions, yes, I think your mother is dying and has only a short time to live. I also know that she wishes to leave the bulk of her estate in trust for her granddaughter. She has not ignored your needs, but has left you a sizable bequest as well." Hollis took a deep breath. "In turn, she would like your assurance—"

"That I can see Kate on a regular basis," Kiki implored. "Maybe even … maybe she could even stay with me for a week or so."

Alicia blanched.

Hollis wondered if she would ever be able to finish a statement between these two. But judging from Alicia's reaction, it might be a good thing.

"Yes, Mrs. Lynch," she said, "your mother would like to have Kate stay with her until … she's physically unable to engage with her."

Alicia's mouth turned down. "You use such fancy words, Ms. Morgan." She stared at her mother. "Basically, you want to buy my daughter to be your pet until you drop dead. I wonder, did you ever—even once—think of me as you do Kate?"

Kiki, chin trembling, said, "Oh, Alicia, I know I did you wrong. I know I left you to parent yourself, but it wasn't for lack of love, it was because I didn't know *how* to love." She looked down at her hands, and when she looked up, there were tears in her eyes. "The men, the alcohol, it was all I thought I deserved. I knew from the very first time I held you in my arms

I didn't *deserve* you. You were an angel, and I was … what I was."

Tears were streaming down Kiki's face, and she carelessly swiped at them with a tissue. Hollis looked at Alicia out of the corner of her eye. She sat stiff and unmoving.

Hollis picked up the file. "Maybe we—"

"Why did you send me away when you married what's-his-name? When you got rich, you were ashamed of me, of having a daughter who could reveal your real age," Alicia shouted with a tremble. "You have always rejected me. You never wanted me, in bad times or in good."

Kiki reached out for Alicia's hand across the table, but her daughter pulled back. Kiki returned her hand to her lap.

"That's not true, Alicia. Don't you understand anything?" Kiki sobbed loudly. "One of the reasons I love Kate is because she reminds me of you."

Alicia put her hand to her mouth and stared at her mother. Tears slipped down her face. "Why did you send me away?"

Kiki took a deep breath and held her head high. "Harold was a nice man, but a self-centered one. We had a good relationship, but I was a trophy, not a wife. I loved him because he saved me from a very bad life. But he had a mean streak and I wasn't sure how he would treat you. You and I didn't have a good relationship. You were a teenager, almost an adult, and I could pay for you to go to a good school. I didn't think you'd miss being around me."

Alicia's chin jutted out, and she said through her tears, "I actually liked not having to see you."

Hollis sat quietly, letting the emotional dynamics play out. While the tension in the room had lessened, she doubted that much had changed. Alicia had started to fidget, and Kiki would not meet her eyes.

Hollis gave a small cough. "Perhaps now would be a good time to get back to the reading of the—"

"No," Alicia said, making a slashing motion with her hand.

"No, I want Derek here. He's Kate's father and my husband. He should be here."

Kiki's smile was sad. "Sweetheart, I really think this is between you and me. Derek has his own agenda, and ... he would only complicate matters."

Hollis knew immediately that those were the wrong words at the wrong time.

Alicia stood abruptly, causing her chair to fall over. "How dare you .... How dare you talk about my husband that way?" Her face reddened as she grabbed her purse and jacket. "He has shown me more love than you ever did, or ever could."

Kiki came around the table with an outstretched hand. Alicia backed up.

"Alicia, I—"

"Do me a favor and don't contact me or Kate ever again," Alicia yelled. "We don't want your money. If you try to give money to Kate, I will burn the check on your grave, on your *grave*." She backed away to the door and screamed, "Do you hear me, Kiki? I hate you!"

Kiki Turner stumbled back into the table, doubling over as she found a chair and collapsed into it. Hollis saw the crying woman's shaking shoulders and went after Alicia, who was already darting through the lobby past curious onlookers. She approached her at the elevator.

"Let me ride down with you."

"You see, I tried. I honestly tried," Alicia said through clenched teeth. "But she doesn't respect me, or my family. It's always about her."

Hollis saw the tears filling the young woman's eyes. The doors opened, and they both got in. Gratefully, no one joined them on the quick ride. When they reached the ground floor lobby, Alicia looked around as if disoriented. Hollis put her arm around her shoulder and led her to a quiet alcove where a walnut veneer coffee table sat between a pair of loveseats.

Hollis sat next to her, and a minute later Alicia's head was on

Hollis' shoulder. She sobbed as if her heart would break. For a while Alicia continued to sob. Hollis shook her head slightly when a security guard came around the corner to check out the commotion.

Finally, Alicia raised her head to dig in her purse for a tissue.

Hollis got up and bought a bottle of water from a lobby kiosk. She handed it to Alicia, who gave her a weak smile as she opened the bottle and took a swallow.

"She can always get to me," Alicia said, wiping at her eyes with the back of her hand. "I practice what I'm going to say, and I swear to myself I won't let her words touch me." She tightened her lips to a thin line. "But they always do."

Hollis said nothing, but she thought about her relationship with her own mother and their inability to communicate.

Alicia took another swallow and then looked at her watch. "I've got to go. Derek is watching Kate, and I have to start dinner." She hesitated long enough to re-gain her footing. "I don't know if you believe me, but I feel sorry for her. It's too bad she's dying. She's had a hard life."

Hollis nodded. "I can't advise you, Mrs. Lynch. Your mother is my client." She moistened her lips. "I need to head back upstairs. She's waiting. What shall I tell her?"

"Tell her, goodbye."

TIFFANY MOTIONED DOWN THE HALL with her head, signaling that Kiki Turner was still waiting. When Hollis entered, the woman was sitting huddled over the table with her head in her hands. She lifted her face to catch Hollis' eyes and turned away after Hollis shook her head, no.

Kiki sighed and said, "I knew she wouldn't change her mind. Didn't you hear her? She hates me. She really hates me." Her eyes filled with tears. "What shall I do, Hollis?"

Hollis took a breath. "You might not like this, but if you want to provide for Kate—and Alicia—you'll have to talk with Derek. I think he's the only one she'll listen to."

Hollis ignored Kiki's groan.

"Kiki, soon you'll be … gone, and what will all your disapproval mean then? She will still be married to him."

Kiki picked up her purse to leave. "All right. Arrange for me to meet with Derek. Not here, maybe at the lake. You be there, too. Make it for next Friday. I have to go into the hospital tomorrow for what the doctors are calling a last-resort treatment. I … I'll be ready next week to meet with him." She paled, putting her hand to her chest. She leaned heavily against the door.

Hollis reached for her. "Are you okay, Kiki?"

Kiki waved her away and nodded. "You know the funny thing? My doctors told me this morning I could go early." She gave a small laugh and walked into the lobby.

Hollis watched her leave and then turned to look out the window. With a deep sigh, she placed a call to Derek Lynch, who sounded like he had already gotten an earful from Alicia. She must have flown home. He agreed to meet his mother-in-law at the Lake Merritt boat house.

"She'd better be ready to talk terms," he said with bluster.

It was all Hollis could do to not click off. *What a way to end the week.*

HOLLIS DIDN'T REALIZE SHE HAD fallen asleep with the television on until the phone jarred her awake. Automatically, she picked it up, noticing it was close to midnight.

"Is this Hollis Morgan?"

She didn't recognize the male voice, and it put her on alert. "Yes, who is this?"

"My name is Edwin Parker," he said, "and I'm a team officer with Homeland Security. I work with John Faber. I'm sorry to call you at this hour, ma'am, but John made me promise that I would get in touch with you if … if anything happened to him and—"

"John? What's wrong with John? Where is he?" She sat up on the sofa, her heart pounding.

"I'm sorry to tell you ... but John has been killed. He was on an undercover assignment and was shot. He was with three other HSD men. They were covered by the team, but the assignment went wrong. There was an explosion, and as they ran out of the building, they were shot, and their bodies taken away by the killers. We traced the criminals and ...."

He wouldn't stop talking, and his words kept coming.

She'd stopped listening.

Hollis stared into the darkness of her living room. The only light came from the white glare of the television, where the movie she'd been watching had ended. She could hear the voice on the other end of the phone droning on, but she couldn't understand the words.

He finally stopped speaking.

"When? When did he die?" She spoke in barely a whisper, trying to hold down the scream that was welling up in her throat.

"On Wednesday," Parker said. "But we just got final confirmation an hour ago."

He'd been out of her life for three days already.

"I know this is a shock. Each officer, before they embark on a mission, leaves instructions in the event ... in the event they don't return. John didn't want a memorial. His only instruction was to inform you as soon as ... well, to inform you. Is there someone I can call to come over and be with you? I can tell them the circumstances and make it easier for you."

Easier?

She mumbled, "No, no one. Thank you for calling."

She heard her voice responding, but it wasn't hers. She saw herself sitting on the sofa, but it wasn't *her*. This must be what it was like to have an out-of-body experience.

He was speaking again. He wanted her to take down his phone number. She scribbled it on a paper napkin.

"Goodbye," Hollis whispered.

She clicked off before he started to talk again.

Hollis sat there for some time, not thinking, not seeing, not feeling. Her senses had shut down. Finally, she picked up her phone and punched in a number. The voice on the other end greeted her over soft jazz in the background.

"Hey, girlfriend, can't sleep? What's up?"

"Stephanie, John's dead."

There was a sharp intake of breath. "I'm on my way over."

CHAPTER TWENTY

Saturday—Thursday

To HOLLIS, TIME PASSED AS though muffled in cotton. Stephanie had come over and put her to bed. When she woke, thin slats of light came into her bedroom from behind the shutters, but the rest of the room was in darkness.

She stared at the ceiling.

Thankfully, Stephanie hadn't tried to force food on her, but had sat in a chair next to the bed, reading. From time to time, Hollis turned her head toward the windows, her eyes raw from the stream of silent tears that soaked her pillow. She couldn't speak. She couldn't sleep. She stared into the darkness. She wondered vaguely if the world was still out there, because her world had stopped.

Much later, she jumped when she felt Stephanie's hand on her shoulder and the smell of her favorite lavender tea.

"Here, drink this and take this pill. You've got to sleep."

Hollis took the pill and drank the tea.

"What day is it? What time?" she said, her voice faltering.

Her throat was scratchy, and she realized she hadn't spoken for a while.

Stephanie sat on the edge of the bed. "It's Sunday afternoon." She patted Hollis on the hand. "You feel like talking?"

Hollis dropped her head back on the pillow and rubbed her eyes with the palms of her hands. She'd given Stephanie an abbreviated version when she arrived, but now, in a flat tone, she recounted the complete conversation with Edwin Parker as best she could remember.

She mumbled, "He left a number to call, but I didn't hear most of what he had to say after he said …" her voice drifted off.

"I'll call him tomorrow and find out … what we need to find out." Stephanie stood. "I'll also call the firm and tell Tiffany you're going to be out for a few days. She can tell Gordon Barrett. Then …."

Hollis closed her eyes and Stephanie stopped.

"What's wrong, hon?"

"Is that all it will take, a few days? In only a few days I'll be getting back to my life?" Hollis' eyes watered. "My life ended six days ago."

Stephanie's lips tightened. "I know." She looked into her friend's red and swollen eyes. "I know you're in pain. Just let it all out, Hollis. If you don't, it will take that much longer to honor John and what you two had."

Hollis held her hand up, warding off her friend's words.

"But my heart …."

She could say nothing more. The sobs came and wouldn't stop coming. Stephanie got up and shut the bedroom door, leaving her friend alone to say her goodbyes.

THERE WAS A LIGHT TAP on the door, and not waiting for an answer, Stephanie walked in with a tray of fruit, two cups of tea, and toast.

"You know I can't cook, but you need to get something into

your stomach." She put the tray on the side of the bed. "At the very least, you've got to get some rest." She helped a silent Hollis maneuver into a sitting position with the tray in her lap. "I made some calls. Are you up to hearing?"

"Yeah, sure," Hollis said, tentatively picking up the fork and taking a bite of fruit.

"I called Edwin Parker yesterday—"

"Yesterday." Hollis frowned. "What day is today?"

Stephanie sighed, sitting on the edge of the bed. "It's Tuesday. I told you, you needed the sleep." She took a swallow from her cup of coffee. "Anyway, Parker gave me the details about … about what happened to John. They're going to have a brief service next week for all the men who … were there. They invite you to … to attend and represent John's family. Do you know if he had any family?"

"I don't want to go." Hollis shook her head. "John didn't want a service. He was adopted and his parents died in a car accident soon after he graduated from college."

"I didn't think you would," Stephanie responded. "I said I would get back to them. Then I called your office. Tiffany was fantastic. She said she'd let the managers know, and she and Penny will call your clients and tell them you'll be out for a while. She also said for you not to worry, because Gordon Barrett said he would keep up with Odelia Larson and handle your client caseload until you returned."

"Now that's a scary thought," Hollis mused. "I won't have any clients left if Gordon handles my cases." She took a bite of toast. "I want to go back to work. I need to do something. Otherwise …" her words faded into the unsaid.

Stephanie smiled. "Good. Tiffany said that mentioning Gordon Barrett working with your clients would get you back to the office quicker than anything. But there's no need to rush."

Hollis gave a small smile, but then tears filled her eyes.

"Do you think I'll ever stop hurting?"

CHAPTER TWENTY-ONE

Friday

HOLLIS WAS GLAD SHE'D CHOSEN Friday to return to the office. As usual, most of the firm's attorneys were working half days or wouldn't come in at all, thus getting an early jump on the weekend. She greeted Tiffany with a small nod and a quick "good morning" when she came in and headed straight to her office, closing the door behind her.

There was a light knock, and the door opened.

Tiffany entered. "Hollis, I'll make sure no one bothers you today," she said in a low voice. "Gordon is traveling and won't be back until next Wednesday. Penny knows you're here, but no one else does, and we'll keep it that way."

"Thank you," Hollis said, not yet ready to remove her sunglasses. She hung up her jacket and put her briefcase on top of her desk. "Can you take my calls? I need to get ready for the meeting with Kiki Turner and her daughter."

Tiffany looked startled. "But Hollis, I thought you might want to cancel that appointment for today. I was going to reschedule."

"No, that's just what I *don't* need. I *need* to keep busy." She coughed to cover up a sob. "Don't baby me. I can take things from here. Do me a favor and ask Penny to see me when she can."

"Sure." Tiffany closed the door behind her.

Hollis leaned back in her chair and swiveled around to look out the window. The sun had chased away the night sky, and slow-moving clouds were sprinkled across the East Bay. A wave of fog rose like a tsunami outside the Golden Gate. She stared at the natural beauty of the sight until she couldn't stop the weight of moisture forming under her eyelids from slipping through.

She pulled the window drapes closed.

OAKLAND'S LAKE MERRITT WAS ADJACENT to downtown. Surrounded by parkland and city neighborhoods, its grassy shores and artificial islands of bird sanctuary were anchored on one end. Not far away was a boat house where sailboats, canoes, and rowboats could be rented and sailing classes were held. It was a peaceful refuge from the hectic streets of business centers and government buildings that encircled the lake.

When Hollis pulled into a parking space, she spotted Kiki Turner sitting on a park bench staring out over the water. She was glad they were meeting outdoors. She could keep her sunglasses on without comment.

She walked up to the bent figure. "Kiki?"

Hollis suppressed a gasp as the woman turned. Her freckles were gone; in their place were ominous-looking brown splotches.

"Hello." Kiki gave her a quick nod of the head and went back to looking out over the water.

Hollis sat next to her and couldn't help but notice the large dark circles under the once clear blue eyes, now covered with a thin haze.

Kiki gave a short laugh. "Don't look so shocked. No, this

didn't happen overnight; this is me without makeup. Add mascara and lots and lots of foundation and I am transformed. But you know, I woke up this morning, and I was just too tired for a false face." She put on her sunglasses and said quietly, "The last-resort treatment didn't take."

"Kiki, I'm so sorry, I—"

"I'm sorry, too," she said, her eyes piercing the dark glasses. "Your assistant told me you might change our meeting because you lost someone close."

Hollis stiffened. She couldn't find words to speak.

Kiki didn't appear to notice. She pulled her purse to her, and with a shaking hand took out a tissue. "Look, I want to get this over with. I'll give Derek whatever he wants. He's still a jerk, but he's Alicia's jerk. I just want to see Kate one last time." She dabbed at her eyes.

Hollis pointed to an approaching figure. "He's here."

Derek was wearing a suit with no tie and loafers with no socks. He wore a wide smile and started talking before reaching them.

"Sorry I'm late. I couldn't get a parking space. Who knew this place was so crowded during the week?"

He held out his hand to Kiki, but she turned away. He passed the snub off and directed his hand to Hollis, who shook it gingerly. Derek, after looking a moment longer at Kiki's face, said nothing and sat across from the two women.

"Ms. Morgan, I understand that you want to make me an offer." He grinned.

Hollis sensed rather than saw Kiki's shoulders and jaw tense. But Kiki remained silent.

"Mr. Lynch, my client would like to reconcile with her daughter, but that does not appear to be possible at this time. She wants to leave her estate to her granddaughter, but that too appears to pose problems." Hollis took a breath. "Therefore, she is asking you to … to discuss with Alicia the possibility of accepting her bequest and allowing Kate to visit her. I have a copy of Mrs. Turner's new notarized trust to show your wife."

"Hmmm, that's going to take some doing." Lynch ran his hands through his hair. "Alicia came back madder than hell after your last meeting," he said, looking at Kiki. "Of course, I know how to calm her down, but like I said, it took some doing."

Now Hollis could feel her own jaw tightening.

"Mr. Lynch, Kiki would appreciate anything you could arrange. She has adjusted the language in her trust to give Alicia—and of course, you—the ability to draw down on Kate's trust fund as needed to ensure her happiness and welfare." Hollis was tempted to roll her eyes at the broadening smile on Derek's face. "Of course, it's stipulated that a certain amount not be touched until Kate reaches the age of thirty."

"That's great," he laughed, and turned to his mother-in-law. "Don't worry, Kiki, I'll talk to Alicia. I'll get her to back down." He looked at Hollis with seriousness, "When do you think we can have the money?"

A chill came over Hollis as her chest filled with red hot anger.

She clenched her teeth so hard, her words came out in a hiss, "Mr. Lynch, the trust takes effect upon the *death* of Mrs. Turner, and *that's* when you can have the money."

"Er, yeah, yeah, sure, I'm sorry," he said vaguely in Kiki's direction. "Look, I'll get Kate over to your house tomorrow morning. That's what you want, right?"

Out of the corner of her eye, Hollis could see Kiki sway slightly as her hands gripped the edge of the table. The brown splotches looked even more startling against her blanched face. She put a hand on Kiki's shoulder to steady her.

But Kiki said nothing.

Hollis locked eyes with Lynch. "That's what she wants, and I think you need to make it happen as soon as you can."

"Tomorrow morning, no problem." Lynch put his hand in his pocket and came out with a pair of sunglasses. He slipped them on and with a wave walked back the way he came.

"I can't stand that man." Kiki gripped Hollis' wrist. "But, Hollis, I'm not feeling right. I think we need to go."

"Hold on to my arm." Hollis braced herself so Kiki could pull herself up to stand. "Kiki, do you want to go to the hospital?"

"No, I do not. I'm … I'm fine. I'm just—"

Kiki slid to the ground, unconscious, and Hollis called 911.

THE EMERGENCY ROOM AT HAYWARD Sunrise Hospital had only a few patients. Hollis tried not to notice a man pressing a rag to his left hand. His injury was only barely quelled by a blood-soaked red towel. A young woman with earphones sat in the corner working her cellphone, and an elderly couple held on to each other waiting to be called.

After a half hour, when only the young woman remained in the room, Hollis went up to the window.

"Excuse me, a Mrs. Kiki Turner was brought in by ambulance. I was with her, and called for it to bring her here. Can I find out how she is doing?"

Without even looking up, the counter clerk swiveled to her computer monitor and tapped some keys.

"You said she came in by ambulance?"

"Yes, she passed out. I told the EMTs to call her doctor. Her doctor's name is Soames and—"

"She's been admitted. Patients with our hospital's doctors go straight to admissions, if only for observation. You'll have to check with the information desk in the lobby." She pointed to a long hallway.

Hollis nodded and gathered her things. She hated hospitals, and they hated her. The worst accident she ever had was in a hospital when she was waiting to take her brother home from getting his vaccinations and her foot was impaled on a nail file she'd just dropped on the floor. Her foot took eight stitches, and she had to use crutches. There were numerous other mishaps that tended to occur whenever she found herself under a hospital's roof. She pushed out of her mind the upcoming transplant surgery.

The woman at the information booth looked to be in her eighties. Her bluish-white hair was complemented by pale blue eyeglasses.

"Kiki Turner ... now that's an interesting name," she said as she scrolled through the lines on her monitor. "Ah, here she is. She was just admitted." She looked over her glasses. "Are you a relative?"

"Yes," Hollis said earnestly, "I'm her niece."

"She's in ICU, but you can't go in there. Go up to the nurse's desk on seventh floor and let them know you're waiting to talk to her doctor. There's a little waiting room, and they'll let the doctor know you're there so she can talk to you."

Hollis went back to her car and retrieved her briefcase before going to the seventh floor. After notifying the desk nurse she was waiting to speak with the doctor, she settled in. An hour passed before the doctor—a middle-aged, gray-haired woman—opened the door.

"Ms. Morgan?" The doctor offered her hand. "I didn't know Mrs. Turner had a niece who was local."

"We don't live near here. I was just visiting when she collapsed." Hollis felt no qualms about lying. "How is she doing?"

"She's dying," said the doctor. "You need to call your cousin, and tell her that her mother may not last the night." The doctor shrugged. "Mrs. Turner told me about their strained relationship, but if the family wants to say goodbye, they need to come now."

Hollis moved like a robot. She wasn't close to Kiki and there was certainly no love lost between her and Kiki's daughter and her husband, but she was vaguely aware that somewhere in her subconscious was another goodbye she had never gotten to say. She hurriedly blinked back her tears.

Derek answered the phone, and she quickly told him what had happened.

"Please, ask Alicia to come and bring Kate."

Derek hesitated. "Er, sure, but it's kind of late. Can we come in the morning? I was going to watch this movie—"

"*Now*, Mr. Lynch." Hollis clicked off.

Kiki Turner lay still with eyes closed, and except for the beeping of the machines tracking her vital signs, the room was eerily silent. From her seat near the head of the bed, Hollis stared at the still figure, a pale shadow of the colorful character of a couple of weeks ago. The brown patches of skin on her face were larger and seemed rough and scaly against the pallor of her face. Her cheeks were sunken and her mouth drawn back as if draped over her teeth.

A nurse came in.

"I understand you're Mrs. Turner's niece. Do you know Alicia?"

Hollis' tone was grim. "Alicia is her daughter. I've already called her to come quickly."

"I hope she makes it in time. Will you stay with her?"

"Er, yes, I'll stay until the family … I mean, the rest of the family, comes." Hollis clasped Kiki's hand in her own.

The nurse took down the numbers from the various screens and left as quietly as she'd come.

Minutes passed, and the beeping of the monitoring machine was lulling Hollis into a drifting state of mind. She jumped when she felt movement in the little finger of the hand she held. Kiki was staring at Hollis.

"Alicia? You came, you came." Kiki's voice was thin and raspy. "I'm sorry I have to leave you alone again." She wrapped her thin fingers around Hollis' wrist. "Please forgive me … for everything."

It was all Hollis could do to smother the sob rising in her throat. Her thoughts flew to John, but she took a breath and said, "Of course, I forgive you, Kiki. Our past is in the past."

"Thank you ... thank you." Kiki laid her head deeper into the pillow and a slight smile crossed her lips. "In the past, good. Kate ... where's Kate, Alicia? She looks so ... so much like ...."

Kiki closed her eyes.

Hollis rose and kissed her on the forehead. Tears slid immediately under Kiki's lids and down her cheeks. Her eyes fluttered open. "I love you, Alicia."

"I love you, too, Kiki," Hollis whispered. She was surprised at the pang she felt for the lost mother-daughter relationship.

Kiki closed her eyes again. Hollis' eyes sought the measurement bars on the machine. The numbers seemed to be getting lower. That couldn't be a good thing. She'd turned toward the door when she heard a bustle of people entering the room.

The nurse came rushing in, followed by Derek, Alicia, and a wide-eyed little Kate.

"Please, Alicia," Hollis implored. "Put Kate next to her. She reminds her of you."

The nurse nodded her assent. "Under the circumstances—"

Alicia stared at her mother with disbelief and fear. "I didn't believe her. I didn't ...." She took a breath and placed her daughter on Kiki's chest.

Kate smiled at her grandmother and snuggled her head into the blanket. Hollis thought she saw Kiki stir, but a moment later the solid sound of the flat-line signal startled them all. Alicia lifted Kate back into her arms.

Another nurse came rushing in and the two women went through the routine of checking Kiki's machines. After only a few minutes, the first nurse left, and the remaining nurse motioned to Derek and Hollis that it was over. As if frozen, Alicia clutched a now sleeping Kate.

"Honey," Derek ventured, putting a hand on his wife's arm, "she's gone. We need to leave."

Hollis moved to the door and turned to say a silent goodbye

to the figure on the bed. She'd confronted death for the second time in the same month. One had left her empty; the other, crestfallen. Taking a deep breath, she forced this dark thought to the back of her mind. She needed to get back to work.

But she didn't go to her car; instead she headed back to the lobby admission desk.

CHAPTER TWENTY-TWO

———∼∼∼———

Saturday

HOLLIS GAVE A SMALL SMILE to the security guard as she signed in at his desk in the ground-floor lobby of her building. It was almost nine, and she'd forgotten how much she enjoyed working on weekends. The quiet was peaceful. By the time she entered Triple D's offices, she felt both relaxed and energized. Stephanie had called her early that morning, concerned that she was facing the weekend alone. But Hollis had reassured her that work would keep her sufficiently busy.

"Stephanie, I have to get through this ... this *thing* in my own way," Hollis said.

"I know, I know, but I just wish I could—"

"Thank you, but you can't."

Now, after turning the lights on in her office, and glancing at the almost full inbox on her table, she went down the hall to fix a cup of tea. She had been right; work would be her salvation.

Penny evidently couldn't help herself and had left a note saying that she'd put the papers in order by date. That way, no matter which way Hollis decided to review them, they would be easy to sort and go through.

Three hours later, Hollis looked around at the stacks of papers scattered on the floor. Bell had been an orderly man. His taxes had been done by an accounting firm and his investments were mostly passive. He didn't appear to be interested in day trading or second-guessing the market. His sister would benefit from his conservative monetary approach.

Her phone trilled.

"Where are you?" Stephanie asked.

"I'm at work, where I told you I'd be. I have a backlog to get through," Hollis said, tossing her pen on top of a stack of papers.

"Hmm, well, I'm calling to invite you out to dinner with Dan and me," Stephanie said. "And before you say no, remember that you have to eat, and you don't have to make conversation." She paused. "We're your friends, Hollis. Please let us in."

Hollis felt a tear forming, which she wiped away with the back of her hand. She didn't look forward to being alone in the house that evening. *Their home.* Going out to dinner would postpone the reality.

Stephanie must have read her thoughts. "You can pull the covers over your head tomorrow."

She sighed. "Okay, but not the StoneAge Grill, please not there."

Stephanie laughed. "Hey, that's Dan's favorite pub. But, okay, if chunks of meat cooked in a simmering broth of ox blood don't appeal to you, we'll go for Chinese food."

"No," Hollis almost yelled, "not Chinese." She lowered her voice, trying to regain control. Stephanie didn't know it was John's favorite food.

Her friend must have sensed the significance.

"Right, no problem, how about Indian?"

"Perfect."

John didn't like Indian food.

*

AFTER AGREEING TO BE PICKED up at six, Hollis returned to Bell's bank statements, which went back twelve months. She knew that he disliked online statements—online anything, really—and had insisted on receiving paper copies. What she would love to have were the companion statements of his victims; then she could track who was paying what, and when.

He actually had accounts at two different banks. Both had large deposits made on a monthly basis but on different dates. She copied down the various amounts and then stared at the results.

There were *five* different amounts. That meant *five* victims, not four.

And all five were in existence at the beginning of the year. She would need to see his past statements in order to evaluate when each victim had started to pay. The amounts varied from fifteen hundred to ten thousand.

It was almost four o'clock. She smiled in satisfaction as she got her things together. She would be back tomorrow.

DINNER HAD A FORCED AIR of enjoyment that caused Hollis to feel gratitude and compassion for her friends. Dan made only one reference to questioning the police progress on the Bell case, and Hollis held his curiosity at bay with San Lucian anecdotes that brought them all to forced laughter. Again, she found herself looking at their scene as if from across the room—seeing herself in this most ordinary of circumstances. None of it touched her.

Stephanie was staring at Hollis as she had been all evening, looking for cracks in the wall. Hollis was just as determined that she not find them, because they were definitely there.

"How's your mom doing?" Stephanie asked. "Have they scheduled the transplant yet?"

Dan added, "Yeah, Stephanie told me. Are you nervous at all?"

Hollis shook her head. "No, not really. A kidney transplant is no longer cutting-edge surgery. My mother's doctor tells me that she has an excellent chance of recovery and that I won't miss a thing." She took a sip of wine. "Right now we're just waiting for my mother to say that she's mentally ready to go forward."

Dan raised his eyebrows. "*Mentally* ready? What does that mean?"

Stephanie put her hand over his. "Hollis' mother is something of a character. She may be trying to get used to the fact that she needs her daughter to give up her kidney."

"Stephanie is being tactful," Hollis said. "My mother is trying to get used to the fact that she needs the kidney from *me*."

HOLLIS SPENT MOST OF SUNDAY verifying that indeed there must have been five victims. With Bell's account numbers, she created the online access to seven years of his statements and could trace the deposits as far back as five years. The smallest blackmail payment came first, then about six months later there were two payments, and within the next three months there were a total of four. Finally, about a year ago, there were five payments showing monthly deposits.

CHAPTER TWENTY-THREE

———

Monday

WHEN MONDAY CAME, HOLLIS WENT early into the office. She smelled the coffee Tiffany had started to brew in the lunchroom and closed her office door. The floor was littered with papers, but that was a good thing. She was pleased with her discovery. She pulled out her legal pad and flipped to her first delivered package: Anthony Cantone. Her next task was to go through her interview notes and see if she could link the payment to the victim. When Gordon came in the next day, she would hand over her findings, and even he would be impressed with her work.

There was a tap on her door.

"Come in," she called out.

"Hey, Hollis, mornin'," Vince said, a wide grin spreading on his face. "I've got good news. I found Naomi Eaton." He glanced at the clutter on the floor. "You okay?"

"I'm fine," she said quickly. She watched him. "Please don't tell me you worked on the weekend again." She pointed for him to sit. "I thought you were going to wait and get started today."

"Yeah, I think she did, too," he said smugly. "I figured that she would think she was okay to move about on weekends, 'cause she would think we wouldn't be working. So, on Saturday I went back to those townhomes, brought a stack of my school books and just waited. I didn't see nothin' that day, but I came back on Sunday anyway."

Hollis looked at him with resignation. "Of course you did. And, you saw her?"

"Yep, about eight o'clock in the morning; I'd just gotten settled in. She came out of the townhouse on the end of the row—not the one we went to. She was wearing a jogging suit and off she went, running."

She sat up. "You're sure, Vince?"

"Oh, yeah, because I verified it was her this time."

"How exactly did you do that?"

He grinned. "This is the cool part. They have these mailboxes across from the townhomes next to the curb. I thought: hey, maybe her name is on the box." He tapped the side of his head. "But they only have numbers on them, right? They're only big enough to hold regular mail. If you get a package, they leave you a slip, and you have to go to the post office to pick it up."

"Ah, the mail carrier left a notice on the outside of the mailbox?"

Vince chuckled. "No, it was FedEx and they left it taped to her front door. It's white, and her door is dark brown, and I could see it from where the mailboxes were. It was just dumb luck, Hollis. She didn't see it when she left to go running, but I knew she would when she got back. So, I went up to her front door and read the slip. It was her name."

She cocked her head in amazement, and then halted. "Vince, you're telling me the whole truth, right? You didn't break into her mailbox and violate federal law, did you? Or do something criminal I can't guess right now?"

"Oh no, Hollis, it's all the truth." He looked offended. "I would have made up something a lot better than that."

Hollis' smile became a frown. "Wait a minute. The mail doesn't get delivered on Sunday. She would have gotten her mail on Saturday and seen the slip on her door. You found her on Saturday, didn't you? Why didn't you call me?"

"You're a good detective." He flushed. "Because I knew you needed to rest." He looked away. "Please don't be mad, but Tiffany told me about John."

The sound of his name, said out loud, caused her to gasp. She closed her eyes and took a deep breath.

"I'm sorry," Vince said. "You okay? I didn't mean to—"

"I'm okay," she said softly. "Maybe not all the way, but enough to get me through one hour at a time. If you want to help me, then talk to me about work. Give me something to puzzle out, to pass the time, to get me through that hour."

Vince nodded with understanding.

He went on, "We can catch her around seven tomorrow morning. I went out there about six this morning, and at seven, there she was in her jogging suit. I bet she runs every day." He paused. "I'm just not sure it's always at seven."

Hollis pursed her lips. "I'll pick you up at six tomorrow. We'll either catch her leaving or coming back home. Otherwise, we can always try again the next day."

A CUP OF STEAMING JASMINE tea later, Hollis sat back in her chair with a slight smile on her lips. She looked at the list of payment amounts made by Bell's victims—five, not four. Based on their earlier admissions, she was able to put the names of Cantone next to the five-thousand-dollar entry and Griffin next to the twenty-five hundred amount. That left three payments: ten thousand, three thousand, and fifteen hundred dollars.

She would bet it all that one of them was the killer's blackmail payment.

CHAPTER TWENTY-FOUR

Tuesday

FORTUNATELY HOLLIS AND VINCE WERE both morning people. They agreed to meet at six a.m. at the office and take Hollis' car to sit outside Naomi Eaton's townhome. The lingering morning fog would give them some cover and the early vestiges of the sun would provide enough light. Evidently this time of the morning was attractive to several runners. The pair sipped hot beverages as they watched them go by. Vince was hooked on Peet's, and Hollis gripped an insulated cup of steaming tea.

She looked at Vince, who stared out the passenger window, focused on proving he had cornered Eaton for sure this time.

Gazing straight ahead, Hollis said casually, "So, tell me, are you and Tiffany seeing each other?"

A red flush crawled immediately up his neck. "Aw, Hollis …." As he turned to look at her, he seemed to regain his confidence. "Yeah, yeah, we are. It took a long while to convince her. She was bothered 'cause she's older than me—not by much, but women … well, I think it can make a difference to them."

"But you persuaded her that it wouldn't make a difference in your case."

He shrugged. "I asked her, what if I was her 'one,' and she was my 'one'?" He looked down at his hands. "I told her what AA taught me—that anything can happen tomorrow, but it's today that matters. We only get one shot, and—"

"Vince, look." She pointed to the figure locking the townhouse door and heading down the steps to the sidewalk. She took a breath to push back the feeling of heaviness in her chest that his words had conjured and the tears that threatened to follow.

"That's her," he said, excited. "Let's go." He started to open the door.

Hollis grabbed his arm to stop him. "Are you kidding me? Knowing Eaton, she's probably a sprinter. We'll drive past her, park, and cut her off."

"Yeah, okay."

Hollis drove past the running Eaton, and less than a half mile away, turned into a parking space. Quickly, they got out of the car. Hollis sat on a bench next to the running path, and Vince positioned himself a few yards farther up the way.

Moments later, Naomi Eaton made the curve in the road and saw Hollis. She slowed and gave her a resigned smile. "Well, Ms. Morgan, I didn't know you were a detective, too." She sounded only slightly winded as she sat down next to Hollis.

"I'm not. I'm representing the woman who's accused of killing Matthias Bell."

Vince, seeing the two conversing, walked back and sat on the far side of Hollis.

Eaton nodded. "Yeah, I read about her in the paper. I don't want to get mixed up in any murder investigation. I figured, knowing you that the police might start looking for me. So, are you going to tell them you found me?" Eaton's strong features turned stony, and she ran her fingers through her hair. "I didn't take the money for myself. I needed cash for my grandmother. She lives at the other end of the street from me." She raised her voice so that Vince could hear. "She told me you came by."

He gave her an awkward smile.

Eaton turned back to Hollis. "She has to have a twenty-four-hour caregiver. Do you have any idea how much those people cost?"

Hollis frowned. "I don't think you have anything to worry about. Chief Brennan needs you to answer some questions so he can tick you off his list."

Naomi Eaton gave a short laugh of disbelief. "Really? Well, we'll see. But I'm tired of ducking and dodging. And now my family's being bothered." She sighed. "Bell bled me like the leech he was, and I'm glad he's dead, but I didn't kill him."

"Miss Eaton, can you tell me how much you were paying Matthias Bell?"

"Three thousand a month," she said bitterly. "He almost ruined me, and he didn't care." She slapped her thighs and stood. "I'm not going to run anymore. You can tell Brennan where to find me."

She took off, resuming her former pace.

Watching Eaton disappear into the next curve, Vince ran his hand over his head. "Do you think she killed Bell?"

Hollis tilted her head and said, "No, no, I don't. But that's the chief's problem. My job is to provide Gordon with enough other suspects that our client will be freed due to overwhelming reasonable doubt." She gestured to Vince. "Let's head back to the office; our work here is done."

BACK AT THE FIRM, SHE picked up a message from Rita and returned her call right away.

"It's mother. Dr. Lowe wants to move the surgery date up."

Hollis frowned. "Is she worse?"

She could hear Rita take a breath. "Yes and no. She's still a prime candidate for the transplant, but her blood work came back less robust than the previous time and Dr. Lowe is concerned it may be a trend."

"Okay, well, thanks for letting me know. I assume Lowe will be calling me, too?"

Rita cleared her throat. "Yes, of course. He wanted someone from the family—me—to call you and let you know about Mother. He didn't think it appropriate that he call you first like the last time."

Hollis recalled his awkwardness during the last call. He knew that Hollis was the black sheep and that their family circle, although it needed her, did not include her.

"Well, then, thanks for the call, Rita. I've already started to get my work in order and off my desk. I'll wait to get the new date from Dr. Lowe."

"Becca ..." Rita began, then stopped. Finally she said, "I don't think I ever thanked you for saving Mother's life. Because that's what you're doing. And even if she ... well, she knows it too. It's just that—"

"I know, Ri," Hollis murmured. "Thanks for calling."

HOLLIS RAN HER FINGERS OVER the top of the envelopes. Except for the Pittmans, they were all there, and in place of the original Pittmans' envelope, there was the thinner manila version that Penny had pulled together. She compiled all the papers and polished off a summary of her conclusions and final recommendation. Gordon was counting on her to have made substantive progress on the Bell case. She wouldn't disappoint. He'd made it clear he didn't like to lose. She didn't either.

Hollis rubbed her forehead as she glanced down at Bell's scrawl. After examining it closer, she pulled out Matthias Bell's detailed trust instructions. He had written them out when he first signed his trust, hoping to save on legal fees. Penny had entered them on the computer, but Hollis had kept the original in his file. Frowning, she dug into her briefcase and pulled out the letter Bell had written directing her to distribute the envelopes.

The handwriting on the envelopes and letter were close to the original, but side by side, it was clear that one hadn't quite managed to mimic Bell's bold strokes.

The letter was a forgery.

She leaned back in her chair and stared out the window.

Bell had never intended to return the blackmail material to his victims.

A cough from the doorway broke her concentration. Penny took a seat in front of her desk. "I'm not one to gossip," she whispered, "but did you hear about Vince and Tiffany?"

Hollis raised her eyebrows. "Now is not a good time."

Obviously eager to get the story out, Penny didn't acknowledge Hollis' comment or catch the tone in her voice.

"I'll be brief," Penny said. "Evidently they're dating. Everyone in the office is shocked. And not only that—"

"Penny, do you suppose we could get back to work on our client's case?" Hollis stacked the Bell material on the edge of her desk.

"Absolutely, I didn't mean to spread chatter, but he is your protégé." She stood. "There's one other thing. I want you to know I'm ... I mean we're ... we were all sorry to hear about your boyfriend."

Hollis froze. "That is none of your business."

"No, of course not." Penny took a step backward, finally hearing the warning tone in Hollis' voice. "I didn't mean to ... I mean—"

"Do me a favor and tell everyone in this gossiping, interfering firm—starting with yourself—that my private life is not open for general discussion, and please—*please*—don't bring it up again."

Penny was forced to step back to the door as Hollis stepped forward. When she'd crossed the threshold into the hallway, Hollis slammed the door. It was that same door that she leaned against as she slid down to the floor in a fetal position, grasping her legs to her chest. She sobbed silently. The tears wouldn't stop flowing.

It seemed like an hour, but when she looked at the clock, less than thirty minutes had passed. She rose stiffly and smoothed her clothing. Her nose was stuffy, and she knew if she looked in a mirror it would be red, along with her eyes. She had cried herself out; now there was only hollowness and shame. She regretted her harsh words in response to Penny's fumbling attempts at sympathy.

She put on her sunglasses, slung her purse over her shoulder, and headed quickly down the hall.

Hollis stood outside Penny's open door. The woman's head was bent down as she pored over fine print with a hand magnifying glass.

"Er … Penny," Hollis began, "I'm sorry for my rude and totally unacceptable behavior. I never should have yelled at you like that and I want to say … to say thank you for your sympathy." Hollis tapped the stem on her sunglasses. "I went out and got a cup of tea, and … uh … I didn't realize how bright—"

"Hollis," Penny interrupted her. "You don't have to apologize. I should have known that … well, I should have known."

The women exchanged weak smiles, and Hollis could tell from the look in Penny's eyes that she hadn't bought her sunglasses story. She nodded and motioned that she was returning to her office.

Hollis dashed down the hallway.

She moved to lock her office door, and after taking a deep breath, settled in behind her desk. She took a sheet of paper from her purse and re-read the email from John's friend. As Stephanie had said, there was going to be a memorial ceremony and they wanted her to come. Well, that wasn't going to happen. John didn't want a memorial and she wasn't ready to share her grief with strangers.

She took several deep breaths and then proceeded to empty her inbox. Her phone trilled, and when she saw the name, she froze.

"Dr. Lowe, is everything all right?"

He cleared his throat. "Everything is fine, Hollis," he said. "I'm calling to let you know that I've scheduled your mother's surgery for two weeks from today. You'll need to come in one more time for re-testing, but it's pretty routine. I'm going to be mailing you some information on the surgery and diet restrictions. There are also more forms for you to complete. Feel free to call me after you've read them through, but for now, do you have any questions?"

"No, you answered them all." She paused. "How is my mother?"

"Ava is fine. I think she thought she would have more time before the surgery, but the last few days have been difficult for her. She's been exhausted doing even minor tasks, and I think it scared her into calling me."

Hollis said, "She must be terrified."

After she hung up, she leaned her elbows on the desk and put her head in her hands. The surgery would coincide with the new numbness in her life. Maybe that was a good thing. Her nervousness with hospitals seem to fade when considered next to her sorrow over her loss.

As least with her mother, she could do something.

She picked up the Bell material and took another deep breath, once more attempting to puzzle it through. If Bell hadn't released his victims, who had?

HOLLIS SAT IN HER CAR across the street from the condo complex. Odelia Larson's unit was on the top floor, and if she remembered correctly, the light she saw on was in the kitchen. She opened the car door and stepped out onto wet pavement. Despite the drought watering restrictions, sprinklers had done their best to maintain a green lawn.

At the door, she steeled herself and ignored a pre-printed index card instructing visitors to knock first and then ring the bell. She supposed it was Odelia's belt and suspenders approach. Lips twitching with amusement, she rang the bell.

Odelia answered. She was wearing a long, floral house dress, circa 1960s. Her steel-gray hair was styled in a page boy and bifocals covered her eyes. She craned her neck to see if Hollis had brought anyone with her.

"Ms. Morgan, what are you doing here?" Odelia asked, surprised. "Why the urgency? Why couldn't you tell me what you wanted when you called? Although, you were right to call first; I haven't been answering the door. I've been harassed by those annoying reporters."

Hollis moved past the woman into the hallway.

"I'm concerned about something," she said. "I didn't think it was appropriate to speak about it over the phone." Hollis positioned herself to view the woman's face.

Odelia clenched and unclenched her hands.

"Then come to the sun porch. It's this way."

Larson led her to a solarium-type room. It was modest in size and held an overabundance of needlepoint pillows, footstools, and wall hangings.

"Did you do this?" Hollis said, sitting and picking up a blue and white plump pillow displaying a collage of butterflies and flowers.

"Yes," Larson said. She remained standing.

Hollis ran her fingers over the threads in the footstool at her feet. "It's pretty. Everything is quite ... artistic."

"Thank you, but why are you here?"

Hollis held her eyes and took in their uneasy look.

"I know you forged Bell's letter to me, and I'm pretty sure you're the one who made up the envelopes to return the goods to his victims. What I want to know is, did you kill him?"

Larson gave a small cry and slumped heavily into a tufted velvet chair next to the one where Hollis sat. She reached into the bodice of her dress and pulled out a neatly folded handkerchief to wipe her forehead.

"Thank goodness it's over. How … how did you find out?" She choked back a wail. "Yes, I did the letter and the envelopes, but I didn't kill him."

"I thought so." Hollis peered at her. "It was the designation of the church that gave you away. Bell was as selfish and cheap as any person I'd ever met. The church didn't make sense; it raised too many red flags."

Finally, this could all come together.

She felt sorry for the woeful-looking woman before her, whose skin had turned a pale gray to match her hair and whose hands shook visibly. The bold, obnoxious Odelia had disappeared, leaving this small, vague woman.

"Odelia," Hollis urged gently, "you've got to tell me the complete truth. What happened?"

"You and Mr. Barrett will still defend me, won't you? I swear I didn't kill Mr. Bell."

Hollis leaned over and patted the woman on her shoulder. "Of course, we will continue to defend you, even if you did kill Mr. Bell, but we can't do our job unless you tell us everything."

"I'm telling you, I didn't kill him." Odelia took a deep breath and dabbed at her forehead again. "It was Saturday, and I was watching a special on public television in my room upstairs. I usually couldn't hear any noise coming from the den because it's on the far end of the house, and it has that thick door. But I did hear what sounded like a loud thump, and I turned the volume on the TV down in case there was more to come. There wasn't, and after a minute or so, I turned it up again."

Hollis' forehead puckered. "You knew Mr. Bell was home?"

"Yes, and I knew he would call me if he wanted something." She moistened her lips. "Like I told you before, he would often take his, uh, guests from the side entrance into his den, and I usually never met them. Anyway, my show finished, and I came downstairs to see if Angie had started dinner. Mr. Bell had asked for his favorite dish, and I wanted to see if she'd remembered his request."

"Was he expecting someone for dinner?"

Odelia frowned. "You see, that's what I thought at first, but I don't know why I did, because he didn't say he was. But later—I mean when … when … I found him—I remembered the thump." She stared out the window.

"So you came downstairs and …" Hollis prodded.

"He was on the floor on his back, and the safe was wide open. There were papers, wrappers, and bank statements scattered on the floor all around him." She shuddered. "I didn't scream, but I did call out. I ran to him and took his pulse. He was breathing, but it was very shallow. I ran to the phone and called 911. There wasn't blood or anything, so I thought he'd had a heart attack while he was going through his safe." She put her hand to her brow, covering her eyes. "I didn't want to move him because I didn't want to do more harm. I closed the safe door—but not all the way. Then I went to tell Angie."

At that, Hollis gave her a curious glance but said nothing and continued to take notes.

Larson continued looking down at her hands, as she continued, "When the paramedics came, they said they thought it was a heart attack, and that they would take him to Hayward Sunrise Medical Center. I gave them his doctor's name and told them I would meet them there. Angie was a wreck and said she was leaving; she was going to stay with a friend."

"So, at what point did you go through the safe?"

Odelia Larson jerked her head up and flushed. "Mr. Bell passed away about two hours after I got to the hospital. I … I … came back to the house. It was late, and then I remembered the safe." Her voice dropped and she ran her fingers through her hair. "Ms. Morgan, would you like some coffee or tea? I think I would."

What she would like was for Odelia to finish the story. But she didn't want to antagonize her.

"Yes, whatever you're having."

Odelia nodded. "Tea then. The water is already lukewarm."

Fortunately, it didn't take long for the kettle to boil.

Or for her to get her story together, Hollis thought cynically.

The kitchen was partially open to the sitting room and Odelia went about putting the tea service on a tray. In only a few moments, she was back, placing a mug of green tea in front of Hollis.

"It's … it's hard for me to talk about, but I may as well get it over with." Odelia took a sip. "I put all his papers and paraphernalia on the floor into a paper bag, then like I said, I remembered the safe was open, and I was just going to close the cabinet but … but—"

"But your curiosity got the best of you?" Hollis offered.

"Yes, it was full of these thick envelopes with names on them. I didn't see any with my or staff's names, but I did recognize a couple of the names as being people Mr. Bell had over to the house." She paused. "So … So, I couldn't stop myself. I opened one envelope and immediately I could see that it contained scurrilous material. I think the first was Mr. Cantone's envelope. The pictures were shocking, and I … well, I went through the rest of them and I had a pretty good idea what was going on. Mr. Bell was … was blackmailing them."

Stating the crime out loud seemed to drain her face of its remaining color, and Hollis wondered if she were going to faint. But Odelia pulled herself together and continued on.

"I'm a church-going woman, Ms. Morgan. I know it's not popular today, but if nothing else, I know that good and evil are not for me to judge. I'll leave that to the one who knows what he's doing. But I do know that these people were suffering at the hands of a greedy and manipulative man." She took another sip of tea.

That sounded pretty judgmental to Hollis, but she remained silent.

"Well, I got fresh envelopes and sorted each person's pictures and papers. I imitated Mr. Bell's handwriting and wrote the contact information on the outside and put the whole batch back in the safe. The church is one I go to over in the city. They do real good work, and well … I knew his family wouldn't miss the money. Then I wrote that letter, in what I knew would be Mr. Bell's tone and … and that was that."

Hollis pursed her lips remembering Bell's—or Odelia's, she knew now—mocking words in the instruction letter. She had captured her boss' voice very convincingly. And the forging had been done with skill as well, for an amateur, with the same attention to detail as the needlework on the pillows.

"Odelia, did you think Mr. Bell was murdered? I mean, last time I asked, you told me that you went into his desk for the black case before you went to the hospital. Frankly, I'm on your legal team, but I can see how the prosecution might say you were rifling through his house after you killed him for cheating you. What is the truth?"

The elderly woman shifted uncomfortably in her seat. "Er, I didn't give you all my keys," she mumbled.

"What did you say?" Hollis asked.

"I had another key." Odelia rubbed her forehead. "I didn't like your attitude, and I didn't know that Mr. Bell thought so little of me all those years to leave me that paltry sum. I knew he had millions."

Hollis looked at her, wide-eyed. "So you came back into the house after I left."

Odelia nodded. "I wasn't going to take anything. I had already fixed things up for those poor people. But I remembered I'd left the bag of papers I'd found on the floor in my room upstairs, and there was a beautiful vase in the kitchen I wanted back." Drawing herself up and looking more like her old self, she added, "It was mine."

Hollis kept her expression neutral. It was a long way from the kitchen to Bell's den.

Odelia was clearly set on getting her whole story out. "I happened to pass by the den and I noticed that a couple of chairs were out of order." She looked pointedly at Hollis. "I guess you didn't return things to their proper position when you opened the safe."

Hollis shook her head. "I returned the chairs, Odelia."

"Then who pulled them out? They weren't where they were supposed to be." Odelia's voice rose. "I'm telling you the truth when I say that I don't know who killed Mr. Bell. I swear it wasn't me."

Hollis pressed her lips into a thin line. There was something nagging at her, actually two somethings.

"Odelia, where's the bag with Bell's papers now?"

"In my bedroom. I was going to … to get rid of it." She mumbled, "I didn't want it to incriminate me."

Hollis raised her eyebrows. "I'd like to have it. It may do just the opposite."

While visiting Odelia Larson, Hollis had received a text indicating that Gordon was waiting to see her as soon as she got back to the office. She was glad; there was a lot she needed to tell him, and there was a chance their defense strategy would require a reshuffle.

"Congratulate me, I won my case." Gordon beamed. "One trial down, and one to go. How's the Larson case going? I'm able to give it my full attention now."

They sat at his conference table. Hollis put her briefing notes in front of him.

"Congratulations on your win," she said. "I've got big news regarding Larson."

Over the next hour, Gordon listened intently. He let her go over her findings, questioned her on the details, and then asked for her assumptions.

"*My* assumptions?" she responded. "I don't understand."

He leaned back in his chair and crossed his arms over his chest.

"I agree with you: one of Bell's victims is his killer. So, let's for the moment 'assume' it isn't our client. You've gone to some effort to confront Bell's known victims at least once, most of them twice. Clearly, you assumed that one of them was the killer, until you came across evidence that there are five victims—assuming there are no more, of course. Then you assumed that the fifth victim might be our murderer. Do I have it right?"

"Er, yes, I suppose so. But—"

"But then our client confesses to tampering with the evidence and possibly obstructing justice by squirreling away crime scene material to protect herself from incrimination. So, I ask you, what are your assumptions now?"

Hollis paused before replying, "Odelia's intended act of charity by releasing Bell's victims doesn't change my *assumption* that one of his victims killed him. And yes, I'm assuming he had only five victims because after poring over seven years' worth of bank statements, I can state with reasonable assurance that I've seen all his blackmail deposits. Finally, I'm assuming it is in fact his fifth victim who killed him, because as varied as they are, the four victims were hiding things from their pasts and they were willing to continue to pay. But victim five is relatively new and was probably paying for something affecting their present situation, and since the amount paid is the smallest of them all, I am assuming he, or she, couldn't comfortably pay it."

Gordon chuckled and gave a slow clap with his hands. "Well said, Ms. Morgan. Who knows, maybe you should consider coming over to the dark side and taking up criminal law." He picked up a file and tossed it over to her. "And on top of the Larson case, you were still able to take care of Kiki Turner. Well done." His smile disappeared. "Our next step is clear. I want you to set up a meeting with the assistant DA. We are going to share your assumptions with that officer of the court and have the charges dropped against our client. You've turned up enough reasonable doubt to run a fleet of trucks through their case."

Chapter Twenty-Five

———

Wednesday

THE ASSISTANT DA, WHILE EXPRESSING more than a little skepticism, agreed to meet later that afternoon. "The defense may try to conjure reasonable doubt," he said, "but your client has the strongest motive. It's more than likely you're just wasting your time."

Hollis hung up. She hoped Gordon wasn't the one making a wrong assumption.

Penny poked her head in. Ever since their last confrontational conversation, Hollis had noticed that the paralegal was staying clear of her.

"Come on in, Penny. Have a seat. What is it?"

She sat in the farthest chair from Hollis' desk.

"I don't want to bother you, but that reporter called again. He insists that he has to see you today. He said he visited with Odelia Larson, and he thinks he can contribute to the investigation."

Hollis smiled. "You know, this time I think he's right. Call him back and tell him to meet me for lunch in the café downstairs." She took a deep breath and added, "Penny, I'm really sorry about losing it the other day. I know you meant well, and I was wrong to tear into you like that."

"Please, don't apologize. I'm ashamed of myself for acting so ... so callously."

Hollis gave her a smile. "Then let's move on and not mention it again."

"Yes." Penny smiled back. "I'll give Mr. Lyles a call back right now." She hesitated at the door and pointed to the paper bag on Hollis' table. "Do you need help with that?"

"Nope, I got this covered," Hollis said.

This time Penny didn't try to change her mind.

Kip Lyles rose from the café table when Hollis walked up.

"Ms. Morgan, Hollis, thanks for giving me a call. I was a little surprised you'd grant me a special meeting."

"Sit," she said. "I thought it would be good to meet instead of talking on the phone." She put her purse on top of her briefcase on the next chair and gave him a generous smile. "Why did you want to see me?"

"Well, I was wondering if you could let me into Bell's house one last time. I just need to refresh my memory on the room layout as background on my story."

Hollis made a sympathetic face and nodded. "You know, I can imagine that a sharp lone reporter like you must be kept busy with all the stories you could choose to run with."

Lyles peered at her. "Er, yeah. We're just a small paper so I have to screen regional interest stories from local ones. We rarely report on a regional or national story."

"How do you do that ... exactly?" Hollis prodded.

"What do you mean? It's usually by location."

Hollis frowned. "Oh, sure, but I mean the *San Lucian Daily* can't possibly pay enough to support a professional. You could be making more money if you worked for the Bay Area's regional papers."

He began to look irritated. "What's your point? You're jumping all around."

"I'm sorry, bad habit of thinking out loud." She leaned back in her chair. "I'll get to the point. Do you know a Dennis Long?"

Lyles had been playing with the cap from his bottled water. At Hollis' question, he fumbled it, and it shot across the table and onto the floor. He reached to pick it up.

"No. Well, I mean I know he's the new City Council representative for downtown, but I've never met him."

"Really? Well, Dennis Long doesn't know you either. But it seems that on that Saturday—the day you said you were in the emergency room when Matthias Bell came in—Dennis Long was there, too. In fact, he was involved in a drunk driver hit-and-run, and had come in for stitches."

Lyles started to fidget. "What are you trying to say?"

Hollis managed a deadpan expression. "Oh, I'm not *trying* to say, I *am* saying that you did not see Matthias Bell come through the Hayward Sunrise Hospital Emergency Room, because he was admitted directly to the hospital upon his arrival. You weren't in the Emergency Room at all. If you had been, I'm sure that, as our local reporter, you would have seized on the story that one of our three city councilpersons had almost been killed by a drunk driver. That would have made the front page, right?"

"So?" Lyles pushed back. "What difference does it make? Yeah, I missed the Long story. But I nailed it the following week when they caught the driver. The Bell story was a bigger headline anyway."

"How did you know, Kip?

He frowned. "How did I know what?"

Hollis put her chin in her palm. "Bell's doctor ordered him taken straight to admissions, where he died without regaining consciousness. Yet, when I met you, you told me and Odelia Larson the reason you knew to come to his house that night was because you saw him come through Emergency. He didn't, so how did you know?"

"I don't see the big deal." He moved his shoulders as if to shrug off her question. "One of the nurses told me."

"Which nurse in Emergency knew that Bell had been brought in?" Hollis peered at him.

"I can't reveal a source," he said with a smirk. "You know that."

"Uh-huh." Hollis smiled. "Well, I went to Emergency and checked. None of the nurses I talked to that afternoon remember you, and they were the same nurses on shift the day Bell was brought in."

Lyles' eyes narrowed. "They're lying."

"Somebody is. The question is, why?"

"You're just trying to turn the chief's suspicion from your client."

"I don't have to *try*. Odelia Larson didn't do it."

He moistened his lips. "Well, then, she has you fooled. She's my primary suspect. There's evidence that directly points to her, and while I'm not free to divulge what it is, I can assure you it's damning."

Hollis looked down at her nails. "You know what I think, Kip? I'll bet you're a diabetic, or someone in your family is. You had free access to insulin. I think you returned to the Bell house because you'd left a piece of evidence behind that Saturday after you killed him. You watched the house until you thought everyone was gone. You got in somehow, and then you were almost discovered by Odelia, who'd returned for her own reasons. After that, you could never get into the house to retrieve that one little piece of evidence.'"

Lyles looked over his shoulder as if checking to see if they could be overheard. But the only other table in the café that was occupied was in the far corner.

"I know about you, Ms. Rebecca Hollis Morgan Lynley. You're an ex-con trying to pretend you're better than everyone else, and that's a con in itself." Lyles sneered. "You can't afford to have that attorney's license of yours tarnished. I wonder how many clients you'd lose if your background was given full scrutiny?"

Hollis smiled again, only this time it had the desired effect on Lyles. He drew back in his seat and moved his coffee cup in front of him as if for protection.

She spoke through clenched teeth. "Lyles, your threats don't scare me because I've been there. I know what it feels like to lose the faith of family, friends, and society, and worse—in myself. I know what it's like to be shunned, and I know I'm not going to let scum like you hurt an innocent person."

Lyles turned pale, and then sat straighter in his seat. "That'll be for a jury to decide."

Hollis eyes bore into his. "How much were *your* Bell payments, Kip?"

"I didn't pay him anything. He had nothing on me," he snarled. "Not everyone has a past like you do, Ms. Morgan. I have nothing to hide."

"Oh, everyone has something they wouldn't want the world to know about them, and I bet you do too. In fact, I think I found it." Hollis reached into her briefcase and took out two sheets of paper.

Lyles watched her suspiciously. "You're not going to intimidate me. I'm not foolish enough to fall for some fake trick."

"I agree," Hollis said. "I wouldn't waste your time or mine with a fake item. But a real story …. Yes, I would bring that to your attention. You see I found out, through my own … methods, something about your past. It took a little doing because you covered your tracks well."

"I don't know what you're talking about."

"Oh, I think you do." Hollis smiled, placing the papers to the side. "You know, I wondered why a fairly intelligent, energetic young man like yourself would hire on to a weekly, a neighborhood throwaway paper." She took a sip of her tea. "There's no money in it … at all. So I ran a background check on you, and came up with … nothing. There was nothing at all on a Kip Lyles. Now that's more suspicious than finding a heap of information, because everyone has some background, schools, jobs, driver's license, *something*. But there was absolutely nothing on you."

He shifted in his seat, but was silent.

"No comment? I don't blame you." Hollis picked up the top sheet of paper. "You remember that cup of coffee you were drinking in the chief's office the last time we met? I asked Joyce to put it aside for me. She thinks I'm a little strange anyway, so she did. I was just curious about you. Until recently, I forgot I had the cup. But, as your bad luck would have it, I have a friend who works in forensics for the county, and she ran your prints."

He rubbed his chin as if he had a beard. "So? It's not a crime to change your name, as you well know," he added pointedly. "Reporters can attract a lot of weirdos. A name change is a safety net."

Hollis slapped her hand on the table. "From a weekly throwaway? Give me a break." She tilted her head and looked at him. She glanced down at her sheet of paper. "Oh, wait, maybe you mean the weirdos who would be attracted to you if they knew you were Kendall Taub, noted former *San Jose Herald* reporter who took up a life of writing fiction and passed it off as in-depth news. Your last little story caused a woman to commit suicide. Are those the weirdos you mean, Kendall?"

Lyles glared at her.

Hollis pretended not to notice. "So you took your nickname and added it to your mother's maiden name. That was smart, and Kip Lyles was born."

A server stopped by their table to see if they wanted refills. Lyles waved her away.

"Like I said, it's not against the law to change your name."

Hollis nodded. "No, Kip, it's not against the law, but murder is." She picked up the second sheet of paper. "As executor of

Bell's estate, I'm privy to his bank records, and when it became clear that my client had a propensity for blackmail, I reviewed those records, and what do you think I found?"

Lyles ran a hand through his hair. "Okay, okay, he was blackmailing me. The asshole took me for fifteen hundred a month. A month! I only had a small inheritance from my parents, and he was draining it like it was water."

His voice had started to rise, and he checked himself. He inhaled and exhaled deeply.

Hollis felt her heart beating rapidly. She'd been fairly sure that Bell had blackmailed Lyles, but she'd only known the amounts paid, not who paid it.

"And you killed him to stop the payments."

Lyles jerked his head up. "What? No, I'm just a victim like the others."

"No, Kip, you're not. You see, Bell was collecting five payments, and thanks to Odelia, it was clear who four of his victims were. But his fifth victim—you—killed him and took your blackmail material out of his safe. There were no papers that concerned you when Odelia opened it and no reason for me to suspect you. I didn't know for sure he was blackmailing you until you told me just now. But it does explain one thing."

"What?"

Hollis leaned in. "You came back for the needle wrapper, didn't you? You realized that you'd left the wrapper behind, that it might have your prints. That's why you had to get back in the house. Well, I found it. Mrs. Larson had bagged what she thought was trash and was about to throw it away. I called the police, and they have it now."

Lyles blanched and caught his breath. He looked around the café again. There was no one paying attention to their table.

He rubbed his hands over his head. "Damn, I could never find it," he said grudgingly. "Yeah, I killed him. What are you going to do now?"

"You're a reporter. What would you do?"

They locked eyes. Then, without saying a word, he smiled, gathered his car keys, stood, and walked quickly out of the café without looking back.

Hollis leaned back in her seat. Her hands trembled as she left enough money for the bill. She folded up the sheets of paper and put them next to the recording machine running in her purse.

Epilogue

Hollis had spent the past two weeks doing everything she possibly could to fill every minute of every day in an effort to avoid the quiet and the need to think. Still, there had been some moments of satisfaction. As arranged, the police had been waiting for Kip Lyles as he walked out the café's doors. Her statement and evidence should keep him in jail for a long time. Even Gordon was impressed and had recommended her for a bonus.

But eventually she found herself at home, confronted with the silence.

The finality of that—the silence—left her aching and numb. She turned the television upstairs on, and then the television downstairs, and then she flipped on the radio in the kitchen.

Noise filled the house, but it didn't take away the silence.

The hospital room was quiet except for the soft whir of the air conditioner. Hollis glanced over to the bed next to hers and saw that her mother was sleeping, or at least pretending to sleep. She turned her head to stare out the windows.

John was gone.

Stephanie and Rena had visited her in the hospital, talking
with a false gaiety and not mentioning his name, even though
it screamed amongst them. They were fearful she would be
upset going into surgery. They were trying to be her friends.
But she didn't need friends. She needed John.

As if hearing her thoughts, her mother stirred.

"Rebecca, I know you're awake. I want you to listen to me."

Steeling herself for an onslaught, Hollis turned to face her.
"Yes, Mother, I'm listening."

Ava Morgan's pallor was even more pronounced with the
two blots of blush on her cheeks. Gray hair was edging boldly
along her scalp line in contrast to her salon-acquired auburn
tint. Her usually piercing hazel eyes were dull and underscored
by shadows covered in thick foundation. She looked ten years
older than her actual age.

"I don't know why they insist on doing surgeries so early in
the morning," Ava said, "Six a.m. is really too early to ready
oneself. That's one of the reasons I wanted a private room."

Hollis smiled. Since she was the only other person in the
room with her mother, it was clear she would rather be alone.

Again, as if reading her mind, her mother said, "I mean, not
you, of course."

"Of course."

Her mother appeared to be ready to go off on a tirade;
instead she exhaled and spoke softly, "But that's not what I
wanted to talk to you about. Your father thinks I haven't been
fair to you. He made me promise that I would … that I would
reach out to you."

He must have used all his chits for that to happen.

"That's not necessary, Mother. I know that I'm not the
daughter you wanted. I know I've let you down."

"Yes, that's true, but it is also true you've made changes to
your life. You've tried to do better." She moistened her lips.
"I'm not a monster; there are just some mothers and daughters
who never get along. We are one of those pairs. Rita told me

about this young man of yours, that he's dead. I'm sorry to hear that. I would like to have met him. Your choice of that criminal ex-husband fooled me completely. You're not stupid, so I knew you would never make that mistake again. This one had to be better."

Tears started to fill Hollis' eyes. Her mother's attempt to be kind was almost more than she could bear. Her sharp, mean-spirited barbs were more common and easier to block out.

"I ... I—"

"Rebecca, please, I'm speaking." She pointed to the wall clock. "Rita and your father will be here to visit us in a few minutes, and then we'll be off to ... the operating room." She winced as if she had experienced pain.

Hollis leaned up on one arm. "Are you okay?"

"At sixty-three years old, I'm at death's door, in a hospital operating room waiting to have my gut cut open to get a new kidney from a daughter who hates me," her mother spat out. "Does that sound okay to you?"

Hollis stared at her in amazement, and then laughed. Her mother looked startled, then laughed, too. Hollis frowned, trying to remember exactly when she had heard her mother laugh, but she couldn't remember the last time, or the first.

"No, I guess it doesn't sound like you're okay," said Hollis, still chuckling. Then she was serious. "But I don't hate you, Mother."

"You always were a liar, Rebecca, a very good one, too, but I could tell when you were lying." She lay back on her pillow and closed her eyes. "I want to ... to thank you for ... for saving my life by donating your kidney." She held out her hand. "I ... we ... it may be too much to ask to totally heal our relationship in one fell swoop. But maybe we can start by being ... friends?"

Hollis reached across the bed to take her mother's hand and nodded, tears slowly trailing down her face. "Yes, friends."

IT WAS SEVERAL HOURS LATER when Hollis blinked her eyes

open to the soft glare of light slipping through the slats of the window blinds. It slowly registered that she was in the recovery room, and she turned her head to see the bed next to hers.

It was empty.

The slight twist of her neck caused her to wince, and she licked her parched lips. As if on cue, a nurse entered the room and poured her a cup of water.

"Hello there. I'm Nurse McKee. I'm glad to see you awake."

The nurse tipped the cup to her mouth, and Hollis sipped gratefully. "Hello."

"Let me check your vitals." Without waiting for an answer, McKee placed a blood pressure wrap around her arm and took down the figures bleeping on the machine over the bed.

"My mother, where—?"

"She's doing fine. She's in ICU, and that's not uncommon. We want to keep a close eye on her. Doctor Lowe will be making his rounds soon, and you can ask him how things went." The nurse went to the IV bag next to the side of the bed. "Now, you'll have an intravenous line for a while so we can give you fluids to keep you hydrated and administer medications for the pain." She checked the time and marked the readings on her chart. "As soon as your intestines start to work again, you'll be allowed to eat and drink. If you're not nauseous after sipping water, you'll progress to clear fluids and then to a regular diet within the next two days."

"How long will I be here?"

McKee gave her a sympathetic smile. "That's a question for the doctor."

Hollis nodded and let out the breath she'd been unconsciously holding. She lay passively as the nurse finished her monitoring routine and smoothed out her bed. She remembered the conversation with her mother. More than anything, she wanted the hope for their future relationship to be real.

One of Hollis' cellphones sitting on the standing tray vibrated.

The nurse handed it to her, gave a small wave goodbye, and left as quietly as she had entered.

Hollis stared in wide-eyed disbelief at the text on the screen, muffling a sob with her hand.

San Francisco 49ers by ten.

R. Franklin James grew up in the San Francisco Bay Area and flourished in a career of public policy and political advocacy. In 2013, the first book in her Hollis Morgan Mystery Series, *The Fallen Angels Book Club*, was published by Camel Press. *The Bell Tolls* is the fifth book in the series. James resides in Northern California.

For more information please visit:
www.rfranklinjames.com.

THE HOLLIS MORGAN MYSTERY SERIES

All the members of the Fallen Angels Book Club are white-collar criminals. Hollis Morgan is one, thanks to her ex-husband, who set her up. Now all she wants is to clear her name so she can return to law school. After fellow members start dying in scenarios right out of club selections, Hollis becomes a suspect. Can she identify the killer before she herself becomes the next victim?

While awaiting the results of the bar exam, paralegal and pardoned ex-con Hollis Morgan hopes to clear the name of a friend accused of libel by a philanthropist whose charitable giving looks a lot like money-laundering. Only problem: the evidence has disappeared and her friend Catherine is found dead. Can Hollis exonerate her friend without getting killed herself?

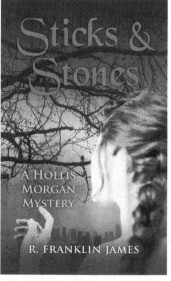

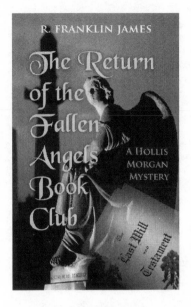

After obtaining a pardon, Hollis is a new probate attorney in the Bay Area. Her first two cases are trials by fire. The first involves a vicious family dispute over a disinheritance. She is also hired to file the will and family trust of her former parole officer. Jeffrey introduced her to the Fallen Angels, his other white-collar ex-parolees, who unite once again to solve his murder.

While Hollis sorts out a dispute over an inheritance for a colleague, she becomes embroiled in a murder case involving a woman she knew in prison. Olivia had a list inculpating many public officials and businessmen, and they believe Hollis has a copy. To solve the mystery and thus stay live, Hollis asks her friends from the Fallen Angels Book Club for help.

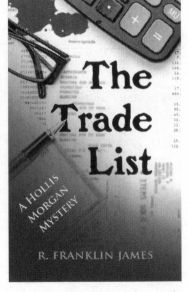

From Camel Press and R. Franklin James

Thank you for reading *The Bell Tolls*. We are so grateful for you, our readers. If you enjoyed this book, here are some steps you can take that could help contribute to its success and the success of this series.

- Post a review on Amazon, BN.com, and/or GoodReads.
- Check out R. Franklin James' website and send a comment or ask to be put on the author's mailing list.
- Spread the word on social media, especially Facebook, Twitter, and Pinterest.
- Like the author page and publisher page.
- Follow the author and publisher on Twitter.
- Ask for this book at your local library or request it on their online portal.

Good books and authors from small presses are often overlooked. Your comments and reviews can make an enormous difference.

Made in the USA
San Bernardino, CA
10 July 2017